PHOENIX OVER THE GALILEE

PHOENIX OVE

Ka-tzetnik 135633

THE GALILEE

Harper & Row, Publishers

NEW YORK, EVANSTON,

AND LONDON

First published in Hebrew, under the title *Phoenix from Ashes,* by Am Oved Ltd., Tel Aviv, 1966.

PHOENIX OVER THE GALILEE. *English Translation copyright* © *1969 by Nina de-Nur. All rights reserved. Printed in the United States of America. No part of this book may be used or reproduced in any manner whatsoever without written permission except in the case of brief quotations embodied in critical articles and reviews. For information address Harper & Row, Publishers, Incorporated, 49 East 33rd Street, New York, N.Y. 10016. Published simultaneously in Canada by Fitzhenry & Whiteside Limited, Toronto.*

LIBRARY OF CONGRESS CATALOG CARD NUMBER: 75-85045

E. d'M. A.

Author's Note

It is not customary for an author to tell his reader about the vicissitudes of his writing, nor to submit to his readers an account of his labor. The relationship between writer and reader is of a totally different order. This time, however, I am moved by a sense of duty to afford the reader some key to the following pages, as to an inaudible background melody.

For twenty years I have been trying to bring myself to write this book. Yet no sooner would I start than I would find myself existing not within the ambits of time as indicated by the hands of our clock but on another planet: the flaming planet of Auschwitz. At moments I am ejected from it, and when I turn my head to look back, there is the planet—burned out. Ashes.

I have seen an entire people, my own people—its infants and its aged, mothers and virgins—become fire and ashes.

And I, pen in hand, myself am become as fire and ashes.

For twenty years I have been struggling with these desperate attempts, yet my pen refused me. Until one dawn, in the wake of an all-night vigil. The window stood open. Outside ranged the citrus groves of the Valley of Sharon, my country's vessel of perfume. Spring was afoot, and the breeze through the window wafted to me the fragrance of the orange blossoms. All at once I was filled with the ancient Sharon, that of the poet of the Song of Songs. I was filled with longing for the days of my childhood, when I was taught the sacred symbols according to which the Song of Songs was composed; those childhood days when I learned that Shulamith's love for the shepherd was really the love of Israel the bride for her Lord.

It was a sudden moment of grace. And the key offered me that dawn for writing this book, I am now passing on to the reader:

. . . Harry Preleshnik, the hero of the story, symbol of what has been left of a people, which in the course of two thousand years of wanderings has been burned at the stakes of every alien land, returns after Auschwitz, like an infant crawling barefoot after an earthquake, to the place where his home, his cradle, once stood.

Galilea, the heroine of the story, symbol of the native soil, is waiting for her beloved to come back to her from exile and redeem her. Many are the nations, tribes and conquerors that have passed her way and coveted her in the course of two thousand years. But Galilea, in whose heart the annals of her beloved are inscribed and sealed like a commandment of destiny, waits.

She knows him, though her eyes have not yet beheld his present face; she remembers him from antiquity, before they were torn asunder. And when he returns, shrouded in his cloak of ashes, none but she, with the power of her love, is capable of resurrecting the spark that survives in his ashes.

On the night of November 29, 1947, upon the consecration of Israel by the United Nations, Harry and Galilea's union is consecrated.

But the long night is not over. All the torments Galilea's beloved has undergone in the millennia from Exile's start to Auschwitz Galilea's soul now takes in, with staggering immediacy. The torments that have been his are now hers to bear.

Tottering on the hairline boundary which separates the living from the dead, Galilea reaches out for a cure for her malady. It is not on the analyst's couch that she finds the long-sought remedy but mirrored in the silent eyes of her beloved: the path he has chosen to cure his Auschwitz malady has not been that of a blood avenger nor of a blood redeemer, but of a seeker of his own redemption.

Standing on the crossroads to Bethlehem and Jerusalem, Galilea now beseeches mercy for her sons falling on both sides of the border, the bleeding border which cuts through her heart.

Ka-tzetnik 135633

K.Z. (German pronunciation *Ka-Tzet*) are the initials of *Konzentration Zenter* (Concentration Camp). Every K.Z. inmate was known as "Ka-tzetnik Number . . ."—the number itself being branded into the flesh of the left arm.
The author of this book is Ka-tzetnik 135633.

PART ONE

Though I said I would die with my nest,
I have, like the Phoenix, multiplied my days.
—Job 29:18

1

"You are running away from yourself! You're escaping!"
Dr. Garden said sharply.

Galilea lifted her eyes with effort. She did not understand why Dr. Garden was suddenly so angry with her. As a rule he treated her tenderly, with patience. What could she have done to make him lose his temper like this? All she had asked was that he send her to a suitable hospital. Mainly for her family's sake, not so much her own. It would be better for them if she were away where she could be treated like a real patient. Harry would never accept the fact that she was really ill, that this was simply an illness like any other whose roots must be dug down to if she were ever to be cured.

Why were they unwilling to believe her? Why was the doctor so angry?

The light in the doctor's office was focused beneath the shade of the lamp on the desk. Dr. Garden always brought his paunchy coffee mug with him when he entered, and now it squatted among the other objects on the desk. She looked at the round pocket watch, at the open appointment book. She looked at Dr. Garden's hands resting on the desk, the hands bathed in a pool of light beneath the lamp shade. The whole dim narrow room seemed to feed on the light reflecting from these hands. She couldn't grasp the words he was directing to her. They simply didn't reach her brain. I must listen to every word he says, she repeated dully to herself.

Dr. Garden abruptly shoved the full coffee mug from the circle of light, tapped the tip of his finger on the desk, each tap reinforcing his every word.

Once, she had been able to absorb even the jumble of talk and prattle going on around her in the crush of a cocktail party, but now no sooner did she feel that someone was angry at her than even words meant for her stopped short at the threshold of her ear as though before a closed door. His finger tapping on the desk rose and fell like a drill boring into the earth. Was he trying to force his words into her brain?

"And the main point, dear lady . . ."

Oh, now it was "dear lady"! Could she have made him that angry?

She knew she could no longer bear the sadness in Harry's eyes, the sorrow which he tried to hide from her. Nor did she have the strength left to continue covering up an illness that had to be brought into the open if it were to be cured. *Dr. Garden, doesn't this make sense?* She wanted to be well, as much as Harry wanted it for her. Harry—her one reason for wanting to live. Was Harry really unable to understand this? Oh God, the same Harry who in his books was capable of penetrating to the very heart of his characters.

"Running away from yourself!"—the button on the lapel

of modern man. As if Tag Day were announced on God's earth, and the sanctimonious fingers of philanthropic ladies pinned this button to your chest.

This much she knew: she had to have faith in Dr. Garden. Once she lost faith in him, she herself would be lost. If only she didn't *know*. It would be better for her to know less. Before man tasted of the fruit of knowledge, he was free from the curse of faith. Today we are lashed to it with an elastic umbilical cord. The further we stray from faith, the more brutal the impact when we are flung back.

She sat on the edge of the couch, both hands in the pockets of her outsize coat. In one of her clenched fists she crumpled the ten-pound note Harry had given her when she left the house, the fee for the session. "Don't pile up debts, precious," Harry had said as he walked her to the stairway. Certainly Harry had no faith in Dr. Garden. You could read it in his eyes. God keep her from such skepticism! Harry didn't even believe she was sick. Or perhaps, deep down, he did and refused to admit it. In her family's eyes such sickness was still a stigma. But Dr. Garden too? Why did he say she was "running away" from herself? Oh, how she hated that inane expression! How did Dr. Garden come to use such nauseating drivel?

She didn't want Dr. Garden to turn against her too. It bothered her to have angered him. She could not bear it if he became one of those who didn't understand her—or who didn't want to—for whom she was nothing but a nuisance. She knew that the moment she was out of this room her hands would reach out for him as for a life buoy. For the present, Dr. Garden was the only point of light in her life.

Through the glass door she could still hear Dr. Garden's little boy crying for his father to sit with him for a little while before he fell asleep.

Dr. Garden had been running late today. Maybe this could account for his touchiness. Feelings of compassion stirred in her. All day long he worked for the Israeli army at a psychiatric consultation center. At evening, the command car returned him to his home. The girl in the waiting room should really have been sitting in her place by now. Today Dr. Garden didn't even have a minute to spend by his little boy's bed. His wife was calling outside, "Go to sleep now! Daddy's busy."

Suddenly within her was that signal—she never knew when it would come or why—ticking like a time bomb, warning of the onrush of the black wave of fear. At first, waiting here for the doctor, she had relaxed completely, like someone suffering with a toothache whose pain lets up the instant he sits down in the dentist's chair. She had felt that a good session was in store for her. Dr. Garden would be pleased with her. Today they would be able to cover a substantial stretch of her past, and for him this was progress. But hearing the boy cry had made her think of home; right now Harry would be putting the children to bed. For a fleeting moment her eyes opened again to see the idyl of her home: Harry sitting between the two little beds in the children's room, their eyes sparkling as he told them about Chum Pum, the legendary hero of the War of Liberation whom Harry had created especially for them, weaving nightly before their eyes a fabric of his daredevil feats. For a glimmering second she belonged again to her family, and they belonged to her. But, immediately, the same black knots of smoke surged back, billowing in her brain. Harry and the children dissolved into the columns of smoke, and the faces of marauders floated in the mists of her imagination, blurry and interchanging—now the faces of the German SS just as they had been burned into her mind's eye when she read Harry's books, now the faces of the Arab *Fedayoun* as she had seen them in newspaper photographs.

"Dr. Garden! Please send me to a hospital. I can't possibly go home . . ." she begged him.

"You have a home. You have a husband. Two children. Your place is there. You belong there. Not in any hospital! It is your home. Yours!" The tapping of his finger on the desk top accompanied his words.

Her puffy lids felt heavy, as though her tears, instead of spilling, had been soaked up in them as in sopping sponges. Before she knew it the hour would be up, and once again she would have to leave the doctor's office, once again walk into the merciless outside.

Dr. Garden was silent. Waiting. She was supposed to go on rummaging in her past now. *Where does one's past begin? To what dim distances does memory reach?*

She couldn't understand why it was Dr. Garden's practice to seat his patients across from him rather than have them lie on the couch. She was too exhausted to sit up. She saw her knees tremble, knocking together. Anxiety held her in its grip. Again, everything seemed unreal. She longed to lie on the couch, to sense Dr. Garden present somewhere behind her head—both present and absent at the same time. To lie like that for eternity. Until final oblivion.

"The source of a plant's rot is in the roots, hidden in the thick of the earth . . ."

Why was he rehashing this old stuff with her now? A murky opaqueness descended upon her memory. She couldn't remember where they had stopped in the previous session, or from what point she was to continue now. It was like groping among the heavy folds of a dark curtain to find the passageway. Her hands shook.

She must cooperate with the doctor. She must help him. She wanted him to succeed. Suddenly she felt like saying: Dr. Garden, why don't you go in to see your son for a minute? Hug him, give him a kiss. The boy misses you. He doesn't see you all day. The moment he feels you close, he'll calm down and stop crying.

Her conscience plagued her for depriving the boy. She was the one robbing him of his father. "You're always worrying about everyone but yourself . . ." Harry kept reproaching her.

She could not control the muscles of her mouth. They were coiled in fat like the rest of her. The terror of that moment when she would be forced to leave the doctor's office seized her again. She feared the marauding danger stalking her beyond the walls of her home. She knew neither the nature of the danger nor the guise it might assume, and that increased her fear sevenfold.

"The point is, Galilea"—their mouths always ready with a foolproof remedy—"you must look reality straight in the eye!"

Harry's face, the faces of her children, the furniture, the walls, the house—all receded in her soul, leaving nothing but the terror of a vacuum soon to be flooded by the black waves of fear. Quickly, she must fill the vacuum with food. The kiosks which she would pass on the way home rose before her eyes. Plenty of food. She must eat until there was no room for anxiety. She pressed the ten-pound note in her fist: this money was the only ledge of safety preventing her plunge into the abyss that gaped within her. No other medicine would work. Just food. Plenty of food.

But Harry had given her the money for Dr. Garden—this same Dr. Garden who was sending her home again. The money was his. *"You must look reality straight in the eye."* The crumpled banknote in her fist now became that reality which must be faced. As she fantasied of kiosks laden with food, the obsessive hunger assailed her all the more ferociously. No shred of resistance was left in her to oppose this unseen adversary.

"Dr. Garden, help me . . ." Heavily, her tongue forced the whimpering words out of her mouth. She strained to get up.

Dr. Garden's voice sounded soft, caressing. "You mustn't strain yourself, Galilea. Stay where you are. I can hear you from there."

She didn't want his pity. She didn't want him to talk to her the way Harry did. She wanted him to *help*. Her hands wiped at her tears. She stared at her hands: fleshy, shapeless with obesity. She stared at her bloated body. *What has happened to me? Why do I destroy myself with my own hands?*

Galilea left Dr. Garden's office and went out to the unpaved road leading to the highway where the Sheroot taxis stopped en route to Tel Aviv. Each step along this road that led her to Dr. Garden's office and back was seared on her soul. A street lamp shone at the end of the road. It was still early evening, but the neighborhood was already encased in the silence of night.

Dr. Garden lived in a new housing development built in a sandy area, inhabited primarily by army regulars who were allowed to return home every evening. She stared at the emptiness of the dark lots spread all around. How far is it to the border? she asked herself. How many hours would the Arab *Fedayoun* need, even on foot, to reach the back windows of these houses?

She remembered the faces of the Arabs who had worked with her in the army camp when she served as a soldier in the Egyptian desert. She felt again the sympathy and mutuality which had bound them to one another, and she wondered why this feeling couldn't exist again—at least between the Jews and Arabs here in Israel. Somewhere within her flared the yearning to recline once again on a straw mat in the shade of an Arab village home, to savor the warmth of their beaming hospitality and to welcome them as guests in her own home. She knew this was a deceptive fantasy that even as she dreamed was seeping away and vanishing somewhere inside her, leaving behind only the tang of a longing mounting to pain; but all the while a bizarre certainty ran through her that if only she could find again the language of understanding with which to speak to the Arabs, sons of this land, the connection between them could be reestablished.

Odd, at night the trees didn't frighten her. Only in the daytime was she in terror of the jutting branches. Like the Auschwitz skeletons, as Harry described them in his books, they thrust out their gnarled hands to strangle her. And she must run for her life. How many times had she reminded herself not to forget to tell this to Dr. Garden, and how many times had she forgotten? She never got to it. There were always a thousand other things to talk about, and the session was over in a flash . . .

She walked along the dim road. Once the session was over, her anxiety seemed to have been coated with a filmy membrane. A temporary anesthesia of sorts for a painful nerve. The terror would return, but now she felt as if she were treading a bridge that had broken off from both shores; even though it was suspended in mid-air, the bridge infused her with some sense of reality beneath her feet, the reality of the coming session. When the hour was over, all she had left was her hope for the hour to come. Just as she couldn't really taste the food that she swallowed, all the pith of its savor remaining in her fantasies of the eating bout to come.

How much time does it take to get here, even on foot, from the Arab Triangle? What rustles in the dark empty wastes stretching all the way to the border? Couldn't the infiltrators come early in the evening, slaughter a whole family, and that same evening vanish across the border?

Last night, according to the papers, they got as far as Herzliya, broke into an outlying house, murdered the entire famliy, including the two infants, and managed to steal back with the cattle they had pillaged. And Tel Aviv was no farther from the border. Were the children sleeping by now? Or was Harry still sitting between their beds, spinning the tales of Chum Pum's adventures? Harry gave her a sorrowful look every time she asked him not to open the door for anyone at night. Did Daniella's crib have to be right next to the window in the nursery? Even though their apartment was on the second floor, the raiders could climb the drainpipes to the window. Every day you read in the papers about burglars breaking in through windows, even as high as the third floor. Before Independence such things were unheard of. When she was a child, there was no need to lock doors in Tel Aviv, not even when people went out. Now she trembled for fear the *Fedayoun* would break into her children's room while they slept.

In one of the houses along the unpaved road, a door opened. The light from within splashed over the hedgerow fencing the house. A boy was coming out of the cottage onto the dusty road, talking in a Slavic language apparently to his mother, who stood in the doorway.

Galilea quickened her pace. It was good now to run into someone. And although she was thoroughly familiar with the way, she asked, "Where do I get the Sheroot taxi to Tel Aviv?"

"Follow me," answered the boy in Hebrew. "See the bend in the road over there? Beyond the bend is the Tel Aviv stop."

The boy didn't look old enough to have graduated yet from elementary school. His accent betrayed his recent arrival in Israel. In his hand he carried a violin case. Probably rushing to a music lesson. The boy raised his eyes to her. "New immigrant?" he asked.

Why, her grandfather had been one of the ten founders

of Tel Aviv. When she visited Harry's publishers in New York or London, they would say, "From your excellent English it's difficult to tell you're Israeli by birth. Really, Galilea, where were you born?" And she would answer, "Isn't my name an identity card? I was born in the Galilee. In Jesus' neighborhood. Practically next door."

"No," Galilea answered the boy, "I'm not a new immigrant. Aren't you afraid to be out now?" she asked.

"Afraid of what?" The boy eyed her in amazement, as if this woman weren't making any sense.

She was breathing heavily. Trying not to lag behind the boy. Because of her corpulence, her gait at his side was like the waddle of a rushing goose. "You know, don't you, what the situation in this country is like these days?" she asked.

"Lady, this is Israel," the boy said in his Slavic Hebrew. "Just around this bend in the highway you'll be able to see a street lamp. That's where the Sheroot taxi stops for Tel Aviv." The boy pointed. "Follow the road, lady, and don't be afraid. We're in the State of Israel now."

The boy faded into a dim stretch of sand. The street lamp illuminated his back. Her jealousy of the boy's self-confidence tightened painfully in her throat. She felt like a baby forsaken by a grownup in a dark room. It occurred to her that she had forgotten to bid him good night.

"Three seats to Tel Aviv!" the driver craned his head out of the taxi window.

Galilea waited her turn. Two girls stood ahead of her in line, two fragile made-up creatures with towering hairdos. They slipped oblique glances at Galilea as if she were someone to keep away from. Twinlike, they turned to face each other. "Barrel of fat!" one hissed to the other. On her account they'd be sitting on top of each other all the way to Tel Aviv. "This Sherman tank will take up more than two seats. After this ride we'll end up looking like two rag dolls."

"Come on! Come on!" the driver prodded.

"No, we'll wait for the next taxi," the two girls twittered coyly.

The Yemenite behind her, his work sack hanging at his side, came up to the open door and paused until Galilea, with great effort, had squeezed herself in. The passengers turned their heads and watched impatiently as Galilea struggled to lodge her body into the seat. The driver kept shifting glances, now out his window, now in the mirror above his eyes, on the chance of a seventh passenger running up from behind. "Let's go!" he gasped.

Reluctantly, the driver released the Chevrolet handbrake with a muffled thud, slamming his foot on the gas so ferociously that the passengers' heads were jolted forward. "Who hasn't paid yet?" he barked at the road. His hand shot back to catch Galilea's fare. Fingering the change blindly, he called out, "Lady, I figured you'd pay for two places. In a cab you pay by weight."

Someone snickered in the dark.

The hunks of flesh around her eyes flushed hot. Like pleading arms, her vaporous thoughts rushed out to Dr. Garden's words: "You must come to terms with yourself. Accept yourself as you are!" She was seized with nausea, a loathing for the heavy warped body she was doomed to drag with her wherever she went.

She saw herself with the eyes of a thousand others. Scorn blazed in those eyes. No longer the Galilea she once was. No one recognizes her any more. No one knows who she is, and so they don't associate this gross thing she is now with what she once was—she must destroy what she is now.

She craved the moment when she could lock herself behind the kitchen door. She couldn't wait to put the big skillet over the flame. Ten eggs would glide over the melted margarine emptied from a whole package. Now the yolks ogle her from the pan like the raping yellow eyes of vampires, their gleamy stare reflecting at once a lust for life and a lust for self-destruction. Yolky eyes popping open, spilling over as she stabs them with swatches of bread. And she gulps both life and self-destruction. All the pity for herself and all the burning self-hatred. Eating to total obliteration of the senses.

WELCOME TO THE CITY OF TEL AVIV, announced the banner at the entrance to the city. Tel Aviv, the city that matured as she did. How she destested this city now. If only she could run away. But where? Harry was in love with the city. He loved the living roar of its masses of Jews. Didn't she feel exactly the same about Tel Aviv as she did about herself? She wanted to run away from herself too. Where could you run to when the curse of God crouches deep in your belly?

"Your husband loves you just the way you are. Your children love you just the way you are. Remember that!" Dr. Garden had said.

Harry was insane if he loved her this way. Maybe he simply pitied her. She must pull her roots out of his life. Then only the old Galilea would live in him. She must never profane that most beautiful miracle ever given to anyone, the love between her and Harry. If she continued living with Harry as she was now, she would kill even his memory of their love.

The taxi entered Tel Aviv by the south road. She couldn't bear the thought that any moment now she would touch her feet to the city. How she hated those espresso-sippers who thronged the sidewalks in front of the cafés, leaving the pedestrians no room to pass except by crawling over each other's backs; who fingered with their glances each and every passer-by like a Moslem toying with his rosary of amber, each bead separately.

"Driver!" Galilea called out. "Could you please stop at the next corner?"

Her Yemenite seatmate opened the door for her. She hauled herself out with greater effort than usual. To the irascible driver, the bulk of her bottom looked like a great eiderdown being tugged through a cramped opening. "Lady, why don't you go on a diet and maybe the government won't put us back on austerity." He was out to prove that his sense of humor was intact.

In front of the lighted kiosk, the evening paper was strung on a pole like a flag, bait for the passers-by, who, in stopping to glance at it, would notice the marble counter stacked with Napoleon pastries and all varieties of sweets. The shelves of the kiosk were stocked with gaily wrapped bars of chocolate, and the neon light illuminated the bold-type front-page headline: NASSER—WE PROMISE TO PUSH JEWS INTO SEA!

A gang of kids loitered around the kiosk. Some sucked on straws stuck in Coke bottles; others, mouths gaping over the *fallafel* in their hands, leaned forward to keep the *tahina* from dripping down their clothes. Their eyes roved indifferently over the front page. You could tell they'd rather be looking at the sports pages inside. The couple serving in the kiosk were frantically working, the woman at the soda fountain and the man squeezing grapefruits.

Galilea sat on a bench opposite the kiosk in a fever of anxiety: Would she be able to keep herself from approaching Betty, the owner of the kiosk? Galilea had no more money left, but Betty would certainly give her credit. Many years had passed since Betty was a cook in her parents' service. Betty remembers their Galilea. But how could she face Betty now, like this?

A fragment of bustling Dizengoff Street intruded on her consciousness. Pedestrians in a bizarre static flow: the congestion and press made them appear to be standing still. In contrast, the neon lights of the cafés skittered over this multiheaded human chunk in dizzying staccato. The glittering signs flashed on and off as if the most illustrious nightclubs in the world had assembled here to compete with the gaudiness of their lights; while across from her, the spotlighted headline of the evening paper glared from the kiosk: NASSER—WE PROMISE . . .

Pastries dripping with cream. Thick sandwiches. Chocolate bars stacked along the walls. The kiosk was stuffed with temptation enough to make her faint. But she hadn't a penny left in her pocket. In every one of the kiosks on her way from the taxi she had spent the money. To the last penny. TO PUSH JEWS INTO SEA. The newspaper headline again kindled the cruel hunger within her—as though it had been days since she had had any food. Somewhere in her mind drifted a thought of the mysterious link between the two. She decided to mention this to Dr. Garden, but she knew she'd forget it the way she forgot everything these days.

In one of the seaside kiosks, instead of a five-pound note they must have given her only a half-pound note as change for the ten pounds. They looked so alike she could never tell the difference. Then again, she might have forgotten to pick up her change. The sight of a pile of sandwiches on display got her all mixed up. She always believed that people wouldn't gyp her, and invariably they did. As if her gullibility were written all over her face: this cow you can take for anything. "When, Galilea, will you learn that you can't believe blindly in everyone's honesty?" Harry was constantly telling her. Harry didn't understand that the trust in human beings was the very air she breathed. After what Harry had gone through in Auschwitz it was a wonder he wasn't sickened by everyone created in the Image.

Her compulsive hunger encircled her like a magnetic hoop. The only escape was through that kiosk. She tore away from the bench, not feeling her feet propel her to the counter.

She stood before the lighted kiosk. She did not raise her eyes to Betty's face. "I was passing by, and I thought I'd pick up some candy for the children," Galilea said, pretending to rummage through her purse. "But it seems I forgot to take my money."

The woman at the soda fountain went on wiping the wet marble counter, saying nothing.

"Miss Betty, you really don't recognize me? I'm Galilea. Galilea Glick . . ."

The woman stared at her as though she were an apparition. She raised the counterboard and leaped out. Clasping Galilea in her arms, she called to the man in the kiosk, "Rolf! Look! This is Galilea, Professor Glick's daughter! My own darling Geegee!"

Like a running spout, Miss Betty poured questions over Galilea while her hands, trembling with devotion, packed slices of cake into a cardboard box.

Wanting to get away as quickly as possible, Galilea tried to answer the stream of questions: "Yes, I have two children. Only one year's difference between them . . . It's a glandular disease. Even if you only have water you get bloated . . . You haven't seen me because I'm abroad most of the time . . . Yes, everyone says Mother hasn't changed at all. She's like a young girl. Papa? Fine, touch wood. You remember them. Like a pair of lovebirds."

Betty's husband, his elbow resting on the juicer, stood with half a grapefruit in his hand, as though he had petrified in midwork. A smile froze on his face: Could this be

Galilea Glick, whom the boys of Tel Aviv used to buzz around like bees at a honey pot? "Geegee" they used to call her, because of her initials. This was Geegee?

"I'll come by to pay you as soon as I can," said Galilea. Miss Betty was offended, and through the gleam of her tears her eyes rebuked Galilea. "God forbid!" she protested. "This is a present from Aunt Betty to the two children of my Geegee. Do you think I've forgotten how you used to treat me? I was a sister to you, not a cook. Rolf, remember our beautiful Geegee?"

She stood hidden in the darkness of the backyard, beside the garbage cans. Here no one could see her. With one arm she hugged the opened cardboard carton, and in the other hand she clutched the two bulging *fallafel* portions, the chocolate bars stuffed in the pockets of her tentlike coat. Her fingers mushed in the pastry cream. She crammed it into her mouth with a ladlelike hand.

Mute and lightless, the backs of the houses closed in on her. Way off in the night sky, the circular airline ads blinked on and off. Feeding her anxiety, she scooped the food in by the mouthful, numb to all taste. Somewhere in the recesses of her mind a limitless insatiable vacuum seemed to gape. The pungent garlic smell of the *fallafel* urged her to bite into the balls although her mouth was still full of sweet cake. Pangs of nausea welled in her throat, but the pain of hunger within her was fiercer still.

Green beads of flame flickered at her in the darkness from among the garbage cans, cats materializing all around her, whining like babies for their portion. She was horrified that she was stealing Betty's gift to her children. She chewed the chocolate with the remaining *fallafel* and tossed away the cardboard box when it was empty. The cats slunk soundlessly away. And in their loneliness and hunger she felt her own loneliness and aching hunger. Now that the food was gone, she was stripped of everything, desolate, haunted again by the curse. She stood like a pariah, enclosed by dark walls, licking sticky empty fingers, unable to bear the thought of being seen by Harry now. An iron band of despair tightened around her head.

She was spent. She leaned against a wall. Tears rolled down her face. *"Rolf, remember our beautiful Geegee?"*

2

Professor Michael Glick turned on the tap and removed the rubber gloves from his hands. The *khamseen* had clotted the talcum powder between his fingers, and he took pleasure in the coolness of the running water. He scrubbed his hands, sliding the soap from hand to hand, as thoroughly as if he were preparing for an operation, although in fact he had just finished his work in the clinic.

Nurse Ilza appeared in the scrub-room door. Out of habit she grabbed a sterile towel and handed it to the surgeon. "Professor," she said, "a second call from the King's palace. Dr. Fawzi diagnosed an extrauterine. They insist on having you come this afternoon for consultation."

"Which means," said Professor Glick, "that for dinner tonight we'll have royal pigeons stuffed with rice out of a roasted lamb's belly, *insh'Allah!*"

"But, Professor, you've forgotten that this is the Arabs' Fast of Ramadan," the nurse said with a smile.

√

"In that case, we'll have to make do with Viennese schnitzel and Czech dumplings, not to mention a knife and fork."

Professor Glick turned and headed for his private quarters where his family was gathered for lunch.

"Hi, Papa!" Galilea gleefully welcomed his entrance to the dining room. Now at last she'd be able to relax; the tribe of women had been after her like a court of inquisitors. "Is this the way a gentleman behaves—making the ladies wait for him at lunch? Huh, Professor?" She grinned impudently at her father.

From the faces of the women seated around the table, Professor Glick had a pretty good idea of what the conversation had been about. He'd be lucky if the cloud hanging over the table didn't burst during the meal, shattering his pleasure in the noon-hour news and making his siesta a doubtful prospect. The stiff silence on one side of the table and Geegee's exclamation of joy on the other—more a cry for help against this united front set up against her—indicated that his chances of emerging in one piece from between these warring camps could be assessed as slim indeed.

Professor Glick sat at the head of the table, and on his face were the characteristic humor and equanimity that never deserted him. "I was told this was a hen party, strictly for ladies. I didn't want to intrude."

Madame Glick reached for the electric bell hanging from the chandelier. She rang three times, a signal that the Professor was seated and the first course was to be served.

"You'd love that, Papa, one eternal hen party. If it weren't for lunch, you wouldn't care if you didn't see your daughter all year round. I've got you figured out, Papa."

"Shh, shh, Galilea. Address your father respectfully!" Mama protested to Galilea.

"Mama" was Madame Glick's mother. But among all the

other family customs, it was established that the grandchildren called her not "Granny" but "Mama." This as a talisman against recalcitrant time.

"If you really wanted your father's company so badly, you wouldn't refuse to attend the tea this afternoon," continued Mama. "I insist that you go. Do you hear me?"

"Mama," replied Galilea, "I've told you a thousand-and-one times that I'm just not interested in those people, and you know it. And don't you worry about me being an old maid. At least wait till I'm twenty."

Madame Glick, always as elegant as a mannequin in an exclusive shop window, aligned her husband's top plate with the bottom one so their gold-painted flowers would match precisely, and noted, *"Bon ton,* my child, indicates that you attend. You know that the Hoffnagels requested this invitation to the tea especially to see you."

"One of the best and wealthiest families in the country," added Mama with relish. "Besides being a lawyer, the son is director of their bank. You don't deserve a young man like that."

Madame Glick wanted to keep Galilea from a hasty reply. She knew her only child well. "Mother"—she deliberately turned to Mama to divert her attention—"I've arranged for the hairdresser to be here for you at four," she said, touching her finger to her mother's temple where the roots showed white through the black dyed hair.

Betty, the cook, set a steaming tureen of soup on the table and, turning to go, winked secretively at Galilea to let her know one of her suitors had called.

Madame Glick scooped up a ladleful of broth and began filling the bowls, which were passed to her in order.

"Thanks, none for me," said Galilea. "I don't feel like eating."

Aunt Anna sat through this in stony straight-backed silence. But on her face was a mute reproach of her sister, Madame Glick, who allowed flocks of boys to make themselves at home in Galilea's room, boys whose origins she couldn't even guess at. A terrible shame! An insult to the entire family! And what if their only daughter should fall in love with a lower-class boy? Why didn't her parents force her to put a stop to all this? They weren't parents but gypsies!

Aunt Anna was unmarried and getting old. Her perfect match had not yet come along. Certainly if her sister could find a husband like Professor Glick there must be one for her too, not a notch lower. So she waited, tight-lipped, in the hope that the wave of refugees from Germany would wash upon her shore some illustrious homeless professor. Meanwhile, the hairdresser who dyed Mama's hair black bleached Aunt Anna's graying head to blond.

"By the time I was your age, I already had three children," Mama continued her tirade against Galilea, "and you're pressing your luck. I say you're pressing it."

"Mother," Madame Glick interposed, "do you remember what Father, may he rest in peace, used to quote from the Talmud? 'Forty days before a man is born a voice from heaven announces, "The son of father X to the daughter of father Y." ' Don't worry, Mother, whoever is destined for Galilea has already been born."

Aunt Anna jerked her head up as if she were wriggling free of an overtight collar. "If a young lady isn't careful with her reputation, even the one heaven destines will turn his back on her."

Galilea pushed the main course away. "I'll just have coffee today," she said.

Professor Glick raised his eyes from his plate to her. "Really this has gone too far."

"I just don't have any appetite today, Papa."

"It's not only today. It's every day," he scolded his daughter. "You're destroying your body when it should be developing. You look like a skeleton."

"Good thing for me you weren't one of the judges who chose me at the Student Ball," Galilea said teasingly.

"That's right, *you* speak to her," Mama said to Professor Glick. "You are her father. She must obey you. Tell her she must be present at the tea this afternoon."

"Galilea isn't a little girl any more," he said. As he spoke, his lighted cigarette moved up and down between his lips. "She'll learn from her own mistakes."

"Long live my Papa!" crowed Galilea. She hugged her father and planted an ardent kiss on the side of his cheek.

Madame Glick pulled Galilea toward her. She loved to sit her daughter on her lap like a little girl. Pressing her face against Galilea's, she turned to Mama and said again, "Don't worry, Mother, whoever is meant for Galilea has already been born. You'll see, Mother, any moment he'll be here. You can be sure he's already coming for her. He's already on his way . . ."

3

He was on his way.

Behind him, the sky still held low a clot of night; ahead, the light of a February dawn was flaring. Harry was headed east.

It is said that a day comes when the murderer returns

to the scene of his crime, but no one knows that the murdered too returns to the place where he was murdered. It
is, perhaps, the spirit of the victim which summons the murdered to this encounter.

He was on his way from Auschwitz, back to the ghetto
from which he had been snatched.

For it was not in Auschwitz but while still in the ghetto
that his soul had been killed. He had passed into the planet
Auschwitz a dead man, as other dead men pass into the ultimate unfathomable. Now he made his way back over the
snowy road, stumbling along it as the ghosts, seen and unseen, stumble into our world from some other to wander
among us. Millions of voices within him wailed at the murderer, summoned him to this encounter.

Dense forests of pines on both sides of the road accompanied him, trees capped by snow turbans. From among
their trunks the German threat still sputtered its final spasms
onto the road. But he could no longer sense it. For Harry,
indeed, that danger was unreal.

By this time, almost all of Polish Upper Silesia had been
taken by the Red Army, but broken remnants of Waffen SS
battalions still lurked here and there in the surrounding
woods, disguised in striped lice-infested Auschwitz garments which they hoped would help them slip away from
the Red Army's iron fist.

Freedom roared in upon Harry like a tidal wave, pounding and surging. Yet, like the drowning man who cannot
see the sea in which he founders, he did not perceive it.
Somewhere inside the shell of his body the pulse of life still
throbbed. Such is the law of nature on this planet. In each
town and village through which he had passed yesterday,
freedom beckoned to him from all the windows, offering
herself to him. But like a space traveler whose ship has dis-
integrated, he had been shot out to a gravity-free nowhere,

unable to reach the earth again, equally unable to find the orb of his destination.

The road was long and empty. A forest of snow standing on both sides. Naked winter trees, naked like the Mussulmen skeletons on the roll-call grounds at Auschwitz, standing with spiny arms raised in the air, their bony gazes fixed on him. He walked between the rows, a bleached and sterile tunnel to the horizon. And their eyes went with him.

He broke into a run, fired by a ray of sun from the east ahead that burst upon his bare skeletal brow. In that instant he felt wings beneath the blades of his back, felt himself rise aloft and hover there, watching his skeleton run beneath on the road surface, a Ka-tzet uniform, borne by the wind. At that split second he seized freedom, hoisted it on his back like a dripping hunk of sun, and raced with it toward the ghetto. For there, only there in the ghetto, could he savor freedom in all its fullness. In the ghetto *she* would run to him with hands outstretched, her hair streaming in the wind. She would fall into his arms, kiss his shaven skull and whisper into his ear, "Beloved, I knew you would come back to this place. I've been waiting for you here . . ."

The ghetto lay silent, beneath a pane of snow. As though purposefully silent. Purposefully white. Shh . . . Nothing has happened here. Nothing has ever been here. The snow isn't hiding anything here.

No one ran to meet him. Somehow, all along, he had known it would be this way. But the glare of liberation had been blinding; it had sparked from some hidden part of his mind—whence, he knew not. Somewhere, on his way here, for a fleeting moment between truth and illusion, there had throbbed inside him the pulse of a new life after Auschwitz, blurring the hairline boundary separating the one from the other.

Vacuum everywhere. Clotted white vacuum.

He lifted his feet with effort and plunged them, one after the other, deep into the snow. He felt like a blotch on the white expanse. As if it had been his doing, this sin of atrocity. Why else should only he remain alive on this bleached and lifeless plain?

Millions of voices wailed within him for the murderer, summoning him to the encounter.

O God! What yardstick to calculate revenge?

He stood in the darkness of the bunker hole in the ghetto. Here he had seen her for the last time. Here they had parted. She to Auschwitz. He to Auschwitz. Separately. He touched the stones of the wall against which she had leaned; he embraced the empty air as if she were in his arms.

Here in this black hole, hands had strangled the infant who didn't know you must not cry when Germans are searching outside for hidden Jews. Eventually, they were all dragged out anyway, the dead and the nearly dead; no one survived.

He knelt to the ground. As he had done once before, he crawled out through the air hole ripped in the bunker wall. Outside, the ladder was still raised to the attic as it had been two years ago, and on it he climbed up again. In the corner, beneath a rafter, lay his sister's notebook exactly where he had hidden it, rotten and mildewed, gnawed by rats. Only the title on the first page was still legible: THE DIARY OF DANIELLA PRELESHNIK.

All at once, reality was forced down on him like the strait jacket on a madman, and the terrible pain of clarity sliced through him, pain like the ripping away of a tooth with a dull instrument.

. . . Preleshnik. Harry Preleshnik. The names he had had were uncountable. Names in the underground. Names on forged identity cards in the ghetto. Names on which his life had hung when, tortured for three sleepless days and nights, he would be shaken out of stupor with the roar "What's your name?" and somehow know at once to utter that name which happened to be on his identity card when they arrested him; names in extermination camps that were simply digits. More than once these names, enfleshed as dread vampires, came back to haunt him in his dreams.

Harry Preleshnik! The only one of his names that let him be, the only one of his names he had long ago forgotten. His own, his real name.

O my beloveds, where have I lost you?

He stood alone in the ghetto's dead white void. Revenge! the voices within him wailed. He lifted his hands to his eyes. Gazed at the splayed stuttering fingers. Skeleton fingers on his hands. Their silhouettes fell across the snow like the footprints of an ailing bird.

He pleaded, "Please, God, light me a way."

The Red Army soldier was standing by the cab of the truck that headed a long military convoy. The massive trucks loaded high, arrayed one after the other beneath the branches of the trees along the roadside, were going to the front. Overhead, machine guns clattered at Messerschmitts, their volleys rapping like hail on empty tin pots. In the wintry skies the planes looked like stray birds who had lost their way back to the nest. The Red Army man rolled a *papirossa* between his fingers, casually observing the battle of planes in the sky. He took a deep drag on his *papirossa* and responded to the man in the Ka-tzet garment, "O.K., I'll take you with me to the front."

The roads of Upper Silesia were filled with the liberated from German labor camps, pushing along in ecstatic caravans: Frenchmen, Yugoslavs, Czechs. Each people with its flag, hastily fabricated from tattered frocks and German bedding; rainbow patchwork banners jouncing in the breeze. On makeshift sleds, swiftly thrown together, they dragged numberless trunks and bundles. The French, wearing black berets, walked in dance, hands raising bottles to the sky. Freedom! Liberation! At home they're awaiting their return. Each one of them knows his home—and where it is. Each wayfarer's lapel is decorated with his national colors. Liberation has come! Singing and dancing, they surged onward, each to his home, his own home.

The truck cut a path through the carnival throng. The Red Army man at the wheel stared ahead through the windshield and let fall a question to the man sitting next to him:

"Where are you from?"

The mob cleaved like waters before the prow blade of a motorboat. Finally the truck emerged. Now the highway ran to meet them.

"Where do you come from?" the Red Army man repeated.

"I come from the White Ghetto," he said.

With one hand, the Red Army man passed a *papirossa* over the tip of his tongue to seal it. "What's your name?" he asked.

The side windows of the cab gulped snatches of forest from both sides of the road. The treetops capped with snow assumed the form of the faces of his family and loved ones.

"My name was burned with all the rest in the crematorium at Auschwitz," he said.

The Red Army man took a deep drag and, staring ahead at the road, said "O.K., I'll give you a machine gun."

They stood face to face: the Nazi naked to the waist, hands upraised, back to the wall, the exposed SS tattoo peering from beneath his armpit.

And opposite him—he, the Jew, in death-camp rags, the gun aimed in his hands.

From outside, through the doorway, the roaring cheers of the Red Army flooding German soil broke upon his ears. Zhukov's troops had reached the Oder; drunk with vodka and victory, they were smashing open the doors of German homes.

On the floor by the Nazi's boots lay a striped Ka-tzet jacket: it has just dropped, on order, from the Nazi's body. In the forest, hiding in a tree, Harry had seen the SS men bury their uniforms in the ground and put on the Auschwitz garments of the prisoners whom they had taken along for liquidation on their retreat. In this disguise, taken from the murdered prisoners, they disbanded, each returning to his home. And, if asked about death in Auschwitz, they could speak of it as eloquently as any survivor.

"*Unschuldig . . . unschuldig . . .*" The SS man begged for his life.

Through a trap door on the floor came the whimper of the German child in the cellar. The SS family had hidden down there. But who better than he, the Jew, could know where to find them? That he had learned from the Germans. The first to emerge from the cellar was a young German woman who immediately displayed an inviting offer on the white teeth of her terrified smile. Confronting the loaded gun pointed at her by a skeleton man from Auschwitz, her trembling hands inched her dress above her white thighs.

Now she was lying in the next room. Soldiers who had stormed into the house like a gale from the steppes of Russia, red *kolpaks* on their heads, their breath the cutting winds of Siberia's tundras, had swept her into the adjoining room, to bed.

"*Unschuldig . . .*"

On the wall, behind the bare upraised SS arms, the pendulum of a clock was swinging—back and forth, back and forth.

And he, all he wanted was to scream at the upraised SS arms, "Look at me! I am the Jew! The filthy Jew, the lice-infested Jew! I am an *Untermensch*! And you are a German. You're a supergod. You decree who shall live and who shall die! Scream that you're human, and I'll be able to see that your blood is as red as all the blood you've spilled. Now roar at me your German roar, as you did yesterday and the day before, and I'll spray you with the fire of your own crematorium . . ."

To drain his soul to its essence was what he wanted. Yet his finger on the trigger held back.

From outside the doorway, a volley of shots slammed into the half-naked body with the uplifted arms. The man in the Ka-tzet garment turned his head. Frenzied soldiers stood in the doorway, one holding a rifle that still smoked. "He was ours," they roared.

The wall in front of him was splotched crimson with a splash of blood. The pendulum of the clock continued swinging over the bloodstain, left-right, left-right. He bent to the floor. He picked up the Ka-tzet jacket. On it, near the dried bloodstain of the Auschwitz prisoner from whose corpse it had been stripped, a fresh blot had begun to spread. In a moment the blood of these two would touch.

He looked at the Auschwitz number on the jacket. Six digits. Like the serial number on his own jacket. For two whole years, its owner had held out in Auschwitz. Probably someone like himself, one of those herded into the forest by the Germans to be liquidated on the death march. And there, on the edge of liberation, death caught him. This Nazi at his feet—was he the one who had shot him before stripping this jacket from his corpse?

He let the jacket drop from his hands. Had not he himself at the last moment escaped from the death march into the forest, his own jacket might now be lying on the floor.

Outside the window, on the sill, stood an empty flowerpot filled with the white of snow. The window was draped with a transparent curtain, and through the pores of the Gothic letters embroidered in its center, "EIN FÜHRER—EIN VOLK," a white sky blanched in.

Outside, the Red Army troops were surging on like mountain cataracts. Armor. Heavy artillery. Giant tank monsters. Cavalry officers charging past on steeds at a lightning gallop, white-red *kolpaks* cockily aslant on their heads, bold faces, inflamed with fire and frost, liquor and victory. Iron. Iron. Iron. Without number. Without respite or hindrance. Onward. Onward. To the storming of Berlin.

He stood there in the chaos and the blood, among the walls of a German home. The cries of the baby rising from deep within the opened cellar sawed at him from one side; the shouts of the soldiers in their orgy with the German fräulein in the next room hammered at him from the other. He could no longer stand it. Suddenly he felt himself excruciatingly alien here. Belonging to no one here; no one here belonging to him. He felt no sense in the victory, no sense in the revenge. He was as lifeless as the corpse lying before him.

The baby in the ghetto bunker had cried exactly this way before they strangled him. He did not know why there was no joy of victory and no joy of revenge within him.

The roads were a mire of slush. His feet stepped on the corpses of German soldiers, run over and flattened by thousands of giant tanks pushing forward. Soldiers' corpses ironed out to paper thinness, impressed like tiles into the muddy snow. The hairy growth on their mangled chests looked heavenward, like the trampled memory of man. The sooty ruins of gaping walls jutted this side and that the whole length of the road. Annihilation and destruction where once there had been human life.

He went on. The wind seeped through the Ka-tzet garment to his bones. The melting snow soaked through to the soles of his feet. And in his hands he bore the heavy load of loneliness and the sealed secret of revenge.

The wail of the Jewish baby from the ghetto bunker rang again in his ears. Not the crying, but its abrupt falling into silence after Jewish hands had strangled it. And he asked himself whether the blood of the German infant in the cellar could have hushed, if only for a moment, the wailing of the Jewish baby in his ears. Only the murderer's blood has the power to wash away the stain of blood borne on the flesh of the blood redeemer. But how will blood wash away blood on a body whose flesh has been burned to ash?

An anguishing void extended around him. No longer was there anyone to whom he could return, his hands soured with the murderer's blood.

He choked with longing for some familiar face, a face from *then*, from a world which had been and was no more. He was crossing a sea of death spreading over the face of this earth. Would his soul's cry for revenge never be stilled?

As though in response to a voice calling him from a hidden beyond, his legs led him on. Where could he seek revenge? And what revenge would it be that could restore to him all he had lost?

Flying high on the houses of Upper Silesia were the red-and-white Polish flags. He knew that more than one Auschwitz SS man had grown up in these very houses. But now, instead of the Führer's portrait, they had hurriedly hung pictures of Polish freedom fighters on their walls. And the women, whose husbands at this very instant were still prodding Auschwitz prisoners in evacuation to the depths of Germany, these same women had suddenly forgotten all about the honor of the Master Race, and brazenly, with choppy Slavic words hauled up from the recesses of their memories, were shoving their naked flesh into the arms of soldiers numb with vodka and victory.

Alone, he walked along desolate roads. Heavy winter skies crouched over the ruins. Evening began to fall over the slushy field of slaughter. In all this vast expanse he no longer had a single stone beckoning him to rest his head.

He lifted his eyes to the pale horizon. In all the world he no longer had a single door waiting for him to come and open it.

The mildewy sky sagged over his shoulders. And, like a submarine eye scanning above the surface, his head cleared a path for him through the murky waters of the sky.

His feet led him, and he followed. Where are the obscured radar ears in man which pick up the voice of destiny calling to him from a hidden beyond?

He left Sodom and Gomorrah behind. He did not turn his head. He was on his way.

4

Splendor of sky above and mirror of sea below converged at the horizon like a giant open conch casting its luminescence up at the sun. They stood facing the water, leaning on the railing of the promenade in Tel Aviv. "David, look!" Galilea exulted, "my wave touched the shore!"

The young man at her side shifted his gaze from her profile to the sea. His feet were shod in sandals, his shorts and rolled-up sleeves bared the solid muscles in his legs and the wispy bronze fuzz on his arms. A shock of hair like a cluster of grapes covered the scar on his forehead. His face was open, clear as the sky above his head. The sky was his, and he was the sky's. Like a child to his parents. That this indeed was so was what David Artzi had to swear when he joined the underground at the age of thirteen.

Why was Galilea suddenly starting her stupid game with the waves? he asked himself. Had she guessed what he wanted to tell her, and was trying to prevent him from saying it?

"Hey, where are you?" Galilea turned his face away from her toward the sea. "Pick yourself a wave at the horizon, and we'll see whose gets here first. Countdown: Three, two . . ."

Tel Aviv. Summertime 1945. Behind them the cafés were packed with men and women in bright garments. They seemed to roll from the verandas and patios down to the promenade like the sea waves rolling from horizon to shore. The Allied Forces, passing through this country, had left a tide of affluence and pseudo festivity behind them. And now the first discharged Palestinian soldiers were beginning to return home.

This morning, when David heard that Galilea was in Tel Aviv, home on furlough from the army, he had called and made a date with her. This time David was determined to get right to the point. But he should have known better than to arrange to meet Galilea in a café. He might have guessed that the kids would be all over their table. No matter where she found herself—whether it was an old folks' home or a kindergarten—life immediately began to bubble around her. With difficulty, he had managed to draw her away from the café.

From his lookout on the beach, the lifeguard bellowed

warnings through the funnel of his megaphone at the horde of bathers splashing in the surf. Not a word of his shouting could be made out, or whether it was meant for the heads swimming farther out or for the board riders struggling with their paddles against the waves. Nor did anyone in the water seem to care.

They stood side by side, leaning their elbows on the promenade railing. He felt her arm brush against his hand. "Geegee." He turned toward her suddenly. "Remember the first time you called me?"

His question stuck in her mind for a moment. It was quite a few years ago. She couldn't even remember what high school grade they had been in. David was one year ahead of her. All the girls had a crush on him, but not one of them could find a way to his heart. A stinger bee with innocence smiling on his lips. A bookworm, made all the more attractive by the girls' breathless whispers about his connection with the underground. It was then that Geegee had bet her friends she could bring this bastion down. Eventually, he found out about the bet. She herself told him. Even so, ever since, David had been her closest friend. He was like a brother to her. Her eyes did not shift from the sea. She concentrated on her wave game with an intensity one would bring to a game of chance. "What made you think of that phone call all of a sudden?" she asked.

Since that first phone call, he had ceased to be a free man. How had she managed to set up such an inhibiting friendship between them, so that he didn't dare reveal his feelings to her? She had turned him into an escort to and from her home on secret rendezvous with the Aussies and New Zealanders. More than once after such a date, he saw the disappointment in her eyes: "He wasn't the one I'm looking for . . ." But who was this restless spirit looking for among those foreign faces? he asked himself.

He looked at her profile. He was determined to tell her that the role she had cast him in since that first call had never fitted him. It was time she learned that David Artzi was not a chaperon. *How did we get to this point, Geegee, that my feelings are invisible to you? And how did things reach the point where David Artzi doesn't have the guts to tell you what you should have known all along by yourself?*

Her eyes were fastened on the sea. Her wave, rushing from the horizon, was coming abreast the paddleboards. A board rider slapped his paddle to break the wave, but the wave dived under and reared its head anew, straightening its back like a blade of silver glittering in the sun. It plunged deep, then rose again, breaking and racing toward the waters near the shore. "David, look how many obstacles are getting in the way of my wave!" she exclaimed. "Now the mob of heads are hemming him in, like guards in a prison compound—but, look, he's sweeping over them, dipping low, and now he comes to the land, falls upon her in a wide arc, and in her is absorbed." Triumphant, she turned to him. "There's a strangeness in you today, David. How come our first phone call popped into your mind?"

"Because ever since that call I've been hearing the same old questions being whispered around me, and I'm sick and tired of them: Who is Geegee waiting for? What's he supposed to look like? Or maybe Geegee is waiting for her mummy to decide who shall have the privilege of becoming part of Professor Glick's family?" Suddenly it rankled that this time once again he couldn't look her in the eye for fear his inner turmoil would become obvious.

Galilea blew a long whistle into his face. "David, you too? Of all the people I'd have expected to swallow this bit of gossip, you're the last. But if you insist on sticking me with your stinking mood, I'll tell you once and for all that I don't know who I'm waiting for. Honestly."

She looked at the tip of the scar usually hidden by the forelock on his brow, now uncovered by the wind. His hair was the color of a ripened orange. Her fingers caressed the fuzz on his arm. She felt close to him, a faithful older brother.

She turned her eyes to the horizon of the sea. And he saw her face traced with inexplicable longing. Each wave arriving from the horizon seemed to bring her a message of promise, laying it on the beach at her feet. On her face was a smile suffused with longing, a smile which lured all hearts, yet put her beyond their grasp. She clasped the railing with both hands, her body tossing back. She stood with eyes closed, her lips slightly parted, surrendering to the passion gripping her. It was clear to him that today, again, he would not speak. All at once he felt that their pathways were not divergent but, rather, were like two parallel rivers flowing to meet a single sea. He wondered whether the man she dreamed of would ever come to take his place.

5

Harry was sitting on the rotting straw. The stable was bare, open to the winds, its doors missing, wrenched off. So much had been taken for firewood during these last winter days it was a wonder that the three wooden walls were left intact.

Moist grimy snow fell outside. Seemingly endless open ground stretched before his eyes. Every now and then it seemed the falling rain was transformed in mid-air into murky stagnant pools. The sky appeared to have sagged earthward after the extinction of the last spark of hope.

The girl was sitting beside him on the straw, silently following his outturned gaze. On the ground near the opening of the stable lay the corpses of four Auschwitz survivors. Before dawn the last of them had relinquished life, and his screams for help had died with him. All night long they had lingered in their death agonies. It seemed as if their wailing would never end. Now—stillness.

Four Auschwitz survivors. They had fled the death march during the retreat from Auschwitz. Once the shooting subsided, they crawled out of the forest. Perhaps they had hidden under the heaps of bullet-ridden bodies in the forest, and were thus spared the Nazi bullet. As if sniffing at the footsteps of their own death, they had made their way to this place. Outside the stable, two days ago, a Red Army field kitchen had been still in operation. Field Marshal Zhukov had a makeshift bunker hastily dug for himself and his staff officers. Then he had gone on to the final storming of Berlin.

Four Auschwitz survivors. Starved, they had fallen ravenously upon the cauldrons with their floating chunks of pork, gulping more and more of the melted pork fat into their taut cobwebbed bowels. They had scrambled after the kitchen truck as it pulled away, the cooks throwing chunks of pork to them as they ran. As long as they gulped —they lived. With nightfall, they screamed in agony.

Now—stillness. Outside, the horizon pressed against the stable. It was impossible to tell the hour. Time, like the rain, stood still between heaven and earth. The girl's eyes followed his gaze fixed upon the grayness without. From here the tanker train that stood on the tracks opposite was blotted out. Everything was shrouded, as though underwater. But she knew: no sooner would the engine blow its first whistle than he would leap from the straw to slip into the oil car and vanish as suddenly as he had appeared.

He felt the touch of her hand on his arm. "Don't leave me alone," she whispered.

He looked at her as though he were now seeing her for the first time. The wisps of straw tangled here and there in her golden hair aroused his pity. From behind two blue eyes, her young and fluttering life begged mercy. He did not know from which death camp she had come, just as she did not know from which death camp he had come. But both knew well the "where" they had come from and the "whither" they had reached. They recognized each other like a pair of arms recognizing the body from which it has grown. He did not know her name; she did not know his. Nor did it cross their minds to ask. Both had fallen from that planet where men have no names. Now the two met here in this world. They were the first. One male and one female in this new world into which they had fallen. Next to them the four corpses, who had just returned to the place from which they had come.

"Don't leave me by myself," she pleaded.

He looked at her. "I no longer belong to this place," he said.

Her lips trembled. Her voice was low. "There is no one on this earth who can understand us, except ourselves. Only we can understand each other, we who do not talk in the language of speech. But with the others? The outsiders? In what language could we explain to them? What could we say that they could possibly understand? And if it is now decreed for us to go out among the living, then we must hold on to each . . ."

She did not finish. She looked at him with a world in her eyes that, except for her, only he knew. The gates of that world stood open in her eyes, and through them he entered and was back. Once more he was *there*. He did not see her now. It was as if she had gone.

Slowly, she lowered her head to the straw. She whispered to him as a doctor murmurs to a consultant at the bedside of a dying man, in a language intelligible only to themselves. "Now there is nothing I am afraid of any more," she said, "except living as a woman with a man. That is what terrifies me most. Because what can we give them? And how can either of us lie beside a woman or a man and at the same time exist in a world which they cannot ever enter and we cannot ever leave?"

He felt her hand reaching for his arm. How overwhelming was the lonely hurt of this charred leftover of a life, cast into an empty world of chaos, yearning to cling to another of its kind, finding no one! He had no word for her that she did not know. Now she was more than he. Chastened and pure. A chastity purer than Eve's before the Sin.

She was the blessing in the curse of God.

Outside, the pale rain fell harder. The torrential rains swept the body of one of the men from the opening to the lake which had formed outside. Only the dead man's face and his bare toes jutted above the water. The rain washed over the corpse, giving it the appearance of an exhausted swimmer floating supine who lets the water carry him on its back.

On the siding in the distance, the tanker train could not yet be distinguished; but, on the left, the plank ends jutting from Zhukov's abandoned bunker could already be made out, their tips like fingers of a hand thrust skyward by someone crying for help.

"What can we offer them," she continued softly, "when our souls are ash and our bodies are as ravaged as scorched earth? The climate of our souls will stifle them. And we too, will any of us be able to breathe without another like us by our side to whom we can return, the way a weary bird comes home to its nest at evening?"

His eyes were on her face. He saw her blue eyes, her golden hair. For a moment he imagined it was his sister Daniella lying near him on the straw. Before him now was the face of Daniella as she had been in the ghetto and as he had seen her, later, in the nightmare of Niederwalden. He shivered. He was cold. He was still wrapped in the Katzet tatters, and his skull was shaven and bare. He could have helped himself to the finest clothes in the houses he had passed on his way; there was not a thing the Germans would not now have eagerly given him, just so he would deign to stay the night in their home. Many German families were scuttling about nowadays to find themselves a Jewish survivor; a Jew in a German home was as good as a charm against evil.

She noticed the shudder running through him and did not understand what it came from. She got up and rushed to the opening of the stable. From one of the corpses she pulled off a full-length Waffen SS officer's coat whose collar and lapel pins had been ripped away. She returned to Harry and put the coat around his shoulders. "Don't go in the tank car," she said. "Let's go together to Gliwice. There you can decide the rest of your journey."

"I will not take one backward step on this soil," he said. "Only onward. And you know where my road leads. My destiny and revenge are somewhere else now. That's where I must go."

She tried to dissuade him. "Do you have to set out at once on such a long journey in the state you are in now?" But she knew that the tank cars, going as far as Rumania, were his only chance to push on toward the east, a chance he would not miss. "Take me with you," she begged.

"The trip is too risky, and you won't be able to stand the ride inside the oil tanker," he said.

She did not reply. They both knew that no risk could match the conflux of dangers from which she had emerged. In her mute forlornness he felt the full pain of his own. As if he were now abandoning his own flesh and blood to this cruel loneliness. His hands reached for her. "My sister," his lips whispered the slip.

Her eyes rose to him. The words "my sister" blasted at her from dim distances a scent of belonging and familial warmth which had long since been wrenched from her world. She inhaled this scent; she clung to it. She did not want to lose it again. "Where shall I find you?" she whispered.

"You know the end of my journey," he said.

She wept softly.

The rain had almost stopped. "I must be on my way at once," he said.

"As soon as I find transportation, I'll follow you," she said quickly. "For now, I'll head toward Katowice. From there, I may even be able to reach Palestine before you."

She walked behind him to the stable opening. In the corner, by her feet, lay the Auschwitz cap of one of the dead. She picked it up to cover his skull. He held out his hand to her. "We part here," he said, and went out to face the wind.

The engine, encoiled in white smoke, was almost hidden from sight. The smoke, in the dense grayness, slithered from the chimney, heavy and viscous, not lifting but overflowing, like milk boiling over the rim of a pot. In all, four tank cars were hitched to the engine. Harry glanced at the ladder girding the tank's round belly. He mustn't be seen climbing it. Last night he had loosened the screws of the manhole lid on the last tank car so it would be ready for him when the moment came. The engine was stoked, but he didn't know when the train would move. According to the Red Army man in the next village, the train had to leave today. One way or another, he must not lose any time getting himself inside.

The tanker's back was wet and slick from oil and rain. His clambering hands clutched at the tanker as it might clutch at the slippery back of a whale floating in fog. He lifted the lid of the manhole and squeezed into the tanker, down the rungs of the inner ladder. A rancid black puddle covered the floor. How many days would he have to hang on to this narrow ladder? And what if he should doze off? He didn't even have rope to lash himself to it to prevent his falling into the rank oil.

The slow train, he had been told by the Red Army man, would likely take days to reach the Rumanian border. He stared down at the bottom. From the black puddle below, a human skeleton peered back at him, climbing a ladder upside down whose top dangled into skies of ash. For days and weeks he'd have to manage this way. What of it? After Auschwitz he perceived time like a beggar who in his dream sees bank notes by the millions suddenly his by inheritance, and he scoops and rakes them in, gathering them into his arms. Mints of time have suddenly become his. A millionaire of time. Millionaire and beggar, both.

Suspended on the ladder, his body was hidden in the tank up to his chin, only his head protruding. Now the other side of that barren stretch spread before his eyes, but the stable was out of sight. Although the rain had stopped, the sky was still a dense humid grayness pressing down over the earth. A lone thin sapling jutted above the surface as if it had sprouted from the ashen void. His hands gripped the topmost rung of the ladder. He thought of the forest into which he had fled a few seconds before the SS men began shooting the prisoners. Now he clung to the ladder as he had to the treetop in the forest, huddled in the crook of its naked branches for nearly twenty-four hours. And again as in the forest, the voice of his beloved Sanya rang in his ears, the voice he heard in the depths of his being whenever he was in danger: "Hold tight, my love, because you will live, Harry, you'll live! . . ."

From the thick of the smoke before him a figure emerged, moving closer in his direction. He recognized the light-colored raincoat. The girl from the stable! Her shoes were catching in the boggy ground, interfering with her walk. Bending down, she removed them and continued barefoot. On her arm was a bundle tied in a kerchief. She was ready to set out. Her eyes searched the train; she did not see his head just above the tanker.

He signaled her with an upraised hand. She noticed him. Then she suddenly sprang back as though to hide from unwelcome eyes. She hurried behind the meager sapling and clung to it.

The brakeman stepped from the thick milky smoke engulfing the engine. He tapped and puttered around the wheels with a long iron rod. The girl watched his every move, fearful that he would catch sight of her.

Forlorn, she stood there, and the hurt of her desolation constricted his throat. But he knew he couldn't take her along. The only ladder was too narrow for even his own skeleton, and he couldn't afford another minute's delay; this train was a unique chance, not to be missed. It occurred to him that he didn't even know her name.

In their world, they were no longer accustomed to names. In Auschwitz you did not even know the name of your shelfmate whose body touched yours on the boards. Nor was anyone insulted when, on turning his head toward you, he found that your call of "Hey, *Heftling!*" was meant for someone else. Quite the contrary, there was solace of sorts in the sound of a voice seeming to address you, even if it turned out to be a mistake. Crazed by loneliness, many had gone off to the crematorium without having had one taste of a word taken from the language humans used in the lost world of the past.

He recalled his own name, and was filled with pity for this name once borne by a human being; now there was no one anywhere whose heart this name could gladden if he should bring it back.

The engine blew a whistle into the emptiness of a burned-out universe. The girl pressed her face against the sapling. Gradually the scene blurred, receding from his eyes. Except for the lone silhouette in the light-colored raincoat still limned against an ashen world.

6

The shiny Cadillac glided softly up Ben Yehuda Street in Tel Aviv, turned left, and the sea opened before them, the setting sun reddening their faces. Dr. Semmering, a paragon of complacency, extended an effeminate pampered hand to the sun visor in front of Galilea, pulled it down, then lowered his own to match. Now they were both submerged to their lips in the deep glow of the sun.

Heavy with dignity, the Semmering banking firm had been established by the family founder in nineteenth-century Frankfurt. But young Semmering had been attracted more to the manipulations of the scalpel than to the intricacies of commerce and finance. At the moment he was one of Professor Glick's junior assistants at the Municipal Hospital.

"Would you care for an *apéritif* at the Plaza Bar before dinner, Miss Glick?" Dr. Semmering asked her.

Thank God he didn't call me Geegee, she thought. But somehow, coming from him, "Miss Glick" took on a sanctimonious odor. His type loved to attach titles to people like sales tickets.

"I really can't stand the British officers who hang around there," she said.

"My dear lady, if only you'd met these gentlemen at Yorkshire, Oxford or London! I must say, the English do have qualities which, if they disappeared, would leave the world looking like Hitler's Berlin or a Baghdad bazaar."

"As a matter of fact," Galilea retorted, "I'd be delighted to see these 'gentlemen' in Yorkshire or London—so long as they're not here. It seems to me it's precisely because of their esteemed 'qualities' that the world achieved Hitler's Berlin in the first place. And, as for the Arab bazaar, I can't see a thing wrong with it, except that these nice 'gentlemen' creep around there too instead of staying put in Yorkshire. Dr. Semmering, please remember that I am a daughter of the Orient, and my loyalties are with the sons of the Orient."

"My dear Miss Glick, I fear you've misconstrued what I've said. My remarks were not at all meant to refer to our legitimate complaints with the British Colonial Office. I was simply attempting to observe the situation from a purely historical perspective. Then again, my words may have been spoken in the high spirits inspired by my present company."

Oh, now I'm supposed to incline my head gracefully in gratitude for that delicious compliment, she thought, just as your future "dear Mrs. Semmering" will have to acknowledge all the other idiocies you come out with, no doubt from a purely historical perspective. "And I, Dr. Semmering," she returned, "said what I did inspired by the light streaming from our Oriental sky at this hour. This is the time of day I love best. I don't think I'll ever have enough of the sunset colors in our country."

"I am delighted to give you such pleasure," Dr. Semmering said, radiating the superiority and self-importance endowed him by virtue of his position among the elite of society. He was just like those British officers she was constantly clashing with in the army and whom she couldn't stomach. It wasn't hard to imagine how this doctor dealt with his patients from the Yemenite slum.

"Dr. Semmering, how is your work at the hospital coming along?" she asked.

He shot her a surprised glance as he turned the car parallel to the sea. He had expected the conversation to take a slightly different turn. Clearly, she only wanted to distract him from what he was casting for. "Well—if all this really interests you—I must come up with a confession: every time your father performs an operation I am beset by feelings of inferiority. I have had the opportunity to observe quite a few famous surgeons at the operating table, but with none of them did I feel as excited as when I watch your father operate. When we surgeons confront the opened body of a living person, we are blind to everything but the one purpose for which we are there. This, obviously, is where we get our extraordinary balance, like an acrobat who doesn't slip when he walks the tightrope because the circuits to his brain have been disconnected and all his energies flow to his feet. With your father, however, you feel the circuits to the brain are never cut off. Watching your father with the scalpel in his hand, you feel that here is Man about to uncover a secret sealed away by God. The hands of Man challenge what was defectively created. And you cannot help shaking."

Incredulous, Galilea stared at him. "Dr. Semmering, how amazing to hear all this from you. I'm beginning to change my mind about you. Please stop here." He pulled up the handbrake, his eyes smiling. Everyone had an Achilles' heel, all you had to do was find it.

"I've been waiting to hear you say that for a long time." His face beamed.

Look at the snobbish smirk smeared on his stupid face! "I envy you," she said. "Would you believe that you see my father more than I do?"

The car had stopped along the road which opened to the sea. Before her eyes, the sinking sun stepped behind a milky screen of clouds, as though wishing to undress before plunginging into her bath, her fiery rays rising from behind the screen, setting the skies and windows of Tel Aviv ablaze.

"I would have assumed that the Chief has always been master of his time, no less than we his assistants." Dr. Semmering was speaking to her profile.

" 'The Chief,' when he was your age, didn't drive around Tel Aviv in a shiny Cadillac," Galilea said quietly. "He dragged himself around on a donkey in the hottest sun to perform his complicated operations, even in Arab mud hovels and under the most primitive conditions. That's where he got those godly hands you respect so much. On more than one such occasion, with those same hands, he'd have to do a Caesarean on a cow that was having trouble giving birth—or else, the Arab sheikh would hint, he could not guarantee that the doctor would return through the wadis to his wife alive and in one piece. On more than one night, my mother, heavy with child, would stand on the outskirts of the village in the wilds of the Galilee anxiously waiting for her husband, who had gone out to his patients at daybreak and had not yet returned. On more than one night, your Chief chased away a poisonous snake slithering out from under his wife's bed. And, you should also know, dear Dr. Semmering, that even then, had he wanted to, your Chief could have set himself up very nicely in Tel Aviv or Jerusalem. They were begging him to. But he preferred to serve those pioneers who paved the first roads in the country. And when your Chief did eventually come to Tel Aviv, they still didn't know that a woman in childbirth needs hospital care. All they knew was Professor Glick's address. All day and all night long. Meanwhile the 'barefoot Galilean'—that's me—grew up without a father. That was how it was while I was in school, and that's how it is now that I'm in the army. *Ma'alesh!*" She tossed her hand in dismissal. "It's better not thought about. Do you mind if I ask you a question? Why haven't you joined the army?"

Dr. Semmering smiled. "I have fulfilled my national obligation *in situ.* Certainly, you haven't forgotten Professor Glick's famous slogan: 'Let us fight the British immigration laws with "internal immigration"!' So I have done my duty here in the hospital, at the gynecological outpost. But as a well-disciplined soldier of Professor Glick's, I'd be delighted were I provided the opportunity to extend his slogan beyond the hospital walls . . ." He offered her a cigarette from his pack of Players, tensely awaiting her reaction to his clever, unmistakable hint.

The gallows in Acre would be preferable to his assistance in increasing the population by "internal immigration"! "That sounds like a good enough reason to dodge the army, though, of course, there is no shortage of older doctors here who could have taken your place," she said, her eyes on the horizon.

The sea's back was inlaid with glistening scales, like a

quivering skin. Each scale radiated a maroon phosphores-
cence, as if the sea were shuddering in anticipation of his
union with the sun. The horizon flamed carmine and mauve,
bedded on glowing dust, while the sea sprawled, pulsating
hot and shimmering. Soon now, the sun would descend to
touch the sea, sink into him, be quenched in him.

Roars of laughter and carousing drifted from a nearby
bar. A gang of drunken army men sped by in command
cars. *"Apéritif?"* Dr. Semmering suggested again.

She did not hear him. The sun at the horizon, half immersed in the sea, seemed like an arched gate opening into
a fireland. From the gateway a carpet of iridescence unrolled to the shore. Someone, now, she imagined, will appear in the fiery gate; he'll linger there a moment before
he steps along the carpet. She caught her breath. Who was
he, the man of fire about to cross that luminous carpet on
his way to shore? And who here was expecting him? She
turned her eyes from the horizon to the beach: two children, like cherubim by Rubens, were playing in the sand. A
boy and a girl. From the distance she could distinguish the
boy's bud of masculinity. Their hands poured out stalag-
mites of sea sand as they built a magic castle. Their little
heads were almost touching. The sandy streams filtered
through their funneled hands, the castle growing taller as
though it were safe on solid ground.

"Miss Glick!"

Dazed, she turned her head. But how did Dr. Semmering
pop up here beside her? What did he want with her?

"Would you kindly allow me one question?" he continued courteously.

"Please," she said at once.

"In love?" He dropped the question with a searching
glance.

If only it were true, she thought. "Exactly, Dr. Semmering," she replied without a pause. "If I didn't think it tactless, I'd ask you to drive me home right away. I have a headache."

When the car stopped at her house, Professor and Madame Glick were on their way out of the foyer. "Not a word about my headache!" Galilea hurriedly blurted. "My mother would think nothing of giving up the concert and alarming half the doctors in Tel Aviv."

When Madame Glick noticed Dr. Semmering's car beside the house, her expression changed into one of suppressed bewilderment, and Galilea saw her mother's mouth purse like the dot under a big question mark. She knew that by turning down Dr. Semmering she was making a shambles of the dream her mother had been nurturing: a huge and elegant wedding in the city park, grander than anything this country had ever seen. Professor Glick's only daughter, the bride—and the groom, the family Semmering.

"How wonderful you look, Mother!" Galilea spoke quickly to divert her. "We had a great time, but my appetite's still at subzero, so I didn't accept my cavalier's invitation to dinner." As Galilea spoke, Dr. Semmering began to confer with the Chief about a difficult case at the hospital.

"Mike," Madame Glick turned to her husband, "we must do something about the child's appetite!"

Professor Glick, who from his assistant's face had immediately read the situation, gave his daughter a quick glance of complicity. "Don't let it worry you, dear girl," he offered, to ease her predicament. "If you insist on a movie star's figure, unhappily you must give up dining like a queen, even in Dr. Semmering's company." Father and daughter understood each other.

Galilea was up the stairs to their apartment by the time Dr. Semmering offered to drive his mentor to Philharmonic

Hall. "Thank you, Semmering," the professor said, pointing to his Buick parked a short way off. "That's my horse over there, but I suspect it won't hurt us to walk."

Professor Glick took his wife's arm. It was impossible to guess who of the couple would be the first to speak.

"Geegee!" called Betty, the cook, from behind the closed door of her room at the sound of muffled steps stealing along the corridor. "Is that you in the nursery?" Betty, who was a refugee from Hitler, had kept the habit of locking her door, even in Tel Aviv, whenever she was left alone in the Glicks' sprawling apartment. "Yes, Betty, it's me in the *nursery*," Galilea called back, and to herself she added: Even when I'm falling apart with old age, in this house they'll still refer to it as "Galilea's nursery."

She put on the light at the head of her couch, Mama's remonstrations passing through her mind. Mama—who for thirty years had never tired of repeating to every man who chanced to take her spinster daughter Anna to the movies: "You should bring my girl up the stairs to the door so, God forbid, nothing bad should happen to her!" It wasn't hard to imagine how Mama must have terrified the boys coming to take Aunt Anna out. Maybe that was why nothing "bad" had happened to Mama's "girl." Aunt Anna was supposed to have been a beauty in her youth. Galilea's heart warmed with pity for her aunt on whom life had turned its back. And what if Aunt Anna, like herself, had secretly nursed a love for a man she had never seen except in her dreams; and, like her, had become blind and deaf to all suitors? Why, then, couldn't Aunt Anna feel for her now? Why did they make her go through such torture as today's fiasco with Dr. Semmering? Suddenly she realized that the pity she felt for her aunt was actually pity for herself.

Who actually was she looking for? What did he look like,

that mysterious stranger she'd been searching for among the motley crew of Australians and New Zealanders who used to hang around the house as though it were a servicemen's club? Who was this man disturbing her dreams?

Worn out, she dropped back on the couch. Reaching into the pile of books on the shelf behind her head, she pulled one out and tried to lose herself in it. Her eyes wandered over line after line of senseless print. She let the book drop from her hands.

She shut her eyes. Betty was playing the Ninth Symphony on the piano in her room; so by now, she would already have smeared her middle-aged cheeks with layers of rouge. It wouldn't be long before Rolf sounded his troubador whistle under her window, and the two would be off to their regular table at the German café.

Miss Betty had fled Germany at the very last minute with only the clothes on her back. But her Rolf, she insisted, must come every evening in his one woolen European suit, no matter whether it was as hot as the desert outside. All day long Rolf wore out his feet dragging his wares from door to door, to the top floors of Tel Aviv's apartment houses: toothbrushes, shaving cream! His elongated bony face made him look years younger than he was. The dream of his life was to rent a kiosk to sell sweets and pastries, then marry Betty. "They'll come from every part of the city to buy Betty's cream puffs!" Rolf confidently predicted. Betty really was a superb baker, and Galilea had promised her that when the time came she'd talk her parents into helping them with the necessary funds. They'd probably get married soon. An odd jealousy stabbed at her.

She heard the front doorbell. That couldn't be a patient, she thought; it wasn't the clinic bell. Betty stopped playing the piano and hurried to open the door. "Glichen!" she called from the hall. "It's young Daavid here to see you!"

Galilea sprang from the couch. "Tell him to come to my room," she called back as she rushed to her closet for a robe.

Miss Betty, who had a nickname for each of Galilea's friends, had dubbed David Artzi "Young Daavid" after the Michelangelo sculpture. And indeed, as he appeared now in the doorway of Galilea's room, his chiseled features fraught with mystery, the resemblance was precise.

"I came to say good-by," he said.

She looked at him and knew it was true. After their last talk she had had a foreboding of a change in their relationship. The pain of decision had been reflected in his eyes. She was quite aware that she was the cause of both the pain and the decision, but felt helpless to prevent either. *Please, David, you can't leave Tel Aviv, not now!* she entreated silently. *Now I need you more than ever.*

"Oh, what a dramatic scene!" her voice trembled with strained laughter. "I'm so happy you came. Why don't you sit down first. We'll discuss it tomorrow, at the café on the beach."

"In a few hours I'll be out of the country, Geegee," he spoke softly. "I came here at the very last minute on purpose."

Her laughter had not succeeded in dispelling the solemnity with which he was regarding her; it hung in mid-air, dangling and contrived. She should have remembered that nothing was as diametrically opposed to David Artzi as a theatrical pose.

The wailing sirens of the armored cars of the British Sixth Airborne Division speeding by outside broke through the open window into the room. Out hunting again for terrorists, or perhaps refugees. She knew that even while David was in the British army, he carried out the riskiest and most audacious missions for the Jewish underground. Although they had been friends for years, this had never been mentioned. Yet now she asked, "Where are you headed?"

"Europe," he said immediately.

"For how long?" she asked.

He blew a puff of smoke from the corner of his mouth. "The hour of departure is always known; the hour of return never."

"What assignment are you off on this time?" She heard her own question escaping, certain she would hear no answer.

"Refugees," was his reply. "Refugees who wait at night to cross the sea. It will be best for me to stay there. I will be like a bridge for feet crossing shore to shore, a bridge which stays put. I have asked my superiors for this transfer myself, because here . . ."

She was shaken. Neither the words nor the style were David Artzi's. His despair cried out to her. Now, for the first time, she felt him reaching for her help. "I don't know what's the matter with me, David," she said quietly.

"Tell me at least that you're secretly in love! That you're caught up in some tragic love affair! Tell me you're waiting for him to poison the woman he's married to! Then maybe I'll understand you and your crazy behavior. But if there's no reason for it—and I know there isn't—at the very least give me some sign of hope."

"You've guessed it, David," she said. "I am in love—with someone who doesn't seem to exist. I'm waiting for someone, not knowing if he'll ever come or where he's to come from. I wait for him night and day. Like you, I too am asking for a sign of hope. Just a sign."

His head sank. He covered his face with his hands. "After our last talk I tried so hard to understand you," he said. "But I can't. No matter how hard I try, I just can't make you out . . ."

She took his hands away from his face, and said gently, "You must have asked yourself who it is that Geegee keeps looking for among all those men? But I can't explain it, not to myself and not to you." Her fingertips ran over the scar that the shrapnel fragment had cut into his forehead during one of the underground operations.

They were standing in her doorway. There was a new honesty between them. "I won't see you to the door," she said. Their hands pressed in farewell. They looked into each other's eyes; then he turned and left her in the corridor. She heard the front door close behind him.

She shook free of her immobility in the doorway. She crossed over to the balcony. Outside, night had come to rest among the treetops. Not a leaf moved. Brine-spiced air was wafted to her from the sea, from unknown foreign shores. "Refugees!" The word rang in her consciousness with a new, personal meaning; tonight, under cover of darkness, David would be making his way to them.

7

Harry stood in the back of the truck at the rectangular opening into the driver's cab. The army truck, racing along the narrow mountain road, was covered by a tarpaulin on all sides. Harry's eyes were riveted on the Star of David painted on the hood, and his whole body trembled. His knees gave way, and to keep from collapsing he clutched the iron rail with both hands.

Survivors—charred sticks—lay on the floor of the truck, no longer grasping the nature of that somewhere out of which they had been spewed. Chips flown off in the hewing of a forest now lost and vanished, bearing within themselves the terrible secret of wood and forest alike.

He was staring at the Star of David, and the roots of his hair stung into his scalp. In trucks just like this one they had been shunted from ghetto to ghetto, from the railway siding to the opening of the crematorium. Into trucks like this one the ghetto babies had been tossed during a Children's *Aktion*. You never knew what face death would have at the end of the journey. Invariably, the trucks took you; invariably, because sewn over your heart was the Star of David. The very same Star of David painted on the hood of this truck.

To begin with, they marked you with a Star of David. Thereafter, like a law of nature, as day appears and as day disappears, so everyone marked with the Star of David was bound to vanish in trucks exactly like this one.

Two soldiers from the land of Israel. In British uniform. Driving the truck through the Brenner Pass between Austria and Italy.

The narrow road the truck sped along girded the flank of the mammoth mountain like a rope. One side of the truck was almost rubbing against the belly of the mountain and the wheels of the other side rimmed along the edge of a chasm.

Two soldiers from the land of Israel. One, a dark-skinned Yemenite, little more than a boy, handling the wheel. An army jacket over his shoulders, its empty sleeves clasped about his neck as though he were carrying a wounded man on his back. Smoldering eyes fixed on the serpentine road, like an eagle in flight following the lightning flashing by its eyes.

And the second, outside on the hood. Red-haired. In a full-length army coat. No telling why he was riding outside. As if he were making a point of demonstrating his calm to them, to assure them that on this dangerous road he was leading them along there was no need for fear. They were in good hands. In the strong light of day, his fair head shone as though it were a beacon showing them the way. A scar gleamed on the edge of his brow, like a natural vein within a gem reflecting the light.

Standing at the opening into the driver's cab, Harry looked at the scar on the forehead of this soldier who had saved him from drowning in the frontier river between the Russian and Allied occupied zones. Then, too, when he opened his eyes as consciousness returned, the first thing he had seen was the scar.

For days and nights on end he had made his way, hidden in the tank car, and later on tops of freight cars carrying him across countries and borders eradicated by blood and fire. Months passed, and seasons. He advanced on foot and on any kind of transportation he could find; his body seemed invulnerable to any danger. Until he got to the river.

The frontier guard stationed on the bank had opened fire on them as they crossed the river. Before Harry's eyes, the head of the man swimming next to him sank beneath the water in a swirl of blood. Abrasha, his companion along the escape route, was drowning by his side. With his last strength, Harry had dived under and dragged the drowning man until he lost both breath and consciousness. When he opened his eyes, there was the scar on the smiling face of the soldier on the hood; beside him on the ground lay his comrade Abrasha, shot in the leg.

Where had this Palestinian soldier suddenly appeared from at the river? How had he happened to be there just at the critical moment? At once, he had plunged into the water to rescue Harry and his friend. Then, on his back, he had borne the wounded Abrasha all along that barren rocky road.

Whose hand was this, reaching out to save them at the last moment? From what world did it come to them? From what home was it dispatched? Who was the mother rushing her son to rescue a brother from drowning? What was the source of this breath which blew new life into him?

Two soldiers. The Palestine badge on their uniform. The one brown-skinned, his hands on the wheel. The other golden-skinned, leaning against the yellow Star of David on the hood of the truck.

And suddenly again—that truck, that same Star of David. Leading him off. The two visions spun in his brain, and he had no strength to contain them. He saw the corpses of the four prisoners lying beside the opening of the stable. In Auschwitz they had held on. There they had outfought death. Yet, in the world beyond Auschwitz, the very food which sustains life had been their death. Would he be able to withstand the plethora of spiritual food streaming from this Star of David, flooding his brain? Wasn't his trembling the onset of his mind's death throes?

He tried to calm himself: the hallucinations of his exhausted brain might be no more than a carry-over from the shock at the frontier river. Physical shock. That was the last border, he told himself. Above all, he must keep his spirit strong. For two Auschwitz years, this Mussulman body of his had sustained him because he had guarded his mind to keep from becoming a Mussulman in spirit. In the depths of hell it was his spirit that was in command of his body; therefore, Auschwitz could not break him. But now he could feel his armor falling apart as if it were wax melting around a candlewick in the blazing sun of freedom.

The truck was scaling a mountain back. Soon it would

reach the peak. Wisps of smoky clouds drifted in the chasms between the mountains. The engine ground as it boiled in steep ascent. Any moment, it seemed, the truck would arrive at the gates of heaven and be swallowed up.

With shaking hands he supported himself on the iron rail behind the driver's cab. He must get somewhere quickly, anywhere at all. Once there, he would be able to carry out the vow he had made to them in Auschwitz. They had left him behind on their way to the crematorium. In each one's eyes was the command: Tell it! Do not forget! He had to keep going until he fulfilled his vow. Hold tight, hold tight, he pleaded with himself.

The face of the soldier on the hood broke into a smile. With hand gestures he was explaining to Harry that from this distance he could not hear what Harry's lips were asking of him, and in the same sign language the soldier let him know that they were nearing their destination. It wouldn't be long now.

Treviso.

Perched on top of the Italian boot is Treviso. Here a unit of Jewish soldiers was stationed, here the first cell of the underground's Operation Escape for smuggling out Jewish refugees was planted, and here was where the first waves of survivors streamed in. In Germany the crematoria were still burning, but here, as over all of Italy, it was apparent in the expressions of the soldiers hanging around that the war had long been over.

The redheaded soldier extended his hand in farewell to Harry. "Nobody here owes thanks to anyone," he said in reply to the look in Harry's eyes. "You can call me Felix. And your name?"

What should he say? His name had been consumed in the mountain of ashes. His name remained behind on the other planet—that name he could no longer call to his lips. "And me," he answered, "you can call . . . Phoenix."

"What an odd coincidence, almost the same name," the soldier remarked as he jumped into the jeep. "See you at home," he called out and, releasing the brake, was gone.

Harry stood there. The central square of the camp was bustling with soldiers. Life surged around him in the stir of words and laughter. Everyone had something to say to his fellow; everyone had someone to turn to. For the first time he longed for someone to turn to him, to look at him, to listen to his silence.

"See you at home," the scarred soldier had said to him. Loneliness was choking him. He wanted so to feel the nearness of another human being, to see a familiar face. To be included, if only for a moment, within the circle of life; to taste again what he too had once known. He looked around for someone in whose nearness he might find shelter. No one here stood as alone as he.

At his feet lay the bundle he had carried with him along the route; his Auschwitz garment was in it. All the possessions of a lifetime were crumpled within these rags. No parting with them any more.

He picked up the bundle and headed beyond the barracks. A notice on the wall of the British PX announced that a Palestinian E.N.S.A. troupe would be performing that day for the soldiers. He was thinking of his friend Abrasha, wounded while crossing the river, who had been taken from the truck directly to the hospital. Soldiers passed by him, back and forth. Life billowed and splashed around him, his loneliness tossing in it like a dumb pebble. The language men use with one another had dried up in him as though it never had existed. And he, in his own eyes, seemed not to exist.

He drifted far beyond the barracks to the dusty road

which ran like a ravine between two sloping mountains. His feet, after Auschwitz, could not quench their thirst for walking. Weeks upon weeks he had walked after Auschwitz, day and night. From city to city. From country to country.

At the end of the canyon, a broad plain opened before him. Suddenly he froze as a burst of laughter mingled with German words struck his ears. Walking past the opening of the canyon were two German prisoners of war. Solid shoes on their feet, Wehrmacht jackets slung loosely over their shoulders, mess tins in their hands. Apparently on their way to dinner. Their stride confident, bold, free. Like then. Exactly the way he used to see them through his barbed-wire fence at Camp Niederwalden after they had herded the prisoners back from the hard-labor area, where each German, with a shovel blade, had killed at least one Jew—his minimum for the day. There too in unbuttoned Wehrmacht jackets; there too with mess tins in their hands on their way to the kitchen.

And they laughed like this in Auschwitz. And he standing among the thousands of naked skeletons lined up for a *Selektion* for the crematorium. The same laughter, language, and smell of smoke rising.

Ahead of him in the distance lay an area surrounded by barbed wire. In high stacks within the compound, huge truck tires were piled one on top of the other. Countless tires. German prisoners of war were busy sorting and stacking them. Probably their POW camp, though it was evident at first glance that the barbed-wire fence had been erected not so much to imprison the Germans as to safeguard the tires against theft.

He could walk no farther. His knees buckled. He sagged to the ground, leaning against the mountain flank, the bundle between his upraised knees, his eyes staring at the barbed-wire compound. The columns of tires towered like

black chimneys against the ashen horizon, and at their base
—the workshops, which looked to him like the structures
housing the gas chambers in Auschwitz. And around them
Germans, at work.

He observed their every move. Everything looked right to
him. Exactly the way it should. Familiar. The way he had
seen them there. The same smell rose to his nostrils. He
sank into the smell, was submerged in it to its bottom. He
was back in the world from which he had come. Suddenly it
struck him: Why didn't a Jew here make a run for it?
The gate in the barbed-wire fence was open, and if he didn't
run, those crematorium chimneys over there were ready for
him. He felt the rush of blood in his veins, tensing him for
flight. Then his senses sobered and he recognized the ab-
surdity of his hallucination. Why, he himself was free, and
it was the Germans who were imprisoned! He struggled
to absorb this; yet the painful reality of Auschwitz for some
reason persisted in him, as if he had not been the slightest
bit mistaken. He was gaping at the barbed-wire compound,
and he felt the frantic mix of time and sights and con-
ceptions in one maelstrom of the mind.

His head was shaded by the cliff. Mute, sealed, furrowed
mountain, preserving within its strata in eternal chromo-
script the secret of the chronicles of time, the secret of shifting ancient dust, pulverizer of eons. He was sitting at the
foot of the mountain as if he were part of its strata. He
thought about the trailing dust of time that would cover
both him and the visions of crematorium chimneys etched
upon the pupils of his eyes.

He lost all sense of time, as though he had been withdrawn from its spheres. He looked around. Soon day would
be gone. He rose, went back to the ravine between the
mountains. Their twin slopes almost touched beneath his
feet. He saw the ravine as the letter *V*, now the sign of

victory. And he in its notch, dragging his feet, broken and alone.

He came back to the campgrounds near the end of the troupe's performance. He stood at the fringes of the crowd. At his back he could feel the barbed-wire compound swarming with Germans. He turned his head toward where the Germans were. His eyes were fastened on the horizon. White clouds, like smoky veils, drifted across the fading sky. Time blurred, trickling through the sockets of his eyes. Opposite him, chimney stacks spewing red-sparked smoke towered among the ashen clouds. He had withdrawn to another time. He stood and stood in it, until he felt a hand tenderly touching his shoulder. He turned his head. A soldier was standing there. Kindly eyes were looking at him. The soldier addressed him in a hushed, gentle voice: "I'd like to help you if you'll let me."

Harry could say nothing.

"I'm the director of the Palestinian E.N.S.A. troupe," he said. "My name is Eli. I know what brought you here. Permit me to help you until you get home."

Home. He felt drained. His only desire was that his strength should last until he fulfilled his Auschwitz vow to tell the story. He was afraid he might collapse before he managed to reach his destination. "Get me a place, any place. Isolated. Just a table. A chair," he said.

"I know how you feel," Eli said. "I'll try to get you what you want."

The cubicle in Naples, which was on the top floor, had three walls. The fourth wall, from the roof to the basement, had been sliced off by a German bomb. Harry was given everything he had asked for. And more. There was a field cot too. But if he had imagined that this was all he needed to carry out his pledge, he now realized that what he needed most was still beyond his grasp.

How many weeks had passed since Eli, in Treviso, had said he would bring him here? He didn't know; nor did he know how much more time would still go by while he sat hunched over the desk, staring at the blank notebook before him. No longer were his days divided into the measurable units of calendar or clock. Time had become one solid mass, and like an amorphous body it stood opposite him, across the desk, its palm covering the blankness of the notebook page. They looked directly at each other. He and time. Two foes. The death of his past world on the one side; his life in present suspension on the other.

"I'll drive you to Naples," Eli had said to him in Treviso. "One of the Palestinian units is stationed there. I know a few of them. They're our boys. I'll tell them and they'll help you out."

In the absence of the fourth wall, a gray rectangle from ceiling to floor gleamed at him like polished steel—the breach gaping at the sky. It could have been sea or sky on the horizon, there was no way of telling. How long had he been sitting here like this, and for how much longer could he go on? When night dropped a curtain of darkness over the breach, he would light the lamp on the desk. Now and then, a star sparkled on the black curtain. He stared at the halo of darkness encompassing the spark until the curtain changed into a filmy blue veil. Then he would put out the desk lamp. A new day.

"At this desk, Phoenix, you'll be able to carry out your mission. The boys here will see to all your needs." So Eli had said in parting. As if this were all he needed to carry it out.

Where was the word with which he could begin if that word itself was cremated within him together with them all? How could he voice the muted scream of those who were no more if he himself virtually was no more?

In Auschwitz, the world from which he had been ripped

and his dream of return to that world had lived before his eyes. Now that he had returned, he saw that both his dream and his world had become ashes in Auschwitz. His yearning for the world of the living and the illusion of finding his beloved ones there—both were denied him. Even to dream the dream of return was no longer possible. Reality stared back at him like a face within a mirror. Existing, yet not existing; himself suspended in between, existence behind and anti-existence ahead.

"At this desk here, Phoenix . . ." they had said to him. They introduced themselves. "My name is Felix . . ." "My name is Eli . . ." "My name is Sander . . ." And he would say "Phoenix." Suddenly he was assaulted by the pain of the name Harry Preleshnik, the pain of the world in which that name had existed. A racking pain so horrendous that only a shattering howl would free him of it. The tentacles of terror coiled about him. The name, his very own in the past, was strangling him. And to save himself his hand shot out in reflex for the pen, as, at that moment, the first words screamed themselves out of him onto the page. He saw the letters of the words. They were flaming before his eyes. He connected them: HARRY PRELESHNIK. Then swept on: Harry Preleshnik was Harry Preleshnik, as every man is someone, with a name all his own, a face of his own, a body of his own. For such is the law of nature that, even though all men are created in one image, no two faces are alike. This is how it was before the train took Harry Preleshnik away . . .

No longer did he see the sky paling with the rise of day or darkening when night descended. As though that other world, where neither day nor night held sway, had spread over the pages under his pen. He wrote without respite. Without cease. He had shed his here-and-now. Passed into the planet Auschwitz, which moves in orbits beyond the boundaries of time.

8

Galilea was startled by the harshness of her own voice: "Sergeant, get that blasted whip out of your hand! You treat your house pets better than this in your British Isles. Look at these people. They are human beings, like me and like you!" The sternness in her eyes had softened, but her voice resounded with the authority of a male nurse addressing a violent lunatic who has broken out of his cage. She held out her hand. "Let me have the whip, Sergeant!"

The Arab workers, a labor contingent in the British army camp south of Cairo, were crouched on all fours, their foreheads to the burning desert sand; beside them on the sand were the loads they had thrown off their backs while hauling them from the train to the storehouse. Nature's sudden upheaval, breaking loose at high noon in the desert—the thickened blood-red sky and the darkened crimson enshrouding the yellow sea of sand—had brought them to their knees in a prayer of terror, and Sergeant Climp's whip, usually an effective prod, was utterly without power.

"Private Glick!" By this indication of her rank, he was, in no small way, hinting at his own. "You can't get no donkey to work unless you beat 'im, and wif'out this 'ere whip, you won't get this pack of asses off the ground!"

The dull sadism of a slave driver spoke to her from Sergeant Climp's watery eyes. Galilea stood opposite him, the supply lists in her hands. "I will guarantee you the freight cars will be unloaded today," she said softly. "Let me take care of it my own way. Doesn't the traffic in London come to a stop when it's this foggy?"

A battle of colors was raging in the wasteland air between

the crimson plunging from the sky and the waves of yellow sand frothing heavenward. The maw of the desert gaped like a wounded beast's, wheezing from its depths a dark thirst. All around, welded by the flame of scarlet, the horizon was hardening into walls. A flushed vault of sky plummeted down upon them, locking the fury within the burning desert. It appeared as though God were again smiting Egypt with blood and darkness in order to redeem the slaves from bondage.

Once Private Glick had undertaken the responsibility for unloading the freight cars, Sergeant Climp left. Opposite her, on all fours, the Arab laborers remained crouched as in a ritual of prayer to this God who was so alien to their enslaving master. *Who today had the right to enslave his fellow man?* Two days ago, V Day had been celebrated, but here Sergeant Climp's whip continued to rule as ruthlessly as during the most bitter battles of El Alamein. As out of inertia, the supply transports continued to arrive from the Dominions to the warehouses; as out of inertia, the whip continued to crack across the bodies of the slaves.

The light in the sky was struggling against the fury of the desert. Galilea looked at the bodies hunched over on the sand, enshrouded in their galabia robes, encysted within themselves like the sealed bales at their sides. Under each galabia, a human being. And she had volunteered for the army to fight for human beings—to check the brown beast that had burst across the German borders to fire more ovens of death. "Now what am I to do with an extra million Jews?" asked Sergeant Climp's Big Boss, as millions of people waited before the flaming pyres for his response, while he, arbiter of their fate, tried to make up his mind what should be done about this excess. As if the word "Jew" were a wrapping under which no human being breathed. Like Sergeant Climp, in whose eyes the galabias covered only a pack of asses. Where was the freedom that should have followed the day of victory? And what sort of freedom awaited her in her own land if there too the Sergeant Climps were still in charge?

Slowly, the Arab workers lifted their heads. Like a good angel, their "Gulea" materialized every time the whip of the Ingleez was raised over them. Gulea—they called her by her first name. As she had asked them to. She sat before them on the sand, an offshoot from their own tree, daughter of a tribe migrated from their tents long, long ago. She exuded the scent of their own climate, the family climate.

"*Yallah!*" Muhammad was the first to shake free and jump to his feet. "Let's get to work!" he called. Every last bale would be unloaded today, just as Gulea had promised the Ingleez. Their eyes regarded her with warmth. As one man, they were up from their crouch on the sand, possessed by the goodness of Gulea's concern for them. In her presence the paths of hope were opened again in their hearts.

Bit by bit, the wasteland began to absorb the red-veiled haze. The Arabs, humps of bales on their backs, trudged from the freight cars to the storehouse in a long caravan against the waning glow of the horizon. Galilea stood wearily with the lists in her hands, longing for the day of her discharge from the army she had lied about her age to join. How different she had felt when she entered the army. Now, the aridity of the desert permeated her soul, as though she had come here full and were returning empty. And what was she returning to? In the parched glare of the sands Dr. Semmering's Cadillac gleamed at her. She could see him at the wheel, she could hear his pompous jabbering, and the aridity tautened within her like the barren skyline. Suddenly she realized that here in this hot desert an unspoken covenant had sprung up between her and these humble

Arabs. Here she had come to love human beings in all their shackled simplicity. A direct line ran within her from the suffering of the Jews in Europe to the humiliation of these people here. The fate of both was her fate. And, like members of one family, they would henceforth have to fight shoulder to shoulder for a common freedom in this area where they must live together. Would the burning bush of the desert continue to show her the way, or would it turn out to be only a mirage playing desert tricks on her mind?

Absorbed in her thoughts, she reached the storehouse and sat down at her desk. She was hardly able to marshal her thoughts—now wandering to her home in Tel Aviv, now to the future and what it held for her. A monotonous unending melody, rising from the column of Arabs still lugging their burdens across the desert from the freight cars to the storehouse, trickled past her ears—a song as unremitting and endless as the wasteland sands. She put down the pen and rested her head on her palms, her eyes falling on the letter she had begun to write to David Artzi earlier that day. For several weeks now, she'd been meaning to write him, but being the camp busybody devoured all her time. If she didn't finish it today at her desk, she'd certainly never get it done in the barracks.

Muhammad suddenly popped up beside her. He stared at her with the white-coated pupil of his one good eye. "*Ya-Sitti* Gulea, can I make for you a cup of coffee very, very sweet?" he offered diffidently, baring his remaining teeth, which were rotten with hashish.

She refused him gently, so as not to hurt his Oriental male pride. "Thank you, Muhammad, but not today. The Ingleez might show up any minute. And you know . . ."

Before he turned to leave, his bleary eye scanned the pile of papers on the desk for a letter of agreement to his proposal of long standing to *Sitt* Gulea's father. Once, after a backbreaking workday, Muhammad had suddenly said to her, "*Ya-Sitti* Gulea, I want you, to buy for my wife."

She knew enough to appreciate the honor bestowed upon her, and she had responded, with suitable humility, "My father is a miser, as stubborn as a mule, and very bad tempered, and he asks much too high a price for me. It will break you, *ya*-Muhammad, because you'll never be able to satisfy his demands."

Not backing off, he had made his offer. "Two young donkeys and eight lambs I'm ready to pay your father for you. I'll get me some land beside the Nile for sharecropping."

"I will write my father of your generous offer," she had answered. "But I'm sure the price he asks for me is really too high, and I am unworthy of the great honor you have given me, *ya*-Muhammad."

From then on, at every opportunity, his one bulbous eye avidly skimmed the papers on her desk on the chance that an answer had already arrived from her miserly, stubborn, and very bad-tempered father.

She watched him as he walked away toward the storehouse exit, her mind festering with questions: This fellah, with his proposal, with the land he would sharecrop by the Nile—weren't they both products of the same enslavement? How much time would have to pass before this fellah realized that two donkeys, even young ones, were not equal in value to a woman with whom he would be founding the future generation, a generation with eyes wiped clean of trachoma, a generation which would refuse to bend its back like a blinded ass for profit-seeking foreigners? And the most important question: If the eyes of this fellah should indeed be opened, would he also see his sister nation in the neighboring country, *Sitt* Gulea's nation, scourged in its struggle for independence?

"Now what am I to do with an extra million Jews? . . ."

She was unable to still the thoughts sifting like a sandstorm through her brain. She was sick and tired of the papers piled on her desk and of the exuberant V-Day celebrations in the barracks. When would that army discharge come through? When would she finally be able to get rid of this damned desert and the boss in charge of it? In Tel Aviv too, the Sergeant Climps would be waiting for her. She rubbed her face with the towel, as if to wipe off with the sweat all traces of her simmering thoughts. Of its own accord, her hand reached for the pen.

Dear David,

As you can tell by the insignia on the envelope, I'm still stuck in the army, waiting impatiently for my discharge papers, just as I am for a letter from you.

I can't make out the reason for your silence. I thought for a while you might have sent letters to my Tel Aviv address and that they deliberately haven't been forwarding the mail to me. But whatever the reason, this time I expect to hear from you without delay.

Two days ago we celebrated the victory we've been praying for so hard. My God! If the kissing that went on here could be measured in miles, I'm sure it would come out longer than the Nile. I don't know why, but I myself felt none of the joy. I'm ashamed to admit it, but that's the honest truth. During the past few days we've been getting more definite word about the Jews in Europe, and the news from the homeland is nothing to cheer about either. I felt ashamed of not being touched by the joy of victory, and I tried to keep it from showing.

As for my future plans—I hope to go to Columbia University right after my discharge. Remember Dr. Levitan, the *Middle East* editor, how stubborn he was? He managed to punch a small hole for me in the G.I. Bill of Rights, the Americans' law for rehabilitating soldiers. And that was no easy feat. In his letters to the administration of the university, he attached some of the articles I published recently in his paper. The most miserable ones, as far as I'm concerned. Apparently they didn't read them, because they answered him in the affirmative and everything is now taken care of. In others words, I'm going to go a long way away. No matter what, I can't stay in Tel Aviv. I've got to break away from that nursery of mine.

I've given a lot of thought lately to your work in Italy to help our old mother in her troubles at home. You must have concluded you can do it more effectively by remote control. Today I decided to follow your lead. So my trip to the United States has a double purpose: first, studies; second, and the most crucial, to do the same kind of work you're doing in Italy, but in public relations, for which America is particularly fertile ground. Every product, no matter how vital, needs a good salesman. And I seem to have been born for it.

The E.N.S.A. troupe has meanwhile come to Cairo, and their director won't leave me alone. As chance would have it, he came to one of my Sabbath-evening performances for our unit. And for some reason he's convinced that he has discovered a new Sarah Bernhardt. The man won't be put off. I, he says, must be the leading lady in his troupe's new show. He even managed to shove the script into my hands, and as far as he was concerned the deal was clinched. Can you picture the new star, with a name like *Geegee*, splashing across the Middle Eastern sky? Actually I did appear once in a regular show in Cairo sponsored by the army, a benefit performance to get winter clothes for our refugees. I walked onstage with a volume of Bialik's poems in my hand, accompanied by a storm of wolfish whistles. It took me a moment to realize that their reception was not provoked by Bialik's "City of the Slaughter," which I intended reading to them, but was in honor of my abbreviated civilian hemline, which exposed a fair amount of legs. I have a sneaking suspicion that all the E.N.S.A. director has discovered is the dramatic potential of my legs.

I must close now, and I'll expect to hear from you right away. I'm truly worried about you. And what if you're not even in Italy?

Your sister,
G.G.

9

"And now, my friend," Felix said to Harry, "let's go down to the mess hall. It's time for lunch. I want you to meet Masha, who runs the household here, an ex-prisoner like yourself. She happens to be my wife," he said with a smile. "By the looks of you, I'd say you could use some extra nourishment. I'll see to it that you get proper treatment from my wife. By the way, is there any address you can go to in Palestine as soon as you land? It's extremely important for all the illegals. You understand?"

Harry was at a loss. Then he remembered the E.N.S.A. director, who had said to him as they parted, "I'd be more than willing to give you my address in Palestine, but unfortunately I still don't have an apartment. But my wife is staying in Haifa with my aunt. Go see her there for a start, and when I get to Cairo with the troupe, I'll come up to Palestine for a couple of days. We can meet again then and make further plans."

"Yes, I have an address in Palestine," Harry answered.

"Fine then," Felix spoke rapidly. "I'm on my way to Rome now. Good thing we ran into each other. I stopped by here to see my wife. There's a good chance I'll be around when the boat sails, and I'll try to get you included on the list for the next sailing. You can feel safe leaving your manuscript with one of the Jewish Agency envoys from Palestine." He looked at Harry's silent, steely eyes. "O.K., let's go down to the mess hall," he said, his glance dropping to the paper on the desk in front of him which had been put aside when Harry entered. He knew that if he did not finish the letter and mail it right away, he might wander around with it for weeks. "Just let me finish off a few more lines, and then we can go down together and get some food." Pen in hand, he leaned over his letter:

. . . Well, as I was saying, dear Geegee, I'm involved over my head. This trite phrase admittedly says very little, but it's all I can tell you in a letter. Basically, I'm living a vagabond's life; I never sleep where I spent the day and don't stay the day where I slept the night before. I did, however, find time to do something which will surprise you.

I can't help telling you again how excited I am about the second goal you have set for yourself in the United States, and I hope to see you in Tel Aviv before you leave for Columbia. It simply can't be otherwise! I await with much impatience the moment when I can see you face to face and show you my surprise.

Good thing you reminded me of V Day. I wasn't even aware of it when it happened. I don't know who actually ought to be ashamed that, of all peoples, we Jews cannot be happy about it and join in the celebrations.

In anticipation of our meeting in Tel Aviv soon.

Yours,
David

Felix slipped the letter into a stamped envelope and put it in his pocket. "All set," he said.

They descended the marble staircase of the bombed-out ruin of a castle somewhere in southern Italy. Felix, on this occasion, was dressed in the uniform of an American UNRRA officer. "Really," he said, "I'd advise you to entrust your manuscript either to an envoy or to one of the soldiers about to return to Palestine for discharge. I'm sure it will reach trustworthy hands in Palestine. Don't worry about it. On the trip ahead of you, your hands must be completely free. You may need them for swimming."

Harry's arm tightened instinctively over the folder holding his manuscript, the folder he wouldn't let go of, day or night. He did not answer.

They entered the first halls. The floors, wall to wall, were covered with straw pallets and army blankets. This was the refugees' last stop before their embarkation on the besieged sea from the shores of Italy to Palestine. For the most part, they were the surviving partisans—the first to emerge from the forests while the crematoria in the heart of Germany were still burning.

The two went into the dining hall. At long wooden tables the refugees sat already eating, silent and withdrawn, each into himself. Before the kitchen window through which the meal was being dished out was a short line. Harry joined the queue, while Felix went on through the door into the kitchen.

It was Harry's turn at the window; looking into the kitchen, he saw the back of a girl whose golden hair flowed onto the nape of her neck from beneath a white cap. By her side stood Felix, whispering into her ear, his hand resting tenderly on her shoulder as she filled two bowls from the cauldrons.

"Come, Masha, meet Phoenix," he heard Felix say. She turned around to the people waiting in line, the two bowls in her hands, and drew close to the window. Their eyes met. Her face was the face of the girl in the tumbledown stable, and her eyes his sister Daniella's. With trembling hands, he took the bowls she offered him.

10

Eli, director of the E.N.S.A. troupe, took Harry by the arm. "Dear Phoenix," he said in his soft mellifluous voice, "if you wish, you may come with me on an appointment I've arranged in Tel Aviv. There you'll be able to meet a Jewish family with roots in this country."

The day before Harry had stammered, almost as though he were talking to himself, "Sometimes I'm overcome with a desire just to see a Jewish family inside its own home again, a whole, intact Jewish family living a normal, well-ordered life—a home with linen ironed and stacked in the closets; a home where . . ." He didn't finish.

Despite the early hour, a long line was queued up for the bus. No chance they'd get on this one. Only Eli, a soldier in uniform, was exempted from waiting in line. Eli approached the people up front and whispered something to them. Their eyes at once shifted discreetly toward Harry, who stood to one side, and their stares mutely accompanied him as he and Eli were allowed to board the bus ahead of the others.

Refugee . . . he's a refugee from the Holocaust . . . Harry could read it in their eyes. The horror crawled through his guts. Why did Eli do this to him? How could he explain that all he wanted was to escape such pitying stares? The bus ride was torture. As if his festering sores had been laid bare for everyone to see.

Tel Aviv. Morning. Two-story white buildings soaked in azure skies. You don't need to lift your eyes to the sky. Hold out your hands, and you will see it spread out on your open palms.

Harry's first morning in Tel Aviv. His soul was divided—
like a field of slaughter sodden with the blood of the dead
yet blooming with succulent corn. Around him people
rushed by, each intent on his own affairs. The sidewalks
were swarming with people, and he shimmered and tingled
at their touch on his body, right and left. He gorged himself
on the crush and pressure of the crowd, this friction of the
flesh for which he was starved against his own. All, all,
brother Jews! He was alive in each one of them now. He
was each one of them. And they were all alive within him.
He alone was not within himself. He was empty of himself.

He was astonished to see how annoyed Eli was, struggling
to pull free of the eddying rush-hour crowds. Didn't he feel
the blast of pure oxygen from this wall of humanity surrounding him? They turned onto a quiet uphill street. Eli
was holding his notebook in hand, searching for the number of the house. "Here we are," he said.

They walked up wide marble stairs. The door of the
apartment stood open. It was morning cleaning time, and
two maids were bent over a long runner, unrolling it along
the length of the hall. One maid opened the first of the
doors along the hallway for them. "Please wait," she offered.
"Madam will be here in a moment."

A heavy oval table surrounded by leather chairs stood in
the center of the salon. Eli sat down in one of the chairs,
and Harry seated himself on the edge of a blue divan in the
corner, some distance from the table. Eli's face was tense,
as though he were not sure that this visit would accomplish
anything.

The door opened. Eli rose from his chair. The lady entering was tall and elegantly dressed. Harry, both hands clutching the worn leather pouch that contained the manuscript,
which was wrapped in his only pair of underwear, remained
seated on the edge of the blue divan, present and not present.

He could not take his eyes off the chandelier suspended from the ceiling over the oval table. Daylight glistened through the crystal raindrops hanging around its many lights. In what previous life had he seen that chandelier? Was he back again at Solomon Schmidt's, the home of his beloved Sanya's parents? He saw the lady's blond coiffure on one side of the table and Eli's military haircut on the other. The two were talking. Now the man's voice was audible, now the woman's. What were they talking about?

The lady rose. Tiny crimson blossoms on her pale dress. Still talking, she took back the photograph from Eli's hand. Now she walked toward him. Why was she coming to him? Had she actually noticed him? Did he really exist here? Her hand held out the photograph to Harry. He heard her say, "There you are, sir, this is the girl. Are you also of the opinion, sir, that such a child should be allowed to perform for soldiers?"

The photograph was half the size of a postcard. Harry held it in his hand. He looked at the flowers on the lady's dress and saw the crystal drops shining from a chandelier hanging in that other home, in that other world. He saw her hand offering him the photograph. He remembered where he was and darted a glance at it to be polite. Only the crystal glare of the chandelier stared at him from the picture. Immediately he returned the photograph to the waiting hand. The lady walked back to the table. What was it they were arguing about?

"Sir," the lady continued to Eli, "she's our only child. We have no one else. Our child enlisted against our wishes. She lied about her age so they would take her. She tricked her father into giving her his signature. We were at the movies when she came in and in an excited whisper told us that a hemorrhaging woman had been brought to our clinic. In the darkness, my husband signed what he thought was an authorization to admit the woman to the hospital. But what he had actually signed was a permission slip for his daughter to enter the army."

Eli was attempting to win her over. He called to his aid the military Rabbinate in Cairo, guardian of the purity and morals of the Daughters of Israel who volunteer for the Auxiliary Territorial Service; he spoke of the moral obligation the community owed its soldiers. He used every dramatic and theatrical gimmick within the range of his velvety voice, but the lady opposite him would have none of it.

"I'm afraid not, sir," she ruled. "My husband and I will never agree to it. Thank God the war is finally over. My husband and I feel that it's about time our daughter was at home with us. She's all we have."

Harry had no idea what they were talking about. He didn't know what Eli was pleading for, or what it was the fine lady refused to grant him. He only felt sorry that this good man Eli was not succeeding. The way Eli kept on, it must be extremely important to him. And there was nothing Harry could do to help. He hadn't even looked at the face in the picture, the object of all this stormy bargaining. Snatches of sentences were all that reached his ears.

"I do understand you, sir," the lady was saying. "I also understand how important it is for our soldiers. Therefore, instead of my daughter, I am willing to give a few readings to the soldiers myself. From time to time, I lecture before various groups. My topics include Ben Yehuda, the reviver of the Hebrew language, the Prophets or, if you wish, the Book of Job. You may, sir, choose any subject which seems appropriate to you."

As they went down the stairs, Eli could not stop grinding his teeth. "What an idiot I was! What demon prompted me to go up there! They warned me not to go near her parents for permission. Now I've just screwed up the whole thing completely. God, what stupidity! The bird was as good as in my hand. What devil dragged me to her parents? 'A lecture on the Book of Job for the boys'! . . ."

11

Galilea walked over to the door of her room and locked it. A civilian again, she said to herself. If only they'll leave me alone tonight!

She switched on the lamp. Just a few days as a civilian and you forgot all about the annoyances of barracks life. For how long could you get excited over soft toilet paper? And for how long could kicking off your khakis thrill you? After a few days, you were swamped by all the petty concerns of everyday life.

She sat down at the desk and rested her head on her hands. The rows of typewriter letters gleamed up at her. Yesterday's sheet was still on the machine, and on the desk next to it was the typewritten list of ideas for an article, numbered in order of priority. They leapt out at her now, throwing her into confusion.

It crossed her mind that this might be the moment to take care of the stack of letters that had piled up on her desk over the past few months. But she'd never felt quite so lazy. First thing tomorrow morning she must go over to the American Consulate—which meant that the best hours of the morning would once again be lost. Levitan would be furious if she didn't bring him the article she promised.

Outside, it was already pitch black. She grabbed a cigarette from the pack on the desk and struck a match with such force that the tip flew off and burned a hole in the carpet. Again she pulled the typewriter toward her. She stared at the sheet inserted in the typewriter before her: white and blank. She got up from the desk and opened the door to the balcony. She drew a deep breath. Thank God the *khamseen* was over.

It occurred to her that she had been supposed to go to the dressmaker that morning for a fitting. After khaki she just couldn't get enough of red dresses. This time it was a dress with red flowers. *"Oh, the lady in red . . ."*

She was sorry now that she'd told Betty to say to anyone who called that she was out. She got a real kick out of hearing the boys who had come back from the army tell about how word of her court-martial for wearing the "Palestine" insignia had gotten around. "Private Glick, do you admit to the charge that, against King's Regulations, you have worn the Palestine insignia on your shoulders?" the British lieutenant had asked during the trial. And Galilea, standing at attention between a guard of two military policewomen, had answered, "I do not! You, ma'am, have a country. You have a flag and an identity by which you are recognized. I have only this piece of cloth with 'Palestine' embroidered on it. And this is my country, my flag, and my identity. Please bear in mind that it wasn't by order of the King that I enlisted. It was the word Palestine on this piece of cloth that made me volunteer."

She threw open the window. After the stifling *khamseen*, the breeze that blew in now was cool and refreshing. Turning on the lamp at the head of the couch, she decided she'd lie down for a while before going back to the article. It was getting started that was always so tough. After the first page, the machine would clatter along like an express train on its rails. Just get started.

She lay down on the couch and, out of habit, reached back to the pile of books on the shelf above her head, picking up the Hebrew book that Shaike had given her that day. All she had to do was discover a library in anyone's house and she was already borrowing a book. Terrible habit. Most of the time they put her to sleep, and all she got out of it was the worry of remembering to return it. But invariably she would find herself again standing before someone else's library, and there was always that one book that aroused her curiosity. Occasionally it was worth the trouble.

She held the book in her hand and, too lazy to open it, she eyed the binding, which was scaly like a lizard's skin. The book flipped open to the middle. She didn't bother to turn back to the beginning but read the first sentence that caught her eye. She turned the pages back to the opening lines:

Harry Preleshnik was Harry Preleshnik, as every man is someone, with a name all his own, a face of his own, a body of his own. For such is the law of nature that, even though all men are created in one image, no two faces are alike. This is how it was before the train took Harry Preleshnik . . .

She was no longer aware of her eyes consuming page after page. Nor was she conscious of her hands trembling as they turned the pages. Hour followed hour, and she was still fixed in the same position as when she took down the book. The oddness of the title and the author's name escaped her; nor was she likely to have noticed them. First from indifference, later because she had been sucked into a world from which there was no return.

. . . like Sanya Schmidt, the heroine of the book, Galilea walked into the ghetto's prison, where those marked for Auschwitz were held. Like Sanya Schmidt, Galilea disguised herself as a nurse and, under the eyes of the SS, rescued her family from prison one by one.

. . . like Sanya Schmidt, Galilea went to the private apartment of the Nazi director of Harry's workshop, and, with supernatural strength, commanded him to bring back her beloved Harry Preleshnik from the death camp.

. . . like Sanya Schmidt, Galilea wandered in the streets around Selektion Square, where the Nazis had herded all Jewish males. Like her, Galilea heard the shots. And, like her, she stood on the streets near the Nazi transit camp, her eyes raised to Harry's face looking out at her through the barred window. She knew: any moment now, Harry would be sent to the place from which no one returns. Galilea was seeing his face for the last time. Seeing him . . .

And as the spirit of Sanya's love followed Harry, so Galilea accompanied him on the way to Auschwitz. By his side in the death camp, by his side at every step he took, breathing into him the strength of her fierce love, to protect him and wrest him from each moment's danger. At every *Selektion* for the crematorium Galilea held up his head. And when Harry stood naked before the Nazi doctor whose decree meant life or death by burning, she was the one who lighted the glimmer in his eyes, which kept them from staring like the lifeless eyes of a Mussulman. And when all hope had died in Harry Preleshnik, when all remnants of his spirit had forsaken him and he crossed the borderline between man and Mussulman, the cry came breaking from Galilea as it had from Sanya, like a command:

"Harry, you will live! You'll live! . . ."

When Sanya Schmidt was ordered into the gas chamber, it was as if the life of Harry Preleshnik had been conferred to Galilea as a trust. During the evacuation of Auschwitz, as the SS men herded the survivors out on the death march, Galilea's breath went with him, pleading all the way: Don't give up, Harry! Only a few more moments to freedom! Look at those bodies lying along the roadside; they were shot because their legs gave way, and all they did was slump down for a moment's rest. Hang on. Freedom is only a step away! Keep going! Keep on! Then, like Sanya, her cry broke through: Now, Harry! Run for the woods. Run! Run!

Again and again, Galilea's eyes settled and held fast on the final lines of the book. She drew into her blood the awesome secret rising to her from the final words:

. . . The red glare of the new day set afire the pile of dead in the forest. Harry Preleshnik struggled to his knees and remained motionless among the corpses. Lifting his head to the rising sun, he seemed to have grown from their midst. Only when the Red Army man picked him up in his arms from the pile of corpses did Harry feel there was life in him.

She closed the book, but her hands reopened it. She examined the letters of the title page—the name of the book: SALAMANDRA. Examined the letters forming the author's name: ANONYMOUS. She held the book in her hands like a devout woman clasping a prayer book. She took a few steps. The typewriter stood uncovered on the desk. From the open closet the new red dresses watched her. Though the new day had dawned, the two lamps were still lighted from last night. She turned them off, and now the light of rising day was flawless in the room.

Everyone in the house was still asleep. Galilea stole through the long hallway. Opened the front door. Went out.

The street was suspended in the sleep of dawn. Empty of people. Almost running, she hurried along the road, on her way to the main thoroughfare, anxious to be convinced by her own eyes that somewhere in the world there were still Jews left alive.

Already sitting behind the newsstand on Allenby Road, the Jew with the long white beard was swaying as usual over a thick tome of Talmud. She could not hold back the urgency within her; she had to hear his voice. Here was a

Jew with his long beard. The Nazis didn't slash it off with the flesh of his face. Here was the face—intact. Here was the Jew—intact. Swaying over a thick tome of Talmud. The bushy brows like awnings over his eyes.

She stood in front of the stand. The Jew did not interrupt his study; he took no notice of her. He was used to hands reaching for a paper, then leaving a coin. Galilea did not move or take her eyes off him. The Jew looked up. He saw a frightened girl facing him. "Paper?" he asked.

"A paper, yes," she whispered.

"*Nu?*" The Jew pointed to the stacks of newspapers fresh with the smell of ink.

"Which paper should I take?" she asked, not hearing what she was saying.

The Jew shrugged. "They're all made by Jews," he answered piously.

She remembered that she had come down to the street without any money. She walked a few steps from the stand, then suddenly turned back. "I thank God you're alive . . ." she stammered at the counter, and was gone.

The Jew shrugged, brought his eyes back to the Talmud and resumed his swaying.

The din at Carmel Market was already at its height. Vegetable vendors were trilling the praises of their produce in Oriental accents. From Cornerhouse on Allenby Road the Jew doubled over by a spinal defect stepped out with his cigarette suitcase and makeshift stand, to set up shop. In one hand he carried the folding table and in the other the miserable case of wares. The eyes in his bowed head swept up and down the street to make sure it was safe to cross. Galilea went up to him, took his table and case of wares in one hand, and with the other helped him across to his usual spot. Placing the case on the table she had set up, she went on her way.

The book *Salamandra* was displayed in the center of the Palles Bookshop window, and from behind the letters ANONYMOUS, Harry Preleshnik was looking at her. She saw him. All of him. As he was. As though she knew him, knew him face and soul. She walked on, he walking beside her.

At the end of Allenby Road, the sea opened wide before her—the sea whose horizon her eyes had always searched with a yearning for the unknown. A tremor ran through her. Now she knew.

12

Harry abruptly withdrew his gaze from the sea, turning toward Allenby Road to see whether his friend Abrasha was in sight. They had agreed to meet at this bench on the promenade, and Abrasha had said he would be there sometime in the morning. Perhaps it had not been a good idea to ask him to meet him here.

But then, where else could he have suggested? For almost a week now, one of these benches had been his bed and his home. In a hotel you had to pay by the night, and almost all the money given him this month by the publisher had gone for clothes. Clothes buoyed him and kept his spirits up. Going by his elegance, no one would take him for a homeless refugee. This was his armor against the unnerving stares the local inhabitants reserved for a refugee these days. God keep him from those eyes!

He wondered about the peculiar juxtapositions in this

country: vigorous youths nightly flung their bodies over barbed wire to serve as a living bridge for illegal immigrants, and the first person to greet you, while the sea still roared in your ears, was the Jewish Agency official who persisted in asking, "What political party do you belong to?" The official waited for your answer. He had to fill in his forms. "It doesn't matter, any party at all," he would say. He practically begged you to name a party. He couldn't care less which it was. His job was simply to note it on his form, just as he did your name and the color of your eyes. If you were to enlighten him, if you actually told him that your name and party were burned in Auschwitz, would he understand? Wouldn't he shake his head in dismay over the boys in Operation Escape who had risked their lives to bring back such a crackpot?

Today he should hear from the publisher about the cellar in his home he'd promised to rent him. He would be the happiest of men if that cellar could be his. During the war, they had used it for an air-raid shelter. All it had room for was a small table, a chair and a cot. That was all he wanted. Simply the isolation to continue writing what remained to be said. Without writing, it was impossible to sleep. But for the thousandth time he asked himself why he should be unable to write on this bench, by the light of day or even by moonlight. Why should every single object he saw in this world of freedom encroach upon his mind and prevent him from crossing into that other, barred world? Would he manage to get the cellar? The War Veterans' Association claimed it for their returning soldiers. But how anyone who hadn't been in Auschwitz could live there was inconceivable.

Perhaps the publisher would be home at lunchtime. True, it made him uncomfortable to disturb a person taking his rest, but still it was better than seeing him at the publishing house. He couldn't bear the thought that the employees would identify him as the book's author. Frequently he had questioned his need for anonymity, but unable to account for it, he put it out of his mind. The thing was more than he could handle. If only that cellar were his. There he could lock himself away from all eyes. Only then would he be alone with those who were within him—as he had been within them during their final moments.

Abrasha was approaching in the distance. He looked much worse than when they last met, Harry thought. They had run into each other by the sea a few days ago, and Abrasha had asked to see him again today. Since he couldn't yet manage Hebrew, perhaps Harry would be so good as to come along with him to several places in order to help him settle a certain matter?

They sat on the bench. Abrasha's eyes, staring at him, were an empty cavernous yellow, as if no one lived behind them. The nervous tic that ran toward his nose was constantly in motion.

"And how's the leg?" Harry asked him. "I notice it doesn't bother you when you walk."

"It's not the leg," Abrasha said. His hands were clutching the cardboard folder he had brought along. "I can feel the end coming. I've written a book. After I'm gone, I want it to be a memorial to my whole family. There's nothing else I want."

All those years that Abrasha had hidden in the feces pit on some Polish peasant's farm looked out from his yellow eyes. Only at night, when the peasant was fast asleep, would Abrasha crawl up from the pit like a night rat and prowl the open fields for something to eat. There wasn't enough air in all the world to wash away the stench embedded in his nostrils. With every breath he took, the nerves of his upper lip twitched upward as if to block the passages of his nose. As if for him the air of this world had lost none of its stench.

"Who will give the account of what happened to us there

if we don't?" Abrasha was whispering urgently. "At the river I saw the Auschwitz number on your arm. Don't you feel you have to scream it out of your guts quickly, so long as you're still not dead?" He pulled a scrap of paper scrawled with addresses from his pocket. "These are the places I'd like you to come to with me."

Harry took the slip from his hand. At twelve o'clock, the underground contact would be passing by here, and he had to be back at the appointed hour. "I hope we can manage this at the first place," he said. "But if we can't do it today, we'll go on tomorrow."

The woman listened to them patiently. She was the owner of a publishing house noted for effective distribution. By allotting some of her precious time to them, she was, in fact, making a sincere contribution to the painful matter. She gave them an attentive hearing. Without taking up the folder containing the manuscript, she explained gently that after the recent publication of *Salamandra*, currently on the market, there was nothing to be added to the subject. Previously, this manuscript might have been of interest to her, but now . . .

"But what is in that manuscript in front of you now could have been written by no one but this man," Harry said, trying to reverse her decision.

"My dear sir," the woman turned to Harry, "I don't know whether or not you've read *Salamandra*. I did. And I must reiterate that, on this subject, not one detail could be added which is not already in *Salamandra*. We publishers don't bring out books for our own consumption. We're only an intermediary between author and reader. And these days the market is flooded with *Salamandra*. My advice to you would be to try one of the newspapers. If it's a success in the paper, you'll probably find a publisher who'll undertake to bring it out in book form."

Harry handed the calling card to the receptionist, an introduction of sorts from the publisher they had just seen. With it, she was recommending that the editor of the morning paper, in all probability an acquaintance of hers, grant them an interview. The woman, indeed, had done her utmost.

The receptionist took one look at Abrasha's sallow refugee face and said, "A benchful of people are already waiting to see the editor." Quite obviously, he was ready to put them off to another time. Then his eyes shifted to Harry, whose impeccable dress suggested that he was not someone to be casually dismissed; the receptionist took a second look at the card, and the name registered. "If you please," his manner changed, "you may go into the editor's office. But I'm afraid you will have a long wait."

The editor's large desk was cluttered with papers and files. He spoke in a low voice to those who came up, each in turn, to the chair across from his desk. Bit by bit, the long bench was emptying.

"I meant to tell you," Abrasha whispered beside Harry, "that, in regard to a place to live, I had a miracle happen. I found one of my father's old acquaintances here, on the south side of Tel Aviv. He, his wife and the kid—three of them—live in a room and a kitchen. At night he lets me open a cot in the kitchen. I'd like them to meet you. I'm probably going to have to go into the hospital, and then maybe you'll be able to stay there. The housing situation is getting worse every day with all the returning soldiers. And what about you? Have you found a place to sleep yet?"

"Yes, I have," Harry whispered in reply. "Here nobody lives on the street." He put his hand over his friend's icy one, which didn't loosen its grip on the folder in his lap. Nodding at him in mute response, he squeezed his hand. "Thanks, Abrasha. I appreciate your offer all the same."

Through the window behind the editor's back stretched a wide empty lot. There, among the wild brambles edged with dried-out gray thorns, the sun blazed. In Auschwitz, as they lay on the planks of the hutch, Harry's young mate had once blurted out, "I'd trade all the years I have left for a lifetime in a normal prison just to have one hour in the outside world again. Just one single hour. I'd trade the rest of my life." The next day at dawn they had dragged him onto the pile of corpses outside the barracks. He wasn't even twenty. Many envied him.

At the horizon, framed in the window behind the editor's head, the rays of the sun were ensnared in the spiky twigs of a bramble bush. The dry twigs seemed transformed into tongues of flame. Harry started at the sight. As a child he had seen a similar bush in a Bible picture-book illustrating the passage about Moses and the burning bush. He remembered the ancient story of the bush with a ram's horns entangled in its branches that was revealed to Abraham, that same ram which Abraham offered as sacrifice in place of his son. A sudden tremor ran through him. Again he saw them, the skeletons lined up for the crematorium . . . Were we in Auschwitz the ram? But who was it that was saved from the sacrificial altar? Was it Abrasha, this snuffed-out refugee who offered him his bed before his hollow eyes shut forever? Or was it he himself, the phoenix, with the name Harry Preleshnik burning over his head in unconsumed letters of fire? Or was the survivor this editor, whose shaggy hair with every turn of his head seemed to catch in the bramble twigs flaming within the window frame? Or were the survivors the discharged soldiers—among whom were Felix and others like him, operating the underground?

He thought of the discharged soldier who was competing with him for the cellar. Which of us has the real first claim? he asked himself. Hadn't he too prayed like his shelfmate in Auschwitz for that one hour of reprieve in the outside world, for the price of normal life imprisonment? And here he was, given that freedom—unlike all those others in Auschwitz. He could sit on a bench by the sea in Tel Aviv. He was free to fling himself into the arms of the city streets, to run in the open and gulp the light of day, to embrace the stillness of the nights. What else did he want? What was the secret constitution of that grayish knotty mass in the human skull called *brain*? How could both Auschwitz and this freedom co-exist there? Which of the two flames would consume the other? Or would they burn together forever behind the pupils of his eyes?

"Thank God," Abrasha was whispering to him. "After this soldier it'll be our turn."

The soldier was still in uniform, although he indicated that his discharge was as good as in his pocket. He was about to go abroad to study, he told the editor. Could the editor use his services as a correspondent? The pile of clippings he had deposited on the desk testified to his experience. The editor seemed to have known him prior to his military service. Here you couldn't help overhearing why each had come.

From a side door a man walked in, a glossy leather briefcase under his arm. He was obviously at home in this office. The editor rose, extended a warm hand in welcome. The newcomer pulled up a chair close to the editor's. His face glowed. He had just returned from a trip abroad and he smacked of freshness, like a newly arrived cable. The editor cut short his interview with the soldier. "I'll think about it and let you know," he said.

The soldier left, freeing the chair for those still waiting. But the editor was already deep in conversation with his guest. "Your dispatches had a tremendous impact," he announced. "I ran them daily, like installments of a suspense story."

"I didn't come in as soon as I got back," his guest said,

"because the publisher was on my back, and I only had three days to finish my manuscript. How does *I Came First* strike you for a title? Great, huh? The publisher's advance will pay for a real vacation. I can use a month's break after the whole ordeal. It was ghastly. You can't begin to imagine."

"Yeah," the editor acknowledged with a heavy sigh, as his guest continued to spout like a fountain. He'd evidently been waiting quite a while for an excuse to write a book, and the chance had finally come his way. Most of the work had already been done in the series for the paper. "Now I just have to get the introduction and two more chapters on paper," he went on. "A chapter on Auschwitz which I visited. Actually, there was nothing left to see there. It was mainly in Lublin and Warsaw that I met the survivors. Another chapter I've simply got to have is on Treblinka. Without these two chapters, the book won't be complete. I called the Jewish Agency to get them to find me two or three refugees from the death camps. I'd like them to tell me . . ."

Turning to look, the editor saw Harry grab his friend by the arm and rush him toward the door.

"Tell the receptionist out there that tomorrow you're to be first," Harry heard the editor's apologetic voice behind him.

They reached Pinsker Street. The sun was beating overhead. A treeless street, without a spot of shade. Harry's face was contorted with rage. "I must ask you to forgive me," he shouted at Abrasha, as if not knowing on whom to take out his bitterness. "Maybe it was stupid of me, but I couldn't stomach another minute in that place. I couldn't take any more of that kind of talk. What the blazes is so difficult to grasp? I just couldn't take it!"

"If I don't understand you, who will?" Abrasha said

hoarsely. "The man I'm staying with predicted like a palm-ist all the trouble I'd have. If you don't come with the recommendation of a political party, he told me, you won't get anywhere here. In this country, a baby sucks milk from a party teat. If the teat doesn't belong to a party, it'll be dry as dust."

"That editor made a good impression on me at first," said Harry. "He probably could have helped you. I shouldn't have lost my temper."

"If I had any doubts before about what my host told me, believe me they're all gone now. Did you hear anyone on the bench forget to throw in something like: 'After all, we belong to the same party . . .' It wouldn't surprise me if that receptionist didn't want to let us in simply because we didn't give him the party password."

"No, Abrasha!" Harry declared firmly. "There are other facts as well. What alternative is there for you except to peddle your manuscript door to door?"

"I'd like you to try one more place with me if you would. A party leader. If I'm going to get anywhere, I'll have to have an introduction from a man like that."

They turned onto a side street and proceeded to a quiet, isolated residence. Climbing the stairs to the door, drops of perspiration trickled under Harry's shirt from the back of his neck to his waist, like flies crawling over his spine. A small nameplate was on the door. They took a moment to catch their breath before Harry pressed the doorbell. It was a long time before they heard muffled steps padding inside. The door opened a careful crack.

The woman blocked the narrow opening, addressing the two young men across the threshold in a hushed voice. "My husband isn't seeing anyone today. Since his return from Warsaw, he's virtually been in a state of shock. He saw the barracks in Auschwitz, and now he's writing a book about it.

I'm sure you can understand that in his state he just can't see anyone."

They turned to the stairs leading down. Behind them the door was quietly pulled shut.

13

. . . Lately I've been feeling as though I'm living in a dream. And I haven't yet even set eyes on him! Still, I know everything there is to know about him. He's a *refugee*—with all the implications that has for us these days. But it doesn't put me off in the least. All I know, with every fiber of my being, is that eons ago I lost him, and now that his wanderings are over, he has come back to me.

How it pains me that I still haven't seen Harry in person. I made inquiries at his publisher's, but they wouldn't tell me anything. "The author wouldn't have signed his name 'Anonymous' had he wanted his identity to be known . . ." the president of Pantheon told me with an ambiguous smile, his expression intimating that I wasn't the first to ask.

I'll have to go to Dr. Levitan and tell him I've decided to drop the whole Columbia business. I still don't know what excuse to use. Levitan put in all that time and energy for me, and most of it because I pestered him to try to rush it through.

In less than an hour, the British have announced a three-day curfew will be in force throughout the country. The Sixth Airborne Division is on the loose again in town. It's much more serious than we thought at first. It's amazing how wrapped up I am in my own world these days, so much so that I hardly notice what's going on around me—despite all the promises I

made myself to go to America and involve myself in the same
kind of work David is doing in Italy . . .

14

As Harry left the Rabinows' house, there was a new lift to
his step. He felt as though he were walking on air. In just
two more days, the key to the cellar would be his. A key
that was his. To a door that was his. Outside of the door, he
would tack a small sign: Here lives K. Phoenix. A man with
a name all his own. Each month he would receive a notice
from the municipality, personally addressed to him: "Dear
Mr. Phoenix! You are hereby requested to pay municipal
taxes in the sum of . . ." And electricity bills addressed the
same way. He too would be among the names of all those
in the municipal records.

The key in his trouser pocket would renew his lease on
existence. He would walk among people as an equal among
equals. He would be one of them. He wanted to shout it out
for everyone to hear: All it would take was just two more
days. Then, like someone meandering absentmindedly
along the street, he could, if he felt like it, mumble to himself, "Oh, *at home*, I must have forgotten the . . ."—there-
upon turn on his heels back to his door, insert the key, and
open it. Ah, what a feeling! A skin seemed to re-form over
his body, that body which had felt nonexistent before the
key. That body without reality had an identity again, with
skin to embrace it—as four walls transform thin air into a
home. Home—only those who have none know its value.

And when he had enough money, he would buy another lock for his door. A Yale lock. And he would have two keys. The little Yale key would be more graceful than the old chunky one. He would thread them both on a ring, and as he walked, they would jingle in his pocket.

All this in just two days. Which meant, since today was Friday, that he would have the key on Sunday. "We'll have to sweep the place and clear out the rubbish," Mrs. Rabinow had said. "I couldn't possibly turn the cellar room over to you, sir, in this condition." Had he asked for the key right then and there, Mrs. Rabinow would undoubtedly have given it to him. But could he have brought himself to tell her that for the next two nights he'd be sleeping out on the street on a bench? His damned pride held him back. They were already doing him a great favor. The way things were these days, they could have gotten quite a bundle as key money. Yet all he was asked to pay was two pounds' rent. No, he couldn't let Mrs. Rabinow know how desperate he was to have the key.

An ambulance was parked in front of the gate to the Municipal Hospital. Two white-clad orderlies were sliding out a man on a stretcher. Harry halted. The thought struck him that Abrasha might already have gone into the hospital. Abrasha hadn't been around since they had arranged to meet again at the seaside bench, and in the meantime Harry had moved from that bench to one on Rothschild Boulevard. Lately, it had become unbearable during the midday hours by the sea. Not a bit of shade anywhere to escape from the sun. On the boulevard at least a man could breathe.

Stupid of him not to have taken Abrasha's address. He could visit him now if he had. It might be that their experience the last time had left Abrasha so discouraged that he saw no point in troubling Harry again. At times he could kick himself for rushing away from the editor's office. But, one way or another, it probably wouldn't have made any real difference for Abrasha. The newspaper continued to run the journalist's series on exactly Abrasha's topic. It made a tremendous impact on the reading public.

Why hadn't he thought of taking Abrasha to Pantheon that day, he berated himself. His private aversion to calling on the publishing house wasn't good enough an excuse not to help out a friend he really cared about. Who had more of an obligation than he to find some way to help Abrasha? His word might have carried some weight at Pantheon. Wasn't he just being disgustingly—unreasonably—egocentric? What was this mania for shrouding himself in mystery? What could possibly happen to him if one or two clerks in the publishing house knew that he was the author of *Salamandra*?

He reached Allenby Road and headed for the sea. Maybe he would find Abrasha waiting for him on one of the promenade benches. There was nothing simpler: all he had to do was write the director of the publishing firm and suggest that he consider Abrasha's manuscript.

Approaching the corner of Yarkon and Allenby, he saw a crowd of people on the sidewalk. A woman in a satiny floral house dress, her bleached hair in a crown of curlers, was struggling in a building entrance with two Palestinian soldiers. With her bulk, she was blocking the narrow entrance and attempting to pull back into the foyer a round-mirrored vanity table that the soldiers persisted in dragging outside. The woman was screaming in Yiddish, "Bandits, my apartment you dare to rob from me!" A sofa and two chairs already littered the sidewalk. "We've got an eviction warrant!" the soldiers argued to the onlookers. "We've got no place to live, and upstairs there's only two of them in three rooms and a kitchen. Let her yell! We've got a warrant for one of those rooms." "Murderers! You'll see when my man comes home from the store in a minute! He'll kill you together with this damn land of yours!"

A cluster of kids on their way home from school were jumping on the sofa. The springs flung them high in the air, as though they had wings. With mocking faces, they mimicked the Yiddish words they did not understand: "Laaand! . . . Laaand! . . ." The argument itself made no impression on them. They were used to this kind of scene. It could be seen any day all over Tel Aviv.

Near one of the many hotels scattered in the area stood a group of glum-looking British soldiers. Too preoccupied with their own immediate concern to notice what was going on around them, they were searching for the hotel the girls had taken them to last night. Where the blazes did that hotel disappear to? And no other girls would do. The girls would be out on their Yarkon Street beat tonight anyway, but the soldiers were already looking.

As he turned onto the promenade, his nostrils were struck by a pungent aroma wafting from the kiosks: the smell of the oil in which *fallafel* balls were frying. It was still too early for lunch, but should he buy some *fallafel* anyway? If he ate it now, would it keep him till evening?

The kiosks were crowded. He stopped at one. The *fallafel* vendor was almost invisible behind the press of customers. Only the tip of his red turban showed from among the hands thrust at him.

Glued on the partition between one kiosk and another was the illegal underground bulletin *Action*. Dark-skinned boys, whose youth was masked by the lines of toil and poverty traced on their faces, pushed forward with outstretched arms, ostensibly toward the steaming *fallafel* cauldron, but all the while their smoldering black eyes were stealing glances at the bulletin. Would the coded signal in the bottom lines confirm that their contact was an underground agent and not a plant?

Jonah. Zivah. Auschwitz. Lord Moyne. Massada. Treblinka. Acre. Gallows. There it was! The eyes caught the signal. The hands reaching out toward the *fallafel* vendor trembled with excitement.

"*Falla-fel! . . . Fal-laa-fel! . . .*" the vendor trilled on as he served the *fallafel*-stuffed *peeta*. Their eyes and those of the vendor met, a wordless meeting in which everything was understood. A common destiny united them. Sealed in fire and blood.

"*Fallafel! Fallafel!*" What dark secret was the Yemenite vendor brewing in his cauldron of *fallafel*? What secret did these boys carry away in the pouches of *peeta*? What was the meaning of the new light in their eyes the instant those white teeth bit into the hot balls of *fallafel*?

Harry made his way along the crowded promenade. He was blind to the people brushing against him, to the multitudes swarming along the length of the beach below. The rise and fall of the waves shuffled the images floating before his eyes, superimposing one upon the other: he saw himself at the last assembly point in the Nazi ghetto, just before they were transported to the death camp; he saw himself at the assembly point in Tel Aviv during the recent three-day alert. Here, as there, they had all been herded out of their homes; here, there, herded by identical arms, sleeves rolled up, pointing a bayoneted rifle at the body. Here were the same young faces, the blond hair, the blue eyes:

Here—"Out! Out!"

There—"*Raus! Raus!*"

The same roar, and the same walk on the way to the assembly point.

God no! No! It was not the same walk! He was breathing heavily, with a growing sense of despair. All these people

here in Tel Aviv, herded at gun point to the assembly point
—how did they dare to malign their European brothers with
questions like: "Why did you ghetto Jews go so submis-
sively to the assembly point? Why didn't you resist? Why
did you go like lambs to the slaughter? Crawl into the
freight cars like worms?"

He remembered the black burning eyes of the Yemenite
boys as they stood at the steaming *fallafel* cauldron; he remembered their faces, sealed with the secret as each went
his way after finding the watchword posted on the street
wall and, with that, he saw himself, crouching in ambush
at night in the mountain cave with just such a boy, waiting to wipe out the radar installation—the eyes of the British occupier scanning the sea for illegal immigrants.

The images kept shuffling through his mind: he saw the
face of his comrade, the underground fighter shot during a
failing raid, the boy in his arms breathing his last in the
wadi hideout; and with that the face of his comrade on the
planks of an Auschwitz shelf, he too in his arms, breathing
his last.

God no! *It was not the same death,* just as it was not the
same walk on the way to the assembly point! There had
never been a walk like that one. It had no antecedent, no
precedent from which a lesson could be drawn. In the
ghetto, you did not look back to yesterday but ahead to tomorrow, not one moment back but toward the moment to
come. All dignity and resistance were compressed into the
fervor of your desire to smuggle the spark of your life across
into the moment to come—with every scrap of your strength,
without help from any human being from the outside world.
Always, only the moment to come; that desire to live that,
in the end, turned you to ashes and left nothing behind but
a lesson for future generations to heed, smelted and puri-
fied in the seven oven pyres of Auschwitz like gold refined
of all dross.

Harry's eyes were on the sea. Along the line of the horizon, he seemed to see rickety ships sinking, and on their decks the multitudes from Auschwitz, pressing against the ship railings, their arms reaching out to him, their faces like ash.

The sun had set, and Queen Sabbath on soft bare feet stepped quietly onto the seashore. Harry sat on one of the benches lining the promenade. Not a living soul was in sight as far as his eyes could reach.

When did the promenade empty? Just before, it had been noisy and crowded. On Friday afternoons, the human trafffic was heavier than on any other day of the week. Even devout Jews came to the sea to dip in honor of the Sabbath. And now only the hush of emptiness everywhere. Immersed in his thoughts, he hadn't sensed the change as it came about.

Now the streets leading from the city to the sea resembled dry riverbeds. Everyone had drifted home, each to his family table, set in greeting for the Sabbath. Poor and rich alike, preparing themselves for the festive meal.

Loneliness seized him like a pain. In the hush of emptiness around him, he ached with a longing to sit once more at a Sabbath table. He would sit in silence. Not saying a word. Merely sit and let his eyes drink in the deliverance radiating from the Sabbath candles. Around the table would be a daughter, a son, a mother, a father. He wouldn't have to tell them who he was. Because, in his imagination, he too would be one of the family, whose identity no one need ask. He wouldn't eat. Just sit and watch. Please, let everything at the table be done just as it always was. And when the stranglehold of reality reached his throat, he would rise from the table and leave.

To taste such warmth just once more in his life. He knew it would lie in his belly like a sweet-coated pit of poison. Which was why he would get up from the table and leave as

abruptly as he had come. But where was there such a home,
offering him a shelter, a table at which he could sit where
they would let him see and be unseen, exist and not exist
at one and the same instant?

He sat on the bench, overcome by anguish. The amber
light of dusk dripped like honey into his soul, searing him with a longing as sharp as a scald. Soon Sabbath
Eve would darken the shore. Down on the sand, the con-
cessionaire was fussing over the last of his beach chairs, carrying them back to their storage place. His bare
feet scurried across the deep sand as though, now that his
sunrise-to-sunset workday was nearly over, all his weariness
had evaporated. Soon he too would retire to his family and
to the Sabbath table awaiting his arrival. Sabbath stillness.
The hour of amber encompassing all. Soon no one would be
left.

At his side on the bench, the *fallafel* he had bought for
dinner lay wrapped in paper. All along the promenade, the
shutters of the cafés and kiosks had been lowered. At this
hour, on any other day of the week, these stalls were a busy
hive of people and lights. Now everything was empty and
deserted. Ever since Auschwitz, he had been beset by hunger at twilight. This was the hour that the bread ration had
been distributed. But this time he did not reach for the
fallafel. If only he knew Abrasha's address he could go there.
He would sit with him on the narrow cot. With Abrasha it
was different; with Abrasha he didn't feel he had to talk.
With him he could be silent. The silence would be as under-
standable as speech. But anyone else would be perfectly
justified in asking right away: Why did you come to my
home if not to speak? Or your silence might be understood
—which would make it all the worse for you. Just imagine:
You walk into a man's home, park yourself at his table, and
say nothing. You may. You're a refugee. A miserable, lonely

refugee. You're a tragedy. Whoever takes one look at you will see the Holocaust hiding behind your silence. You'll keep silent—and so will they. Like the silence of mourners whose dead lies on the ground before them. Only now the dead man is sitting at the table. And just as the dead man, even the dearest of the dead, is taken out of the house, so everyone present will wait anxiously for you to get up and take yourself out. That is only natural. It would be contrary to nature for you to visit again, for then you would be regarded as a corpse come back from its grave to the house from which it had been removed.

Something must have happened to Abrasha, Harry thought. The last time they met he had complained that he couldn't find a job. The Jewish Agency would rather give you welfare than a job. "We are not the Labor Exchange," they liked to say. And at the Labor Exchange, there were endless lines of discharged soldiers. Hundreds of them to pounce on every opening, and their rights took precedence over yours. Neither the employers nor the other job-seekers were overjoyed at the prospect of a refugee. The employers because they didn't want a worker to whom they owed pity. Before an employer even set eyes on a refugee, he knew he was bound to have a halo of torment around his head that begged for pity. And to those others, waiting on line for jobs, every new immigrant was like a plague falling from the blue to rob them of their jobs. Perhaps they were right. Certainly there was nothing the discharged soldiers owed to the recent arrivals. Standing in the line along the paint-chipped walls for the employment clerk's window, you could read in their eyes the question: "Where were you until now?"

Where in fact had he been until now? Where had he come from? Where was he now? Suddenly it was the end of summer, 1939 . . . He was reading the last letter Solomon

Schmidt sent from Palestine to his daughter Sanya: ". . . and tell Harry, your future husband, he'd do better to drown you in the sea than bring you to Palestine." Now the words loomed before him on the horizon. Turgid, dark letters, their tips touching the fading sky, their slanting shadows draped over the line of sea, beyond the sunset, into the chasm of the unknowable and the absolute.

Where had he been until now? And now where was he? He imagined that beside him on the bench, Sanya was sitting. She was wearing the same white summer dress she wore their last summer evening together at the Shafrans' in the year 1939. Sanya—he saw her again. He trembled at her nearness. "Beloved," he whispered, "when you are with me I can't think of time or place. Help me, beloved. Tell me where you are so I will know where I am."

As she always did, she put her head on his shoulder, resting her cheek against his: *My love, sitting here alone with you is so good. I don't know where I am either. I only know that where you are I am. You are my country.*

The sea's sooty horizon rose like a wall before his eyes, and on the water at its base floated Sanya's skull. He saw her as he had then, among the corpses after they opened the gas chamber of the Auschwitz crematorium; rising toward him in the air-tight dimness of the gas chamber, her face so close to his that he could see the beauty spot perched like a pepper berry on her cheek.

Wherever he turned his eyes, he saw her. The ashes spread through him, sifted through his being. He was the endless graveyard where they were all buried and where they lived out their unfinished lives. He was the mourner and the burial ground.

The beach-chair man was climbing the stairs to the promenade. A week's work over and done. He was holding his crumpled sombrero as though he were carrying the day's labor in his hand. Weary and sluggish, his bare feet shuffled awkwardly along the concrete pavement of the promenade, as if they were only at home in deep sand. Anticipation of the Sabbath rest smiled from his sunbaked face. His glance met Harry's—the way a man on an isolated island might see another. *"Shabbat shalom!"* His face brightened as he greeted Harry and continued on his way to his shack on Mahlul Hill.

The cafés along the promenade, in preparation for the summer season, were all done up in gaudy colors like make-up on an aging woman's face. But beyond the rooftops of the cafés, Mahlul Hill erupted in a sickening abscess. Tumbledown shacks patched with planks and pitch blended with trash barrels heaped almost as high as the shacks; it was difficult to tell one from the other.

Now the order of things had changed. The cafés resembled bleary eye-sockets, while over Mahlul Hill Queen Sabbath spread her veil just as the Jewish woman in her shack unfolds a modest white veil to cover over the everyday. Sabbath candles in the open windows flickered toward the sea. The beach-chair man trudged up the hill toward one of the flickering candles, to the family table set in anticipation of his arrival.

"Shabbat shalom." Only now did it strike Harry that he hadn't even returned the man's greeting. The man had spoken to him with no pity intended. Had anyone else been sitting in his place, the man would have done the same. Would he ever be able to look anyone in the face without suspecting that they knew he was a refugee? Was he doomed to run like a hunted animal from every kindly, soothing look?

He craved the closeness of others and recoiled from it for fear they would find out who he was and where he had come from. He wanted so much to be like everyone else.

But how could he enter their homes if they didn't know
who he was. And once they did, his life's disaster would be
exposed to their pitying stares. No sleeve could hide the
Auschwitz number on his arm. Like a mark of Cain, the
number would stand out on his forehead.

More than once Harry had resolved to do it—to go to Solomon Schmidt's home. He knew he would seem to them like
a phantom from another world. They were sure he had
been exterminated. He would sit with Sanya's mother for just
a little while, sit and not speak. Then he'd get up and walk
out of that house, never to return. He knew that when he
walked in no one would make a sound, just as no one would
make a sound until he left. The words—"Sanya has gone to
the gas chamber"—would wrap his face like a shroud. The
words burned on his lips would freeze and stick in their
throats. It was his obligation to see Sanya's mother. In the
ghetto, at the last assembly point, Sanya had said to him,
"Harry, if I don't survive, please go to see my mother. Lily
should be a big girl by then . . ." To this day he didn't know
whether Sanya hated her father or pitied him. She had never
talked about it. But it was clear that until the war broke
out, she had thought of her father as a god to be worshiped.
Nor could anyone doubt that Solomon Schmidt's last letter
to Sanya, the apple of his eye, was written with anything
but love and concern to protect his darling daughter from
the hardships of life in Palestine. During her last moments
in Auschwitz, had Sanya hated her father for that?

No hatred for anyone remained in Harry. In Auschwitz
that too had been burned. A fire gone out, no longer shed-
ding light on either good or evil. No trace of hatred was left
in him, either of the monumental or the petty. After Auschwitz, the outside world had ceased to be worthy of hate
or revenge. His hatred was so intense that it crossed beyond
the absolute and was transmuted into pity. Which was why
all the strings of his soul were set in vibration the instant

he had the slightest suspicion that someone, anyone, was looking at him with pity.

More than once he had been determined to go to Solomon Schmidt's, but his feet led him, every time, in the opposite direction. To appear in the home of Sanya's parents he would need the spur of hate or revenge, but there was none of either in him. Sometimes he was terribly afraid of an overpowering moment, a moment of utter loneliness, when, like one bitten by a snake, he would run to the only place on earth where the memory of Sanya Schmidt was still alive, and as an antitoxin against that snakebite, he would inject the memory of Sanya into his poisoned blood.

He was sure that he wouldn't make it through the night here by the sea. Tonight again, pursued by his nightmares, he would run from street to street in search of some place to take refuge from the images of his dreams. But he knew that wherever he ran, he would carry the images on his pupils the way a woman might carry a dead fetus in her womb.

He rose to get away from the sea. He couldn't bear the sight of it. He turned toward Samuel Plaza, then up Allenby Road. At Mograbi Square he mingled with the crowds of people streaming along the street. To be one of them. To be like them.

15

Harry opened the door of his cellar. He could see the mailman's feet climbing the stairs on his way out—must have brought him some mail. He studied the small white sign over the new mailbox affixed to the door: K. Phoenix. His name. He had a name. He existed. He had a door. And the key to that door was in his hand. His hand took hold of the doorknob. The knob of his own door. Beyond the door, inside, was a room. His.

Well then, this was *home*. A man lived in it. A man who owned a name. The mailman came to him. This much was fact. And he himself was that man.

The letter gleamed at him through the perforations in the mailbox. His hand was in no hurry to open the box. This was the first time a letter had been sent to him in the world after Auschwitz. He wanted to feel the concreteness of his existence, to be convinced of it a thousand-and-one times, and then once more.

He was like a man imprisoned in total darkness for many years whose eyes must gradually readjust when he comes out into the light. The harsher the light, the more intense his pain; and the dimmer it is, the easier the pain of adjustment on the eyes.

The harsher the conditions of his life after Auschwitz, the easier he found it to adjust to the air of the new world. Every addition to the arrangements of normal living jarred him anew. This first letter in the mailbox was like an identity card sent him to certify his existence.

He opened the door. He walked into the room to see it, to be convinced of its reality with his own eyes. He wasn't sure whether he would suddenly be jolted out of a dream and find himself lying in the Auschwitz barracks on the boards of a shelf. Exactly like his first nights in Auschwitz, when he had also dreamed over and over that he was back in his elegant Warsaw apartment which was filled with bouquets of flowers. He had at last finished composing "Millennium." After all those years of groping for the key to the finale, it suddenly came to him, in the dreams of his first Auschwitz nights. When he awoke, he could still hear the notes playing in his ears. Like rays, they streamed from his fingertips. Had he pencil and paper in Auschwitz, he could have unerringly set them down. But after a while, the overture was wiped from his memory as if it had never been. And, as time went on, the whole composition left him, as though he himself had never existed in his first world. As though Auschwitz were his beginning and his end.

He was standing in the doorway. The cellar was small and narrow, immaculately clean, its walls washed in a light shade of blue. He looked around: at his right by the wall was a narrow iron cot covered with a white sheet; at his left, a chair and a small table. Menuhin, the senior among Hebrew writers, had given him the table; it had stood on the terrace of the author's home, and he undoubtedly missed it now. "If you use this table, my young friend, for writing more books like *Salamandra* I'll feel that I've helped you somewhat." Menuhin had made light of it. With *Salamandra*, Menuhin had helped more than somewhat. He had been the first to read the manuscript, and, having read it, he wouldn't let it out of his hands. It was he who had submitted it to Pantheon. And it was through Menuhin's recommendation that he had gotten the room.

His room was windowless. The shuttered air-vent facing the yard was blocked by a protective wall, a vestige of the period in which this cellar had been used as an air-raid shelter. A shaft of sunlight, long and pointed, broke in through one of the shutter slits, stabbing the center of the floor like a javelin. Myriad flecks of dust danced in the beam as though newly born with the knowledge that only within its limits could they live out their obscure lives. Were they to pass beyond it, they would cease to be. They struggled, therefore, for survival, wrestling one with another, one on top of the other, not to be pushed out to their doom. Only when the tree in the yard bowed its head before the wind was the shaft of light, and all within it, extinguished, leaving the room in a mixed, absorbent dimness like the jumble of thoughts whirling in his mind.

He turned, went outside, opened the mailbox. He drew out the letter from the envelope addressed to "Mr. K. Phoenix."

Dear Friend,

I received a special-delivery letter from the American publisher just a few moments ago, in which he asks me to hurry with the English translation of your book.

I have a list of questions regarding the exact meanings of certain technical terms, which are insufficiently clear even in the Hebrew original. If you could clarify them for me, it would help the book, and thus aid in the realization of your mission, which is the sole reason I have undertaken to translate your book for the non-Jewish world. We must bear in mind that the topic with which your book deals is completely unknown to the English reader, your book being the first on the subject. In all urgency, I would therefore appreciate a call from you this evening.

In anticipation of your visit,
Dr. Levitan

P.S. The publisher's agent in Tel Aviv has left me an advance for you.

He took the change from his pocket and counted it. If Dr. Levitan had some money for him, he'd be able to go now to Bethlehem market and buy a few household things. He needed a kettle, a knife and fork, a plate. But first he must buy an iron to keep his clothes in shape. He pocketed the letter and left the room. A sense of being alive stirred in his blood.

Walking down Mazah Street, he felt that he was even up to paying Menuhin a short visit. He had stayed away until now. It had always seemed to him that his bench home on

Rothschild Boulevard was stamped on his face. This time it would be different. This time he could sink contentedly into the armchair in Menuhin's study. Nor would it disturb him if Menuhin served him some tea, because now he was going to buy a kettle of his own. From today on, he too would have all the tea he wanted, whenever he felt like it. Even be able to offer some to others. He'd sit opposite Menuhin in that deep armchair, allowing himself to be silent now that he knew he could speak.

He would go to see Dr. Levitan in the evening. He must, for the good of the book. He should have visited him before. He had wanted to, but being homeless he couldn't return the invitation, and every visit would have seemed like alms to him.

At the Municipal Hospital along Mazah Street, near the rear gate through which the dead are taken out for burial, a group of people were standing around. It is here that the passer-by unwittingly slackens his pace, as though a cryptic hand were reaching out from this side door, slowing him, reminding him. As Harry, staying close to the wall, worked his way around the people, his eye fell upon a handwritten announcement among the printed obituaries. The name leaped out: "Abrasha Steinschneider, deceased. Relatives are requested to call at the hospital office."

Harry found himself standing in the office. "You are a relative of the deceased?" the clerk asked.

"An acquaintance of mine," he said.

"Always the same thing," grumbled the clerk. "Afraid to admit it, so they don't have to pay for the burial. What was the address of the deceased?" he asked.

Harry was taken aback. "You don't have his address?" he asked.

"He was brought in unconscious from the street. All we have is the address on the immigration permit we found on him—Immigration House. And there they didn't have anything listed either, not his relatives and not his address. I can't figure out why they run things so sloppily and irregularly over there," the clerk muttered to his colleague at the next desk.

"I'd like to go to the purification room to see my friend," Harry said softly.

"They took him away in the first car. He's already at the graveyard," the clerk said with obvious impatience.

The taxi halted at the cemetery gate. He didn't have much money left after paying the driver. He had rushed there by cab so as not to be late to the burial. Stepping quickly, he went through the open gate. As he entered he was stopped by the cemetery hangers-on, who offered him a skullcap. With one hand he paid, and with the other he kept the black *kipah* on his head from blowing away in the wind. He didn't know which way to go or where to ask. To the left of the first pathway, outside a small building, people stood waiting in separate groups. Harry walked toward them and with hesitant steps went into the building.

Lying on the floor, their bodies covered and their faces bared, the dead waited their turn to be buried. Behind the head of every corpse stood a tall candlestick with a candle burning for his soul. The walls were high and bare to leave room for much stillness here.

Waxen faces sealed in the everlasting contortion which life, not death, had molded. How hard they had endeavored to mask this authentic spasm as long as life still pulsed within them. In a corner lay Abrasha Steinschneider. No candle burned behind his head, as though this dead man had no soul—or as though he had not yet relinquished it. The gravediggers evidently were certain no mourner would attend this man's funeral. After all, it isn't for the dead the candles are lighted, but for the living.

Abrasha stared open-eyed at the ceiling, like a blind man listening to what is being said to him. His face placid, smooth. Abrasha Steinschneider, ghetto fighter at sixteen, who to save his life from the fire hid for two years in feces, now returned his soul like a child. There was nothing death could unmask in his face. He had but one wish: Would this world, which by day had only allowed him a standing place in a pit of feces and by night had offered him the leavings of field rats—would this world be kind enough to accept his cardboard folder with the pages of writing in it?

Where was the folder now? It wasn't at the hospital. The people he was staying with would probably conclude from his absence that he'd found a job in another city. A few more days, and they would throw the folder in with the garbage. Not a trace would remain of the memorial Abrasha had wanted for his dead family, neither a name nor a memory left behind.

"I never knew I had a bad heart," Abrasha had said to him one day. His heart had held out as long as he was living the life of a hunted rat. But in his first days in Tel Aviv, making his rounds from door to door with the folder clasped under his arm, his heart had given out. Now who would ever know what this dead man's eyes had seen in the mirror of feces during those two years of days and nights? Perhaps he had written on those pages what no other human hand had ever set down.

Who would ever know the anguish of those whose one wish was to drain their guts of the excruciating pain in a scream at the universe? And that was not granted them. In the Nazi death camp, at the last moment of life, such a one came running to the sick bay for the medic to help him cry just one tear before his death. Here was that tear—Abrasha's. Under his arm he had carried it, in a folder.

The gravediggers walked in, and one by one they carried

out the bodies for burial to families who hoisted the casket of their dead onto their shoulders. Harry stood beside Abrasha, in a corner. The gravediggers paid them no attention. As if neither of them belonged here. Although Abrasha was evidently the first to be brought here, the gravediggers left him for last.

The day was waning by the time the gravediggers got to Abrasha. They carried him far out, beyond the last tombstones. At the end of a side path a small pit, the size of a child, had been dug, a miserable heap of soil at its edge. The gravediggers worked swiftly, almost angrily. Once they heard that Harry wasn't even a relative of the deceased, they wasted not another word on him. His presence here was only a nuisance. Quickly, they raked the soil back into the pit. The raking done, not even a mound swelled over the grave. As if this dead man, for whom there was not a square yard of space on earth while he was alive, did not take up any space now beneath the earth. No one said Kaddish. No one shed a tear. Then the gravediggers left, turning to glance at the lone man standing immobile over the sealed grave. Soon the watchman would lock the cemetery gate. They didn't even bother to tell him.

Harry walked along the pathways leading to the exit. On either side of him, opulent tombstones stood tall: black mirrors of gleaming granite and white marble lettered in gold. Names. Names. Names. Perpetuating their memories for the living. Abrasha had left no one living behind; not even his name, therefore, would be remembered. He was the last of his family, the last of his town. Now he too was gathered unto them.

Then Harry stopped. His eyes froze on a tombstone. Over and over he read the name shining in newly chiseled letters: Kreindl Schmidt, from Metropoli. Wife of Solomon Schmidt.

Sanya's mother! The date of her birth and the date of her

death. She had died the day after his arrival in Tel Aviv. If he had gone when he first arrived, he might have seen Sanya's mother still alive. "Harry, if I don't survive," Sanya had said to him, "go to see my mother. She loved you so. Lily will be a big girl by then . . ." Now it was no longer within his power to carry out Sanya's last request. Why had he kept putting it off from one day to the next? Why hadn't he gone right away?

He looked at the new stone. The last thread binding his other world to this one snapped before his eyes. Now he would no longer have to put off that fateful visit. The address was crossed out. Sanya's mother was dead. And now it was harder than ever to understand what had stopped him from going to Sanya's parents as soon as he arrived in Tel Aviv.

Dangling a ring of keys from his hand, the watchman was on his way to his shed from the locked gate. Harry turned quickly to leave. The watchman's face indicated his satisfaction that the visitor was not stopping to wash on his way out as was the custom. As the man pushed the gate open for him, Harry handed him the black skullcap so it could be sold again. And he left the graveyard for the streets of the living.

He crossed the road to the opposite sidewalk. A lantern was already lighted in the kiosk. It occurred to him that he hadn't eaten all day. Leaving his cellar this morning for Bethlehem market, he had planned to grab some breakfast at the dairy bar on the way. Now he felt no hunger at all. A fierce need to smoke seized him, to buy a pack of cigarettes and smoke them one after the other, to the last in the pack. He counted his change. Hardly enough left for the bus back to the city. He remembered that Dr. Levitan had some money waiting for him. Levitan must be expecting him by now, he thought. He walked faster. On Haifa Road, he boarded the bus which would take him to Dr. Levitan.

16

Galilea turned onto Yehuda Halevi Street. From here the road led directly to Dr. Levitan's. It was a cool and gentle evening. The fields of the Germans of Sarona were off in the distance to the left. Recent rumors had it that Sarona was where German butcher Adolf Eichmann was born.

By the time she had reached the crossroads, the area between the Jewish city and the German colony was covered with evening, a blanket of mist obscuring the border between the two. In the city streets, life flowed in its regular channels. Almost tangibly, on her way to Dr. Levitan's, she could feel herself walking toward the crossroads of her own life. The cancellation of the trip to America was the first tearing at the thread with which she had been weaving the fabric of her future. She racked her brain for some excuse to offer editor Levitan after having put him to so much trouble. But what could she possibly say that would make any sense?

Lost in her thoughts, she scarcely realized she had arrived at Levitan's home. Just as she was entering the vestibule, the three-minute light, which somebody else had switched on, went dark. But before Galilea could extend her hand to the switch, the light was back, turned on by someone on the stairs. She walked up the three steps to Levitan's apartment. She saw the back of a man who was standing by the door, waiting for it to open. She drew closer, her eyes on the closed door as she stood beside him. "Did you ring?" Galilea asked.

"I've been ringing for some time," the man answered, not taking his eyes off the door.

"If Levitan is roosting on his manuscripts, not even a bomb will budge him," Galilea mumbled.

"Let's try by putting our strengths together," the man said.

"All right." Galilea smiled. "Let's put our strengths together!"

Their fingers met as they pressed the white doorbell. "Now we must say the magic words together. 'Open Sesame!' " she suggested with a laugh.

Inside, the editor could be heard thudding toward the door. The light in the hallway went out. They were standing in the dark when Levitan reached the door and drew it open. The man stepped back to allow Galilea to go first.

Galilea, at home at Levitan's, immediately turned left, into the guest room, while the man was escorted by his host to the den on the right. She had hardly sunk into the armchair when Levitan came in. Facing her, his hands folded behind his back as though hiding a surprise, he eyed her with a mysterious grin. "Do you know who that was with you in the hall?"

She searched her memory, her gaze on Levitan. Why, she hadn't even noticed the face of the stranger. Standing there by the door, deep in thought, she hadn't really seen the man at her side. "No, I can't remember his face."

"He's the 'Anonymous' you've been going to wit's end to meet."

She felt the prickle of goosebumps on her skin. She rose from the armchair. Wordlessly directing the editor to wait there, she tiptoed from the guest room along the dark corridor. The door to the study was open. He was standing in the center of the room. She saw his profile. He was erect, almost proud, and to her he seemed the last descendant of a rare tribe, bearing in his blood the heritage of his race now vanished from the earth.

Harry Preleshnik.

He felt her eyes and turned to face her. For a long moment they looked at each other. At that minute she could not come upon a single word to say. The lambent blue of his eyes obliterated everything she had been saying to him in her mind. She wanted to cry out, "Harry Preleshnik, you will live! . . ." Instead, she blurted out the most stupid banality: "I read your book!" And, almost in flight, she was out of Levitan's apartment.

17

. . . Lately, I've spent every waking moment in Ruth Rabinow's apartment. It's as if I've been hurled back to my school days, when I used to hang around her place day and night. Undoubtedly, they see and know everything that's going on in my heart. No matter what we're talking about, I always manage to bring the conversation around to the cellar dweller under the very floor beneath our feet. No matter how hard I try to hold back, the need to speak of him wins out. I have lost all control.

At moments, I think I must have lost every ounce of respect the Rabinows ever had for me, but I can't help it. Come morning and I'm on their doorstep. Ruth has been a friend through thick and thin, and she's willing to help me all she can. "But this time, Geegee, you don't stand a chance," Ruth says. "He's not like any of the others you've known. He's a monk who has locked himself in his cave. He doesn't want to see anyone and he doesn't want anyone to see him. He won't come up to us either. He lives down there in the dark cellar, completely alone. He and his mission . . ."

Today, at lunch, Ruth's father was telling us: "When they announced that last three-day curfew, I decided to go downstairs and invite him to come up and eat with us, since he probably hadn't stocked up on food. There was no answer to my knock, so I opened the cellar door. The desk lamp was on. I found him writing. His face was not human. I couldn't speak. I withdrew, forgetting what I had come for."

In the evenings, I can see cracks of light filtering out of his cellar through the shutter slits. Will he answer the letter I slipped under his door?

It was Purim, and every home was filled with the holiday joy. I knew he had no one close anywhere who would remember to send him a Purim gift. And I wanted him to know that there was somebody who hadn't forgotten. On my way to Ruth's my eye fell upon it: twinkling at me in the window of a souvenir shop, on a velvet pad covered with trinkets, was a miniature key with three tiny hooks on the back so that it could be pinned on a lapel. I bought the little key, but I didn't know how to get it to him. Ruth's mother looked at me with those kind understanding eyes and said, "It's your life, my child. No one but you can bring him your gift. You must do that yourself." She handed me back the sealed envelope containing the little key and my note to him: "This key is a symbol from the girl who joined her strength with yours to make Dr. Levitan's door open for us."

No matter how hard I try to make sense of the terror that gripped me outside his cellar door, I just can't. I bent down and slipped the envelope through the crack under the door and ran upstairs as fast as my feet could carry me. Sometimes, in my fearfulness, I imagine that there are ghosts from Harry's burned-out world living with him, ghosts who would rise up in a fury against anyone who dared to come close to him or to encroach upon their hermetic world.

Will Harry react to the symbolism of my gift? Will he open his door to me? It's absurd to expect him to respond normally. How amazing is his desire to be dressed so immaculately. And

maybe that's simply a disguise to keep what he really is from the
eyes of outsiders. How will he ever be able to hear new life
knocking at his door if the world of Auschwitz clasps its hands
over his ears? How can he break through the ring of horrors
encircling him all by himself? Doesn't he need a hand from outside if he's to be saved from himself? How can I break through
that Auschwitz wall?

No matter if he answers or not, I'll write him again. Right
away . . .

18

The waiter in the dairy bar on the corner wiped his hands
on the tail of his apron, pulled a pencil from behind his
ear, and set the pad he had drawn from his apron pocket on
the table before Harry to add up the bill: one yoghurt,
one bread-and-butter, one coffee. The waiter's eyes flitted
over the table, to see whether he had missed anything:
that's it. He totaled the bill. Below the sum his pencil scribbled, "Giora cell broken. Better stay away from home today
and tomorrow. Will keep you posted."

He slid the check under Harry's eyes and with the yoghurt cup covered the upper corner of the bill to keep it
from being blown away by the fan. "Please check the total,"
he said briskly, and not waiting to be paid, he rushed off
to the tables of customers impatient for his service.

Harry crumpled the check between his fingers, slowly
rolling the paper pellet till it was no bigger than the fly
perched at that moment on the rim of the coffee cup. The
words on the check bloated in his mind. *Giora cell broken*
. . . which meant that they might be watching his place too.

The others could at least hide with relatives or friends. But if he were to keep writing, he had to have isolation. Where could he find another place like the cellar? The writing had become as necessary to him as the air he breathed. His life revolved around the axis of revenge, feeding on two sources: his writing about the death of a nation, and his fighting in the underground to bring it back to life.

Construction workers who dropped into the restaurant for a quick bite were looking around for an empty table. Harry hurriedly got up, left money on the table and headed for his cellar. As he opened the door, he heard the rustle of an envelope. He picked it up; inside were just a few lines under the sender's address and telephone number. Even these were too much for his patience. ". . . and when you need someone, remember, I'll be waiting for your call."

He was in no state to grasp their meaning; distractedly, he stuffed the note into his pocket. Dashing over to the desk, he pulled two notebooks out of the drawer. One held a handful of pages salvaged from the diary Daniella had written in the Nazi "House of Dolls,"—a brothel for the Nazis— pages her friend Fella had smuggled to him at the Niederwalden labor camp and which he had hidden for safekeeping in the ghetto attic, then brought to Palestine. And in the other, in chapter headings, was an outline of the ordeal inflicted on the boy Monish, who had been used by the block chiefs of Auschwitz for their sexual perversions. He looked at the notebooks. His life had been spared to voice the strangled scream of these two children. Neither the Auschwitz crematorium nor the bullets at the frontier river had managed to kill him. Would a British bullet put an end to his vow?

Quickly, he rolled up the two notebooks and put them in his inside breast pocket. He walked out of the cellar, leaving the door unlocked.

The street was jammed at this hour with clerks emerging from their offices after a day's work, families out shopping together, and young people on an evening date hurrying to cinema ticket windows. Harry submerged himself in the stream of people. He avoided meeting anyone's eyes. Every glance sent a twinge of suspicion through him. No one these days could escape doubt: if he were not an undercover agent himself, he might be a man being followed. He wanted to get to Menuhin as quickly as possible. He would already have been there had he gone the usual way, but this time he preferred to detour onto the main street, where he could lose himself in the crowd.

The senior writer opened the door and showed him into his study. Harry sat in the deep armchair. It struck him that he could easily spend the night in this chair. He was wondering how he could most appropriately explain why he had come. Menuhin did not appear to be in the best of moods. As accustomed as he was to sitting with Menuhin and saying nothing, the silence today was uncomfortable, oppressive. The notebooks in his breast pocket felt hot against his chest. But who could understand him better than Menuhin? These two notebooks were like a sacred last will which had been entrusted to him, a last testament exhumed from a mountain of ashes. And if he had to leave them now with someone, was there any more trustworthy an executor than Menuhin? If he himself were unable to, who better than a Jewish author could establish this monument? And Menuhin was not only his patron, but from the very first had been a father to him.

Harry rose from the armchair, and from his breast pocket he brought out the notebooks. With both hands he held them out to Menuhin, seated at the massive desk. "I entrust these to you," he said. "If I'm gone, you'll know what to do with them."

Heedless of the notebooks placed before him on the desk, the writer lashed out at Harry. "Listen, you!" he exploded, "are you one with the devil too?"

Menuhin got to his feet. His hand slashed through the air, his wrath so overwhelming he could not find words cutting enough to show his utter disgust. "We didn't come to this country to destroy but to build!" he raged. "Every inch of this land is drenched with our sweat! Who do they think they are, these reckless thugs? They got here yesterday, and all they're out to do is drown us in blood! Who are these cutthroat terrorists who want to bring us redemption with bloodshed and murder? Redemption? They can keep their redemption. I don't want their kind of Messiah!"

The writer's face contorted with grief and fury. What was happening these days in the country was obviously racking him. As though all his accumulated bitterness at the waves of terror sweeping the country were now shouting from his heart. Like a caged lion, he strode across his study to the closed veranda door, stopped there, his back to Harry. Then his rage erupted again. "Who are these terrorists actually fighting? The British Empire? No, no! It's us they're fighting! They know very well they can't do a thing to the British! Their terror isn't throwing London into a fright. But the Jew—I can't even step out on my own veranda. These hooligans have turned the country into a battlefield! A prison!"

He pivoted and in a passion of rage lunged at the desk, grabbing up a printed invitation, which he shoved at Harry standing there motionless. It was an invitation from the City of Tel Aviv on behalf of the Authors' Guild to the ceremony of the literary prize. "Here's the result of those terrorists' handiwork!" he fumed. "They've even fouled up our Bialik Award celebration. The writers are too scared to leave their homes. It's as if we're all living under siege.

They've stolen our freedom. You can't walk down the street any more and be sure of your life. Suddenly their bombs start exploding all over the place. Did they ask if it's all right with me? And what have they got in store for us this time? Speak up. What are those murderers cooking up this time? I've had my doubts about you for a long time. Well, we won't let them! Do you hear? We'll oust them from our community like lepers!"

So saying, the writer's eyes fell on the notebooks on his desk, where Harry had placed them. "And what are these things you've given me to hide? I don't take deposits. I'm not a bank." With the back of his hand, he pushed the notebooks at Harry. "I won't be a party to this kind of business." And he returned to his position by the closed veranda door, his back turned on the room in speechless fury.

Harry picked up the black notebooks. He squeezed them between his palms. He did not hear his own footsteps as he walked out of the writer's apartment.

Day was already slipping into evening, and dusk spread among the trees on Rothschild Boulevard. Harry did not know where to turn. He sat on one of the benches; in his fear of being found out, the glances of the passers-by seemed to stab through him like a knife. In the past, before he had a roof over his head, he could have slept here without thinking twice; but now he had an address of his own, and it was just that which ruled out sleeping on a boulevard bench. He was weighing whether or not to steal away to the cemetery as soon as it got dark. Near Abrasha's plot there wasn't much of a fence. He'd be able to slip in on that side and find shelter behind one of the taller stones.

"... *Hoodlums! Gangsters running wild! It's not the Nazis they're fighting, but us. It's us they're out to drown in blood. They can't touch the Germans, but on our heads they'll bring down a holocaust!*" In the very words Menuhin had used, with the same genuine pain, the senior rabbi in the Warsaw ghetto had denounced the ghetto fighters. God of vengeance! Wasn't it time yet? If not now, when? Soon the extermination of the Jewish people in Europe would have become simply one more episode in the Second World War, an episode to be shoved behind the screen of forgetfulness drawn across the conscience of the world. God almighty! If not now, then when?

After Auschwitz, he had turned his back on that accursed soil and walked away, rejecting the revenge he could have taken there. The oath of vengeance was a burden on his heart. But this he knew: his vengeance would not be that of a victor. Like his victory, his vengeance was set apart. Here on the soil of his homeland, he had expected to carry out his oath. Through him, the world would hear the dying cry of the burning ghetto. But no one, it seemed, had heard. No one here had absorbed the lesson of the ghetto in his book of testimony. In his despair, he wondered if he should have burned the book instead of publishing it.

He remembered what Levitan had said when he was working on the English translation of the book: "You've chosen the proper form for your purpose: to bring into the open what, until now, has been deliberately hushed up. This is the only way most people who are not Jews will be able to understand it." If the future proved Levitan right, then there would have been sense to his life after Auschwitz. He suddenly wondered whether Levitan might not treat him the way Menuhin had. He got up from the bench, and, striding away as confidently as he could, to all appearances a respectable citizen hurrying about his affairs, he made his way to Levitan's.

The vestibule was dark. Harry fumbled for the light. He went up the steps and at Levitan's door, his finger about to press the bell, he stopped. The last time he had come, that girl had been standing right here. He couldn't recall her face. All he could conjure up was the outline of her body. And then he remembered the letter he had hastily stuffed into his pocket. His eyes raced over the lines: ". . . and when you need someone, remember, I'll be waiting for your call . . ."

Leaving the building quickly, he went in search of a public phone. A sharp, intimate scent emanated from the words in the letter. A scent from the dim reaches of a forgotten world. Someone passing by told him there was a phone in the drugstore on the next block. He wondered whether he was doing the right thing. He was hesitant, like an adolescent about to take the mysterious step into maturity.

A clear feminine voice rushed at him: "Of course I know who's calling. I've been waiting for your call."

"Is Mademoiselle free to have me visit now?" he asked.

"Totally free."

"May I be permitted to ask you for directions?" Harry asked. "I'm in the vicinity of the bus depot. Where is your home and what would be the shortest way to get to you?"

"A cab is best," she broke in. "The driver will bring you right here. Just say 'Professor Glick's residence.' "

"Sometimes a man can't see the simplest and clearest course open to him . . ."

Before he had finished, her voice at the other end rebounded: "Which is why it's good for a man to have someone point out the simplest and clearest course open to him. I'm waiting."

Slowly, he replaced the receiver. How could such a girl know that, for him, hailing a cab came to as much as a whole day's food? Such considerations were obviously altogether foreign to her. But it would not be wise now to roam the streets in search of an address. Reluctantly, he accepted her suggestion.

The cab pulled up in front of a grand residence. Harry paid the driver and got out. He walked up a broad marble staircase flooded with light. The place looked familiar. As though he had climbed these stairs before. But hard as he tried, he couldn't remember when—just as right now, he couldn't even remember what the stairs to his own house in that world of the past had looked like. This had been happening often lately. Three disparate, alien worlds struggled within him: before Auschwitz, Auschwitz, after Auschwitz. At moments a light ray from one of his worlds would be reflected off an object belonging to another world, projecting an image onto his memory. But from which of the three worlds it came—where should it be placed—he did not know.

He reached the door. Somehow he had stood here before. When had he stood at just such a door? As always, when this unreal feeling gripped him, he was engulfed by a sense-blurring dizziness. Seeking to shake free of it, he reached out for the doorbell, as if by touching it he could grasp reality again.

The door opened at once, and she stood there before him. He was unable to match her to the hazy silhouette in his memory. Last time, he was thinking, her hair had been swept up to the crown of her head. Now her chestnut hair tumbled over one side of her shoulder like a silken screen; her face was glowing, enticing. "Welcome!" The gay ring of her voice received him, calling up distant echoes. Where had he heard this rare voice before—and when? In which of the three worlds? She was opening a door for him.

A crystal chandelier glowed above an oval table. Across from him, a blue divan. His legs, with a will of their own, led him not to the leather chairs around the table but to the divan in the corner, as though he were returning to a familiar spot. He sat down, and the salon in its entirety was there before his eyes. He could not utter a sound. Which of his worlds was projecting this magical scene? Where was he now? In what incarnation had he sat there before?

Silent, she was sitting at the table, in the chair closest to him. As though with her silence she were respecting his.

His thoughts were galloping wildly, and he was dragged along like a carriage hitched behind. He glanced at her. Her folded hands were resting on the table and she gazed silently down at them. Her hair over one side of her face. He looked at her profile, at the exposed cheek for a black beauty mark on its peak. Long ago, somewhere in another world, a black pepper berry had perched on Sanya's profile.

The three worlds of his life flipped through his mind like cards in the hands of a sharp dealer. Suddenly the shuffle stopped. It was all clear. He was shocked by the clarity of the vision: *". . . this is our only child. . . . She's all we have. . . . I'm afraid not, sir, my husband and I would never agree to this . . ."*

Now he identified the salon in which he was sitting. This was the home to which the E.N.S.A. director had taken him. The first Jewish home he had seen after Auschwitz. The chandelier. The curtains draped across the windows. Here was the table: where she was sitting now, Eli had sat then; and opposite him, in a flowered morning dress, the imposing lady of the house. He visualized her now even more clearly than when he had first seen her, and her words were more distinct and intelligible. *"This is our only child . . ."*

This was the divan on which he had sat. He hadn't known what they were arguing about at the table; not a word had really penetrated. The mother had shown him a picture of her daughter, but he hadn't even looked at the face in the picture. Now she was sitting across from him.

"I read your book . . ." she had stammered in Levitan's house. She turned her face to him. Her hand pushed her hair back from her face. She smiled at him tenderly. "I don't want to intrude," she said. "I want you to feel you can be the same in my presence as when you're alone. But please let me fulfill my duties as your hostess. May I get you an *apéritif?*"

"Thank you, Mademoiselle—" He wanted to call her by name but fell silent. It occurred to him that they hadn't even introduced themselves. His fault. His usual evasiveness whenever it came to his name. They smiled at each other. "My name is Galilea," she said. Then, as though she understood, she added, "And I know your name. What may I offer you?"

"Thank you, Mademoiselle Galilea. It's very pleasant sitting here just as I am. I don't want to dilute the pleasure of this moment with a drink." But who was this girl he found himself addressing in the courtly manner of his previous life? What invisible force had brought him to meet this odd girl in front of Levitan's door? Who was she, this girl from the first home he had visited? And why had he come here and not to Sanya's parents?

"No, no other drink," he said.

"It's so good to hear such words from you," she said, with a kind of exultance in her voice. "Nor do I want to dilute the silence of these moments with any words. But may I make a toast to you?" She rose and walked toward him with her hand raised as though she were holding an imaginary glass. "To you, Harry. You will live, you'll live! . . ."

He shuddered. Her words reached him like an echo from the recesses of another world. She was standing at the window, leaning against the white curtain, and now he could no longer distinguish the reality from the dream. He had to convince himself that he wasn't hallucinating. "Would it be possible for me to see your mother?" he asked.

"I would like you to," she said, "but because of the curfew on the highways, my parents have had to stay in Jerusalem, where they went for the weekend—and, as you know, the connections between the cities have been cut. The mayor finally got through to me today to say that a British officer will be dispatched tomorrow to escort them home. My father . . ."

Her words were cut short by an explosion that rocked the house. The casement window behind Galilea flew open with the blast of air—for a moment it seemed that the bomb had fallen right outside the window—and Galilea was propelled toward the divan, almost falling into his arms. Over her shoulder, he saw that the British High Command building, the planning center for curfews and man-hunts, had been the target of the blast. They looked into each other's eyes; her face was very close to his, and he heard her say, "Marry me, Harry . . ."

His mind seemed to rip apart, whirling in shreds among the three worlds. Exactly this way had Sanya Schmidt stood before him; as suddenly and unexpectedly, she had said, "Marry me, Harry . . ." Then too it had been night, and in her parents' home. Then too following the shock of her father's last letter, which had struck Sanya like the blast of a bomb. Now, in the crash of an instant, the images of these two worlds collided, and in the flash of the friction between world and world, he saw a phosphorescent trail extending from one to the other. Shimmering within it was his previous life, his unlived life, demanding continuation and amends. With all his strength, he tried to hold back the storm in his soul. Galilea was looking at him, not saying a word—waiting for him to answer her.

But from whom did that previous life now demand its continuation? From *him*? Who was he? Wasn't he just a part of that world of ashes, even as he stood before her?

"That would be a fatal error," he said quietly. He

slumped down beside her on the divan, took hold of the end of his tie, "You see this tie? The crease in these pants? The light jacket? They don't cover a living body. What can a man like me say to you now other than the truth disguised by this body: except for a desire for revenge, there is nothing alive left in it, only ashes."

Her hand reaching out to cling to him withdrew slowly. She did not dare touch him. The hurt looked out of her eyes. "Revenge is not ashes," she said. "And a body burning for revenge is not a cold ember. Harry, let me help you. Let me be your partner in a true revenge."

"True revenge? What do we know about true revenge? Is there a revenge anywhere which redeems, which consoles?"

"There is, Harry!" she said intensely. "There is! It is the future generation you carry within you; it is the future generations your own will beget. Don't you really see that the hand of destiny has brought us together? That hand holds out revenge to you. This is your revenge: your children, Harry. Our children."

He lifted his eyes to her. He saw the girl the E.N.S.A. director had wanted for his stage, the girl whose photograph had once been handed to him right here, the girl who, with a miniature shiny metal key, drew near to open the ash gates of Auschwitz, to pull him out to life. Who was this girl who answered him as if she were declaiming passages from a trashy sentimental novel, and how did he come to be sucked into such melodramatic talk? He wanted to ask her: Where did you get the right in the first place to burst into the closed world of a stranger? Instead, he let out a whisper: "I sat on this divan once before . . ."

Her face was radiant, as though the answer she sought were coded in the words he had just spoken. The vaguely phrased reply was to be expected. The author of *Salaman-*

dra whose name was Anonymous, would certainly speak in symbols. She could not imagine that he was talking simply, factually, not in hints and symbols: "I sat on this divan once before . . ."

She could no longer contain the surge of her joy. She had an overwhelming urge to kiss him. Frightened by the mere idea, she jumped to her feet. "I'd like to celebrate this evening with a real banquet," she said, extending her hand to him. "Come with me to the kitchen and help me prepare it. Cook Betty must be asleep by now."

Her hand was in his. They walked the length of the corridor to the kitchen. She had to restrain herself to keep from shouting out her happiness.

19

As Galilea left the house on her way to Harry, the sky was as red as the seven poppies Harry had sent her the day after his visit. Seven poppies whose scarlet swam before her eyes. And the words on the card rang in her ears: "For your own good, we'd better not see each other again."

But she had been ready for this battle from the start: it had all been foreseen. A battle not against Harry but against the ghosts from the nether world enclosing him in shadows. She hastened to him now the way one rushes to save a baby from a burning house. She was full of strength. The danger of the flames to her own life—to her soul—had no place in her mind. Her ears echoed with the words Harry had spoken to her in her home: "I sat on this divan once before . . ." As if he were voicing her own feelings. This was what she had felt the first time she saw him; this was the sensation that had throbbed within her, even before she saw him face to face. All her years had been a waiting for him. And now Harry had come.

He had come to her of his own accord. He had come back to his land like a monk returned from his wanderings to the shelter of his home. The hand of fate had guided him to her. His ways were the highways of fire. And she was the first to bless his return. Behind the walls of her house, a promise was sealed between them. He had asked only that they not meet again until he had finished the new book. She had accepted his decision. She knew what the writing meant to him. She knew she was meant to help him carry out his vow. She had told him, "I'll wait six months, a year, even longer—until we meet again." Just as, from her beginning, she had waited for their first meeting. But now in her purse, she carried his verdict: "Don't wait to keep our rendezvous. For your own good, we'd better not see each other again . . ."

As she walked down the steps to his cellar, she felt none of the tremors that had nearly paralyzed her when she had put the little key under his door. Like Sanya, when she had gone to the Nazi workshop director to rescue Harry from the labor camp, her purpose steeled her. This time too, he had to be rescued, brought back to the living.

In her home, he had seemed free of the ghosts from the nether world. But no sooner did he re-enter their realm than life closed over him, like the waters swirling together over the head of a drowning man.

Those evenings, when she had stood across from the light filtering between the slits of his shutter, stirred within her. How desperately she had wanted to penetrate his sanctum. Now she descended to the depth of the cellar as though she were plunging to a root of her soul. Like the nacre forming around a strange particle in the darkness of a conch shell to become a pearl, so was Harry to her in the conch of his cellar. She descended to draw him up to the sunlight—like a pearl, like a tear.

In a corner of the cellar Harry sat hunched over his desk. That was how she found him when she entered. The light from the desk lamp fell across the sheaf of papers before him. There was no room here for another chair. Galilea sat on the narrow iron cot across from him. They looked into each other's eyes.

There was no language to express what each sought to convince the other. She had already said it all to him— "Marry me, Harry . . ."—as he, in his brief note, had said it all. Now they spoke only with their eyes. And the battle raged between their two worlds.

He sat facing her. Opposites—they sat there. When she had come in, the day still chalked white lines of light in the shutter slits. Now night spread darkness through the room. The light reflected from the white pages on his desk cast a glow on the niche in the adjoining wall. Half hidden behind the narrow drape was the striped Auschwitz garment, the pants hanging beneath the jacket; the striped cap above the jacket covering the nail on which it was hung. Like an Auschwitz prisoner it hung there—headless, feet amputated, watching from behind the curtain. The lamp shade made a circle of light around the desk. She was within the circle.

The aura of the room poured into her. All around her, the space was swarming with invisible creatures—faceless, bodiless—spirits from another world. An enraged and hostile world. They glared at her in fury. How dare she break into their circle? This was their world. Who was this intruder in their domain? The enmity between their disparate worlds would last forever; no words could bridge the gap.

No words in her. She could not find the words to say what she must. Everything was understood from the beginning. Understood to the deepest reaches of dread. And yet not understood. She had no language to express this. Whatever words could say, they both knew already. And both had already spoken. But silently, her eyes fastened on his, she spoke again: *Beloved, could you have guessed that I would be sitting here before you? Something I would never have believed I would dare to do, I have done. I came to you uninvited. The words you wrote have brought me to you— to wipe out those words as though they never existed. Look at me, Harry, how poor I am; what could I have sent in answer to your note? But my love has erased your words. Now they are undone. I sit before you and look into the blue of your eyes. Sanya's love sustained you and delivered you from the world of Auschwitz, and led you to the home of my parents. There in that room, our love was made holy. Please don't turn away from the love you have followed, for she has been waiting here for you. The love you need even as much now.*

His gaze did not shift from the light in her eyes. Who was this girl? Was it possible? Here, in his dim cellar, sitting on the edge of his iron cot, was life—mysterious and manifest. Who was she? What hand had brought them together? Now the cup was held to his lips again. Did it hold poison brewed in that deadly world from which he had come? Or grace and reprieve—like the world in that girl's eyes?

She sat before him. Life was gazing at him from that feminine body. A world of life to which he did not belong. And suspended in opposition to hers was his own world, like a star of ashes. A star made of the sparks spewed from the smokestacks of Auschwitz, whose rain of ashes on the soul was deadlier than the effects of radioactivity on the body. But upon the collision of these two worlds, what would happen to this lovely body before him now? What would happen to her soul?

His eyes spoke to her: *See what you are approaching. You do not belong here. Go back to your own life, and do not look back lest you be harmed. Here, lungs breathe cyanide gas. Here, love cries at night from the throats of the crematorium chimneys. Here, the wind carries the ashes of cremated legs, once as long and beautiful as yours; the ashes of a body like yours, lithe and blooming; the ashes of a face like your own and lips like your lips. Only the gaze of eyes, like the gleam in yours, hovers here unconsumed. How could you breathe in this air?*

Unflinching, her eyes answered him: *I know where I'm going. I see clearly what is here. But our worlds are not separate, they are one. A world in which we must account and make amends for Auschwitz, each in our own way. No guilt sent you to Auschwitz, and no guiltlessness kept me out. The vow you have sworn is mine too; I shall not stand in your way. With all my being, I shall help you keep your vow. The same love that protected you there will protect you in this world after Auschwitz; the hand that delivered you from Auschwitz has brought us together here. I know you are trying to shield me. But how can I convince you that I am strong? Stronger than you could possibly imagine. I do not hand you my life on a tray of pity for a lonely refugee. My love is entreating you. How can I explain? Can't you hear what my eyes are telling you?* For my own good, *beloved, I have come to you . . .*

Suddenly she saw that her hands were stretched out to him. Dazed, she withdrew them to her lap.

At her abrupt movement, Harry rose. Only a step or two

lay between them. He walked to the bed—to her. He sat close beside her. The purity of his nearness, uplifting and radiating, enveloped her. She breathed in his closeness. The cellar around her disappeared. The papers on the desk, the light of the dim bulb disappeared. As though Harry had broken free of the circle. She saw only the blue of his eyes, bathing her with grace.

As he looked at her, he shuddered. Over his head his Auschwitz garment was watching him from the niche. As though he himself were hanging there behind her head; as if he were forcing his Auschwitz world down upon this girl's head. He held his hands up to his eyes. He stared at them: smeared with the blood of innocents. He buried his face in his hands. He slumped back on the cot, his eyes freezing upward on the invisible. His head twisted back and forth, back and forth on the bed.

She was terrified. Afraid to turn her face. The cellar was filled with Auschwitz skeletons, crowding toward her from his books. Surrounding her. Insane hunger in the sockets of their eyes, teeth bared, fingers clawing at the walls, biting the empty air in a frenzy of starvation. Pouring their wrath upon her—she, the uninvited, the alien, how dare she cross the threshold into their world?

The chair where Harry had sat stood empty. Its emptiness condemned her. The papers on the desk waited like skeleton mouths gaping for food. Beyond the circle of light from the desk lamp, the dark corners of the cellar expanded, as though all boundaries, all limits had been shattered, and out of the darkness the ghosts of the nether world rushed upon her in fury. Terror washed over her, high breakers crashed down upon her body, swirling through her.

Feverishly, Harry twisted his head back and forth, writhing as in battle with unseen forces.

Oh God, please give me strength, she murmured to herself. Harry has now been flung into his last battle. He can't help me. All by myself I must prove that love is mightier than Auschwitz. Prove it to Harry. Prove that love can withstand even the wrath of the Auschwitz skeletons. Then they too will acknowledge me. Be strong, be strong . . .

She saw the body hanging in the striped Auschwitz garment. Gathering what force was left in her, she pulled free and crossed to the niche. Over the heart side of the jacket, a row of digits was painted. Harry's Auschwitz number. The number branded on the flesh of his left arm. The garment no longer frightened her. It was pain's body, Harry's body. She buried her face in it. And now she felt no more fear. As though it had become a part of her. She was no longer a stranger, no longer alien. Her terror of the skeletons was gone. They were Harry, they were her lot.

She was not conscious of time passing. Harry's closeness was all she knew. Now he was by her side, and his eyes, which had turned as gray as his face when he fell back on the cot, were sheer blue again, gazing at her in wonder and want. Gradually, between the slits of the shutters, pale bands were limned.

She pulled open the shutter. Above the treetops in the neighboring yard, dawn had come. The cellar was blue washed and immaculate. Only in Harry's corner did night and all it enshrouded still linger beneath the shade of the desk lamp—waiting to flow between the lines of the pages. Silent, submissive as when they had stood in line in Auschwitz, the skeletons waited.

I will wait for half a year, even longer, until we can come together, her eyes told him. *I will not violate the secret I bear with me from this night. Let it remain sealed in our joined silence. Look, beloved, I have withstood the test of your silence. Give me a sign that you too have withstood the test of our love.*

She took his letter out of her purse. She laid it on the desk before him. Two lines. He looked at them. He read them. Slowly, his fingers tore the letter into tiny shreds. He shook them off the pages.

Their eyes met. Then she turned wordlessly toward the door. For a split second, deep within her, she felt this night she was bearing away. She shook free. Opening the door, she walked out into the new day.

20

"Your attention please! Your attention! The voting at Lake Success is about to begin!" The announcer's voice over the loudspeaker was pitched high with emotion.

Magen David Square that Saturday night was not wide enough to contain the human sea. In multitudes the inhabitants of Tel Aviv poured into the streets. Crowds of people standing shoulder to shoulder, heads upturned at the loudspeaker over which the radio announcer was narrating the proceedings at United Nations General Assembly. The fate of the land of Israel. At any moment they would be voting.

A full moon hung above the square. Silvery night. A clear and lambent sky. The floodlights played over the crowd: Hasidim in furry hats who had forsaken their rabbis' banquets for the departing Sabbath Queen to be here in the streets squeezed against Orientals who had rushed out in their pajamas from their beds; elegantly coifed matrons pressing shoulders and sides against workmen in cotton sun hats—all eyes focused on the loudspeaker, as if it were a stethoscope held to the heart of the world, through which the throbbing pulse of history could be heard. They were like the maidservants in the Hebrew legend, favored to see God while Moses cleaved the sea, who in their visionary awe were confounded.

Among those massed in Magen David Square were Galilea and her parents. "Little Sabra." Professor Glick turned to his daughter, lost in thought beside him. "Do you know why they postponed the vote from yesterday to November 29th?"

Galilea started and asked distractedly, "Why, Papa?"

"Because the United Nations knew that November 29th is your birthday, and they couldn't think of a better present than the Jewish State."

She wasn't listening. Her mind was not free to grasp her father's joking. Her gaze floated over the sea of faces, and her legs were impatient to get away from her parents—move on, move on. Why wasn't Harry here? Her birthday would be perfect if only he were here. Where was Harry? She knew she couldn't disturb him while he was writing, not even for this. But he of all people should be here to witness this moment.

All around the square, moonlight glinted off the open windows of the houses, packed with the heads of onlookers hanging over the window sills. As Galilea looked toward the loudspeaker on the platform above the crowd, she remembered the time she had stood there urging a similar sea of faces, in a voice edged with emotion, to fight a holy war against Hitler: "*In Europe our nation is going up in flames! Our own flesh and blood. Who among us would refuse to step forth and rush to their rescue?*"

Our own flesh and blood. She had no relatives in Europe. Her family had been rooted in this soil for generations. But could her heart already have known then that Harry was one of those thrown on the pyre?

"Attention! Attention! The balloting . . ." Oh God, why wasn't Harry here?

Harry was among the throng in Magen David Square. He stood pressed against the close-knit clans of fathers and sons, neighbors and friends, who had come out to the streets together; at this inordinate moment of awe and exultation to be near one another, to cling together. Harry stood alone, his eyes raised to the moon above the heads of the crowd. In his mind's eye, he saw the forest into which he had fled on the death march after the evacuation of Auschwitz. The moon had been full that night too. The same light had silvered the tops of the trees in one of which he was hiding. Now, as then, he was asking himself: what will the next moment bring—death or rebirth?

"State! . . . Jewish State! . . ."
In a split second, the human sea, fused in taut attentiveness, divided into rivulets of emotion. One person kissing another, one ecstasy clinging to another, as the eruption of joy swelled through the crowd. And standing solitary and immobile among them was Harry.
The waves of joy heaved and crashed around her as Galilea parted her way through the crowd searching for Harry. She sensed his nearness. Her heart told her that the lonely back she had caught sight of must be Harry's. Now the surge of people pushed them apart, now it swept her almost within reach. Then she was beside him. She did not look at his face. Her body trembled. She felt his hand close to her own, and her fingers touched his open palm. Their hands recognized one another. They clasped in union.
The heart of a nation sang hallelujah around them, as though the very gates of heaven had burst open and the Lord of His People, His liberated wings spread above them, had descended to hover over their dancing heads. Our fa-

thers danced in the streets that night, future generations
would relate; had they but raised their hands, they could
have touched angelic wings.

Through a roar like the surf, they walked away from
Magen David Square. They moved toward the sea. A nation of people flooded the roads and sidewalks; the two
walked in its midst. Only their palms were touching, and
their hands said everything that could that moment be said.

They were standing on top of the hill. Away from the
jubilant celebration of the city. On one side was the wide
open sea at the foot of the hill; on the other the rooftops of
Tel Aviv, luminous in the moonlight.

From the distance the sound of the horas, being sung and
danced under the street lamps in Herbert Samuel Square,
reached their ears—hundreds of dancers, thousands of
dancers. Circle within circle. Like a rustle in the wind the
singing was borne to the top of the hill.

She stood in his embrace, and he could feel the trembling
of her knees against his legs. Incredulous, caught in the
spell of this bewitching night, he held her to him. Through
the stream of hair falling along her cheek, he could see the
heaving moon-veiled sea. As she gazed at him, the depths
of her eyes were like twin stars. Suddenly he knew that this
youthful body had been waiting for him since time im-
memorial. And only tonight had he come back to her. The
journey to her side had been centuries long. And now the
rolling sea would wash his feet of the dust of his final
wanderings.

He felt her mouth quiver under his breath. His lips
touched hers, and they were one. Time dropped at their
feet as did the barriers of clothes with their embrace. All
the force of his potency, his prime preserved within him
like wine in the darkness of a cellar, surged forth to meet

her. Her eyes widened and shut under the dazzling light coming closer. The hill beneath her body seemed to rip free from its roots as she soared to the skies with the taut might of his bow.

They ran downhill to the sea as though they had grown wings. Along the shore she chased him and caught him; along the shore he chased her and caught her. Together, they were alone. Naked and unaware. With faces glowing, they swam in the gentle and benevolent sea, and the sea carried them high in its arms, held them up to heaven like an offering in praise of liberation. They were the first to come to the sea bearing in their bodies the tidings of liberation. The boundless sea was theirs. The sky, their sky—and love, their love.

They lay on their backs, floating toward the shore. Side by side, they rested on the sea, on a bed of spangled light, the waves carrying them close in to shore. Harry planted his feet on the floor of the sea. He spread his hands beneath her back, and her body's length of loveliness was carried on the foam. He stood submerged to his neck in the surf, and the reflection of the moon gleamed from between her breasts. The waves pressed her to him. As their mouths met, the taste of the salt water was like an intoxicating bubbling wine. Now once more, with intensified longing, with the elemental pull of the sea and the still restraint of the stars, and the yearning between the two. Till the sky poured out all its stars into the wells of her eyes. "Beloved . . ." her lips breathed.

They were lying on the hill, her head on his belly. She looked at the drop of sea water gleaming like a diamond in the hair of his chest. She leaned over and touched her tongue to the silver drop. His fingers ran through her hair. All at once she turned to him. "How did we find each other in this place?" she asked, startled herself by the mystery her own question laid bare.

"Ages ago, we had a rendezvous to meet on this hill to-night, my love," he said.

'I want this to be our hill always," she said.

"It has been our hill since the beginning of time," he said.

"Beloved, do you also feel that we have been here before?" she asked.

"How else did our feet know to bring us here tonight?" he said quietly. He held her face between his palms and looked into the shimmering light in the depths of her eyes. "I once dreamed that when I returned to my father's home, I would fall upon the earth and kiss it. But my first steps on this soil were to steal across the barbed wire barriers of the British Coastal Guard in the dark of night. Let me tonight, my love, kiss the soil of this land." He lowered his head to her belly, and kissed it long.

21

Her face looked back at her from the round mirror. Hovering over her, Solange's famous hands shaped her hair into an intricate coiffure. "For this great day in your life, my child," Madame Glick had pleaded with Galilea, "you must let Solange come and make you up for the ceremony. Please. For me."

And Galilea allowed everything to be done to her. As

though she were totally cut off from her own will. Since the moment Harry had insisted that they not see each other for three days before the wedding, reality had lost all substance for her. The hours washed past her like the sea, and she walked among them, straying farther and farther from shore. The house had been made ready for the festive hour. The guests had arrived. And now she was sitting in her mother's chair, in her mother's dressing room, at her mother's vanity, Solange's hands fussing around her, smoothing, caressing, painting. Galilea's eyes were on the mirror, but her thoughts flew beyond the closed door of the room. How long it had been since they had come in to say that the guests were all here. And Harry, when would Harry come?

In a corner of the mirror she could see the white wedding veil on the seamstress' lap. The seamstress and her assistant had come to put the final pleats in the veil and, under Solange's watchful eye, to place it upon her elaborate coiffure. The bride was being prepared just as if the wedding were to be celebrated publicly with great pomp and circumstance. "Harry," she had said to him the last time they were together, "in three more days we will be under the wedding canopy. My heart's prayer will be answered. And everything has been arranged as modestly as you wished, within the privacy of our home. The tables will be spread for a crowd even though only a ten-man minyan has been invited. No one but me knows what my parents have given up, with all the dreams they've had of their only daughter's wedding day. But I could see in their eyes that they understood: the bridegroom will be coming alone to his wedding . . ." Then, for the first time, the question escaped her: "Harry, what is your name?"

Looking at herself in the mirror, she seemed to see a plaster head being molded by a make-up artist for exhibition in a competition. There was no connection between herself and this face. A stranger's face. And she felt as if she were being separated from herself, divided in two. Divided like Harry, whose alter ego was an alien shadow, a shadow she did not know. The Harry of the night on the hill; the Harry of the night in his cellar. Today, under the canopy, she would be joined to them both.

Why had he forbidden her to come to him these three days of his torment? She felt herself reaching out for Harry, the stranger, the inhabitant of Auschwitz; felt herself slipping across to his side of the horizon, lost within that unknown territory. Why wasn't he here yet? Which of the two selves existing side by side in him would prevail? Which of the two would come now to take her to the altar?

Her eyes gazed blankly at her face in the mirror. *Oh beloved, I want to be in your arms. Will the shadow behind you fix me with his stare whenever you hold me in your arms? Oh beloved, prisoner of the nightmare of your past! In which of your two selves shall I find you—what name must I call you so as not to lose you like Lohengrin?* All her attention was fastened on the closed door. Was that Harry now? What upheavals of the soul had he undergone in these three days alone in his cellar? Would anyone ever know the secret of the fire in the heart of the phoenix, rising with him from the flames? And would not his wings fail him if he should turn his back on the flaming pyre?

"The loveliest bride of my career!" Solange chattered away in French. "What exquisite olive skin! What marvelous texture of hair."

She was racked with the pain of the ordeal he must be undergoing in his cellar. Her own anguish revealed his to her. Would it be the man she knew or the invisible other who would be united with her under the bridal canopy?

In the mirror she saw the train of her wedding veil, and

in her mind she saw the Auschwitz garment hanging on the nail in Harry's cellar. The Auschwitz garment was her lot no less than the white wedding veil. Under the canopy she would identify with all who had been draped in the rags of Auschwitz. Like Jeptha's daughter, she would run to meet her beloved's other self and offer him her consummate self-sacrifice of acceptance. *Oh my beloved, shrouded in your terrible secret, you will never know what is churning in my heart. Like you, part of me is crossing to the unknown. I belong with you. I am like you. I want to be near you, to be like you in everything, to share life for life. I shall never again ask you your name. The phoenix must not be made to reveal the secret images of the fire. I want you as you are, beloved, you and your invisible shadow. Oh God, make me strong, keep me whole and let me not lose my inner calm, so that Harry may find his wholeness in me. I implore You for Harry's sake. I must be whole for him whose life has been rent in two. For him.*

Brimming over her lashes, heavy with mascara, black trails of tears trickled down her made-up cheeks. Solange wrung her hands in despair, with the look of an architect whose dam collapses at its public dedication.

Like black pearls, the tears rolled down Galilea's cheeks, on the white lace at the swelling of her breasts. *Beloved, you will live! You'll live!*—the line in his book, the words that had led her to him and had sustained Harry in the death camp—welled up in her throat. *You'll live the way you are, the way you must be, the only way you can be. You'll live in your past. In your fire, like the phoenix in his. Look, beloved, I have accepted your enigma, the silence of ashes within you.*

"He's come!" The boudoir door burst open as her mother rushed in. "He's here!" Like someone struck blind, without turning her head she reached out her hand to her mother.

Her eyes closed. Only now did she realize how intense had been her anxiety that he might not come. Solange bent over her, the cosmetic brush poised in her fingers, anxious to repair the bride's make-up as soon as the lashes reopened. Madame Glick clasped her daughter's clenched fist to her heart, not knowing what she should say to calm her. "Galilea, please let Solange retouch your make-up," she said. "God forbid your bridegroom should see you like this."

Galilea started, as though waking up. In a flash she had risen from the chair. She turned to go out into the corridor to see Harry, even if only from a distance. Then, changing her mind, she stepped back. "Solange, help me with my veil. I want the ceremony to begin at once."

"May the bridegroom and the bride . . . be exceedingly glad and rejoice . . ." The cantor sang the blessing in joyous tones. She did not see the faces crowding around the four posts of the canopy. She was full of the wonder of this moment. The bridal canopy in the center of the balcony was encircled by her family, and against the brilliance of the day, the burning candles in their hands seemed to echo the flickering thoughts in her heart. Harry was standing by her side. "As Your creature made You glad east of Eden . . ." the cantor's chant proceeded. She noticed with a pang Harry's fingers clasping and unclasping beside her; she felt as though she were a needle quivering with his inner vibrations. She herself no longer seemed to exist, no more than the celebration going on around her. She wanted only to breathe joy into Harry, to fill his breast with the essence of her vitality. Yet she dared not look in his face.

"Soon thereafter, there will be heard in the streets the jubilant song of bridegrooms from their nuptial canopies . . ." The cantorial chant reached her ears from far away. Hands took the bride by the arms to lead her in the procession of circles around the groom. She felt the rising tide of her joy, and she focused it on Harry, the hub of the round upon round in which she was led. Would her joy form a ring of life around his past, or would his past, like an axis, pierce through the circle of her life?

A mournful melody, heavy with grief, was suddenly heard: the cantor lamenting *El Malé Rahamim*, the memorial prayer for the dead, never before sounded on the occasion of a wedding. The faces in the circle became like stone, all eyes stricken with fear. Invited now were the cremated of Auschwitz, the groom's invisible relatives, forming a cohort about him. A family tree. Invoked and come to Galilea's wedding.

"Behold you are sanctified to me . . ." Harry was holding her hand, ready to place the sacramental ring on her upraised finger. She gazed into his eyes. Now his eyes were a clear lucent blue. She was alone with him now. Once more with the Harry-of-the-hill by the sea. Together they stood there.

22

Galilea's room had been emptied of most of her personal belongings, and almost all the furniture had been transferred to her new apartment. All sorts of odds and ends were piled in the corners of the nursery, among them memory-teasing trifles which Galilea was now rounding up from the rest of the rooms, as if she sought to take along everything her twenty years had accumulated.

All winter Harry and Galilea had lived in his cellar. That had been Harry's explicit condition before the wedding. Until they returned home one evening after a day of torrential rains to find the iron cot and everything else they owned afloat in a great wash of water. At the sight of the mess, they had collapsed into roars of laughter, then set to work bailing out water by the bucketful into the small hours of the night. As Galilea straightened up to wring out the rag for the umpteenth time, Harry had noticed the gleam of tears in her eyes. There and then, he gave in, and first thing next morning Galilea raced over to tell her parents the good news: "Harry has agreed to move from the cellar!" Yet today, finding herself back in her childhood haven, her heart ached for the cellar. When we have the money, she thought, I'll buy it, and the cellar where I had my first moments with Harry, will be there for me. And when I have children, I'll take them there too, and we'll all crowd onto the narrow iron cot; we'll spread a tablecloth on top of the empty orange crate, and we'll share our meal from the one plate he had . . .

"Glichen!" Betty appeared in the doorway, decked out in her new suit. "Your wedding must have brought me luck. You know my Rolf has finally bought that kiosk, and today we are starting preparations for our own wedding. Rolf and I are so very grateful for the gift from your family that has made our kiosk possible. It may be a bit out of the way, but Rolf says the city is growing and it will come to us. Only you shouldn't forget your Betty out there, Glichen!"

"Of course not, Betty. It's not that far away," Galilea reassured her. "Our own new apartment is outside the city too. Don't worry, I'll come to your kiosk. Not only that, but I'll teach my children that they may only buy candy from Aunt Betty's kiosk!"

The nurse called from the clinic, "Galilea, telephone."

"Oh, maybe it's Harry!" Galilea lunged toward the door. "Don't move, Betty. I'll be right back. I have something else to tell you," and she was off.

"No, I haven't the slightest idea!" Galilea said into the mouthpiece, "and what's more, I'm not in the mood right now to guess who's speaking."

"Geegee," the man's voice continued on the other end, "you mean you weren't even expecting a present from someone when he came back from a certain place?"

David Artzi reverted to his normal voice. "Now I assume you can guess who's calling."

"My God! You good-for-nothing so-and-so! Where are you? Where are you calling from? Why have all my letters been coming back?

"If you're really interested in getting an answer to that barrage of questions, you'll have to take your beautiful legs all the way to the Seaside Café. Waiting for you there will be a host of memories—and the surprise I promised you."

"Forget the surprise, you tramp! I'm just coming to see that silly old face of yours. Wait till I get my hands on you. How many months is it since you wrote? You'd better have an ambulance waiting when I get there!"

The moment she hung up, she began to worry over how to tell David about Harry.

Galilea resolved that to be open and direct would be the best course. The instant they met, she would introduce Harry: David, this is my husband!

She grabbed the phone, dialed their next-door neighbor and asked her to call Harry to the phone.

"My love," she said breathlessly, "tell me, what are you doing right now?"

"You tell me what a husband does whose wife leaves him in a brand-new apartment with an unholy mess of furniture and other junk. What am I doing? Well, let's see now, I'm

hanging up your paintings. And I'm finally finishing with
the ones you did in nursery school. Now you please tell me:
What happened to the ones you did in your diapers? Didn't
your mummy save those too?"

"For some reason, I have a sudden uncontrollable urge
to look into your blue eyes. So I hereby grant you permission to invite me out for coffee on the promenade."

"With your kind permission, Madame, you certainly know
I didn't intend to spend the whole day just putting this
apartment of yours into some kind of shape."

"So just leave all that mess behind and come on over to
the Seaside Café. Almost no one is there at this time of day,
and I'll bet that's what's scaring you away. I'll be waiting
for you!"

"Madame, I would consider it an honor to sit in your
company."

Like Galilea on the way to the café, David Artzi, waiting
for her there with Masha, was nervous at the prospect of
their meeting. How would Galilea react when he introduced them: Geegee, meet my wife! . . . Would Masha
really be received as the gift he had promised her? For
years now, he had had the feeling that Galilea would never
marry. There was no such man as Galilea imagined. She was
in love—if you could call it that—with a man who existed
only in her fantasies, and that was the root of her trouble.
He had spent many a sleepless night before finally resigning
himself to the idea that Galilea was doomed to her Aunt
Anna's fate.

"Here she comes!" He jumped up from his seat, waving
to her in greeting.

"At last I've got you in my clutches, you new immigrant,
you!" Galilea threw her arms around him. "Such an illegal
immigrant, I'll have you deported back to Cyprus!"

He looked her over in wonder. "What's happened to you, Geegee! You look more glorious than ever! What's this new light in your eyes?"

He led her toward Masha. "Here is the gift I promised you. I'd like you, Galilea, to meet my wife."

She was golden-haired—her eyes glowing blue and melancholy. Galilea opened her arms to Masha as though she had always known her: "Just the wife I wanted you to bring over from there, David. From 'there.' I have never felt such respect for you as I do at this moment." She fell silent. Then, almost in a whisper, as she sat down close to Masha: "Tell me, do you have any relatives here?"

Haltingly, in a mixture of Polish-Yiddish and the smattering of Hebrew she had managed to learn from David, Masha tried to evade the question. "I had a very large family, once. They were all—there."

With quick strides, Harry was approaching the café from the other side of the promenade.

Their eyes upon each other, seeing yet somehow disbelieving, they sat now in silence at the table like participants at a séance, wraiths rising around them which a mere word could dispel.

"It all seems like a dream to me," David managed at last.

"Show them the picture, Felix," Masha said, turning to her husband.

"What's this 'Felix' all of a sudden?" Galilea asked David as he pulled the folder from his pocket.

"I can't get used to calling my husband by any other name," Masha said, embarrassed. "For me he'll always be 'Felix.' That was his code name in Italy when we first met. My heart knows only this name. I came back to life when I said the name Felix for the first time."

Galilea's eyes rested on Harry as David put the picture on

the table. Looking up from it was a baby's head, its big eyes two saucers of wonder, a teething ring in its mouth.

Harry looked at the picture, and suddenly before his eyes was the stable where he had stopped the night on his way from Auschwitz. He saw the girl lying beside him on the straw, and his mind transformed her into Masha. The pain of the memory and all it stood for flooded through him. The girl's face in the stable on one side, Masha's face on the other, and between them the face of his sister Daniella, drifting in and fading back into vanishing horizons. Harry's eyes were on the baby's photograph, but in his ears was the voice of the girl pleading in the stable: "Don't leave me alone! Only we can understand each other. Our bodies are as ravaged as scorched earth. How shall we ever lie by the side of strangers? In what language could we explain to them . . ."

"A girl," he heard Masha's voice, "our daughter. We called her Renée." Then, almost as an afterthought: "For Renaissance."

"So that makes me Renée's aunt!" Galilea burst out excitedly. "And for the first time in my life, I'll be called Auntie!"

"Well then, Aunt Geegee," David said, "the Artzi family would like you and Harry to come to our home for lunch a week from today."

"We've just moved in, and our place is still a mess"— Galilea smiled sideways at Harry—"but I want you to come over as soon as possible. And where are you living?"

"In the same building as before, except that now our apartment is on the roof. We've gone up in the world," David said. "It's a great place. You can see the whole of Tel Aviv from our window."

Masha rose apologetically. "I really must go home now. It's time for the baby sitter to leave. Unfortunately, we still can't afford one for the full day."

On the way to the bus, Harry and Masha, her arm in his, walked ahead with Galilea and David following. "We'll never be able to penetrate their inner limits," said David. "They have a language all their own, a secret language we'll never understand. I saw the two of them in Naples, and they spoke to each other in a way that seemed different than any language known to man. Masha wouldn't believe the doctors in Italy when they told her she had a chance of becoming pregnant. And when she actually did become pregnant, she couldn't believe she was carrying new life in her womb."

"And I never saw such an expression on Harry's face as when he was talking to Masha," Galilea said. "I'm so happy to see them together. Oh, I have so much to tell you, David, but right now my tongue feels paralyzed."

"How unreal it seems seeing you and Harry together," he said. "When did it happen? How did you meet?"

"There'll never be enough days and nights for us to tell each other everything."

No sooner had Masha and David boarded the bus than David stuck his head out the window: "Don't forget now, Aunt Geegee, lunch next week at our house!"

They were standing in the center of their empty living room. "So, we finally managed to tidy up a bit," said Galilea, looking around.

Intended for receptions, the room still had no furniture, and now that the mess of construction and painting had been cleared, it seemed to have grown more spacious. Through the bare windows the light streamed in from the sky. Northward from their windows not a house was in sight. Even their own building, at the northernmost end of Tel Aviv, had not yet been completed. The topmost of its three floors was still vacant, and the area around the house, which would eventually be a lawn, was still cluttered with scaffolding and building materials.

The only furniture they had came from Galilea's nursery, and the movers had been directed to place it in the room reserved for their children. "The children have invited us for dinner," Galilea had said gaily as she asked Harry to their first meal in that room, where for the time being they lived, ate and slept.

They stood embraced in the middle of the empty living room, Galilea's head on his shoulder. The smell of new buildings, of beginnings, was everywhere. Beyond the windows was a rocky landscape covered with thorny shrubs which for thousands of years had been waiting for Moskowitz the Builder—if not tomorrow, then the day after—to sink into it the teeth of his steam shovel.

"Tomorrow's Tuesday," she murmured in Harry's ear. "Lucky day, as the good Jews say. Tomorrow I'd like you to go back to your retreat, my love, and begin writing again. I know how you feel, even though you never speak of it. I know now that unless you cut yourself off from this world, you won't be able to return to that other world, to be alone with it to write. So now, I beg you, don't let me delay you another minute. Don't worry about me. I'm much stronger than you think."

Holding her close, he looked through her hair to the barren horizon and saw it as a shaded wood of lofty palms. He inhaled their fragrance. He wondered at the source of energy of this butterfly in his arms—the vitality that had quickened to blossom the wasteland of his life.

"You must go on with your writing . . ." she was murmuring. "For my own happiness, I must make you do it. And if you promise me to go away and not worry, I'll promise you something: I won't worry either! You can't imagine how happy I was when I suddenly saw that to help you I must not mother you. Did anyone mother you when you were in Auschwitz? So now you can stay away as long as you like, even for a year. But promise me you won't come back before the book is finished."

He looked at her. The white light of her teeth tempted him. He leaned toward her parted lips. He drank the light. "Tomorrow, my love," she whispered, "you leave at dawn. Just let me fix you some food for the road. I know it's silly, but I want you to leave with food that I've packed with my own hands."

Pulling free, she left him standing there and dashed off to the kitchen. She grabbed up a wicker basket in each hand. "Harry," she called lightly to him from the corridor, "I'm going to run down to the grocer's. Remember, we're having lunch with David and Masha today."

He watched her from the window. A path had been cleared from the lobby to the street, but instead of taking it her tall legs ran like a schoolgirl's along the rungs of the construction ladders lying about. Sunlight played over the flowers on her summer dress, and her hair fanned out behind her as her breasts bounced to the rhythm of her gait.

The grocery was at the end of a short alley. Walking backward now, she raised her eyes to Harry, blowing kisses up to him. Her heels kicked up dust on the unpaved road. Harry shook his finger at her as though she were a child: Watch out or you'll trip over a rock behind you and fall! God, what a wild creature! She saw his annoyance, but stuck out a disobedient tongue at him. He moved away from the window. If she didn't see him looking, she'd behave.

Inside, he leaned a ladder up to the ceiling loft and brought down a bundle from its hiding place. Wrapped in it was his Auschwitz garment. Whenever he was alone and writing, he kept the garment before his eyes. For two years of Auschwitz days and nights this garment had covered his skeleton. Every thread of it knew him with a knowledge far beyond this place; every thread spoke to him in a language

without which there would be no sense to his writing. He
hid the bundle under Galilea's couch in the nursery to take
with him when he left.

He walked over to her cupboard and took out a sheaf of
paper, estimating its quantity with a quick glance. He knew
that once he was in the cabin among the citrus groves, he
would be as isolated as if he were alone in a desert, and
when he had once entered the world of his writing, he
would not go out in search of writing supplies. The ink
bottle was dry; he regretted not having asked Galilea to
pick some up at the store. He felt the trembling of his knees
that invariably seized him before writing.

In his hands he held the empty ink bottle, and his ears
rang with Galilea's words: "Don't come back before the
book is finished." His mind went limp. A wall of thorns
surrounded his writing, defeating him, cutting him off from
the world of men. What soil did this wild growth spring
from? As hard as he tried, he could not understand why he
was unable to sit at home and write like anyone else. No one
here would be in his way. Why this compulsion to retreat?
Wasn't the subject curse enough? Why should he have to
write like a pariah, ostracized by God and man?

He ached with a terrible ambivalence: his allegiance was
here—and his allegiance was *there*. Both pulled at him, unwilling to yield a piece of him to the other. Each claimed
him totally: unless he brought with him every ounce of his
being when he crossed over to the world of *there*, he could
not write what he had sworn to tell—and unless he returned
wholly to the world of *here*, he could never be like other
men. Between these two poles, in the no man's land separating the two worlds, his life was torn.

Galilea had gone to bring him food! How could she know
that in the place he was returning to they didn't eat food
from grocery stores. It suddenly annoyed him that she was

dragging home those baskets of food for him. Well, he would go help her with them anyway, and while he was there ask for writing supplies at the store.

He went down to the alley. Why had no warning sign been posted for drivers, he wondered, with all this sand around? Once they got stuck, they'd never be able to pull free; the harder they stepped on the gas, the deeper the wheels would sink in.

He had hardly started down the alley when Galilea appeared at the other end. He waved to her to wait. Dropping the packages, Galilea stopped short, seemingly puzzled over why he had come. She held out her arms to him like a mother reaching toward an infant taking its first steps. The wild child was at it again! Harry held back a laugh as he watched her. It was a good thing no one was around to see them. He lowered his head in embarrassment. At that instant, the blast of a bomb flung him into the air, caught him in a whirlpool of sand heaved up from the ground by the force of an explosion.

He was caught at the center of a vortex of dread. He saw death and recognized it, as he had seen and recognized it more than once in his life. And with recognition, a kind of calm lighted his mind as the familiar smell of death rose around him, death which had failed to take him so many times in the past and might fail again. He tumbled up and away from the abyss until the last slowing spins, the earth beneath him subsiding, coming to rest.

He opened his eyes and felt darkness pressing down on his lids. Only now did the danger to Galilea dawn on him, and the terrifying awareness jolted him to his feet. With crazed hands, he ripped the press of darkness off his lids, his eyes straining to penetrate the murky air, until bit by bit he began to make out columns of dense smoke circling upward, intermingled with dust and blue patches of sky.

Little by little he could hear again, and from the distances beyond the smoke, the faint echo of a voice reached him: "Harry! . . . Harry!"

As the sound registered, the image of a second ago was projected out of the darkness onto his brain like an illuminated screen: Galilea, her arms held out to him. He tore free and ran into the thick of the smoke. Their voices called to each other, their hands groping blindly until they stumbled into each other's arms. "I saw the bomb hit you. *Arabs!*" was all Galilea breathed before her body slumped in his arms.

Harry carried her through the gutted alley, emerging into the light after darkness. He carried her pressed against his heart and laid her on the sofa in the nursery. "Everything's all right now," he whispered.

Silent, her eyes wide and glassy, Galilea stared out the window. Outside, the air was thick with flames, a cauldron of dust, smoke and changing colors. In the nursery, the smell of scorching, sulphur and acetone was stifling. "Everything's all right now," he repeated over and over, rushing to get her a wet towel from the bathroom. Her hair was gray with dust, and her face and body were as black as if she had just been exhumed from a grave of ashes. One of her shoes was missing.

As he held the wet towel to her sooty forehead, she suddenly seemed to him to be looking through the eye-holes of a grotesque mask. Quickly, he thrust the towel over her face and began rubbing fiercely to wipe away the mask. At that moment the air around them shook again with a new burst of explosions slamming down in the distance of the city. Her fingers sprang to life and tore the towel away from her face. Her eyes were lucid. "Oh, Harry, how awful you look!" she cried, jumping off the sofa as though she had just awakened from shock, as if what had jerked her to her

feet was the sight of Harry's face and not the thunderous
sounds of the bombs or the lingering wail of the sirens
which might mean alarm or all-clear.

Standing before him now, Galilea was her old self, the
girl whose only concern was Harry, the girl whose enthusi-
asm had sent her off to buy him food just before the bombardment, the long-legged tomboy skipping along the rungs
of the construction ladders. It almost seemed as if what had
happened in the meantime had completely faded from
her mind and had sunk somewhere deep in her subcon-
scious. He looked at her in amazement. She tore off his
jacket, pulled away his tie, unbuttoned his shirt. Ordering
"Don't look in the mirror, my love," she rushed to the bathroom and turned on both shower faucets full force, then
dashed back and sat him on the sofa to remove his shoes.
She stripped him of all his clothes, and, without resisting,
he let her support him on her arm to the shower. He knew
that by allowing her to manipulate him however she
pleased, he was giving her the only cure for her shock
within his means.

As he stood naked under the shower spray, Harry drew
her to him under the jets of water. He held her tight and
watched the grime sloughing off their bodies as though it
were pouring down from above. The mud streamed in rivulets from her hair onto her light-colored summer dress,
pasted to her body and encrusted with filth. He pulled the
dress down over her shoulders, and the water burnished her
body to a tingling nakedness. His hands parted her hair
to reveal her face. She was naked in his arms, surrendering
herself with face uplifted to the spring-clear stream of water.
The whips of water burst into bubbles against her closed
lids, and the tickling on her lips made her smile with the
purity of a sleeping baby when a finger touches its mouth.
It was as if the moment of the explosion had been flushed

away with the grime on their bodies. What connection could there be between the limp body he had placed on the sofa and these glowing eyes he saw now? The link of time joining the *"before"* and the *"now"* dropped at their feet, the singing of their blood rising to fill the gap.

He picked her up in his arms as one would carry a baby to its crib from the bath. Over his shoulder she saw the imprints of his wet feet in the dust of the bombardment, and for a fleeting moment she imagined that they were thumb prints on a coded message received from enemy territory. Suddenly she woke from her reverie: "Harry, the baskets! The food!"

"Forget it."

"But that was the food I bought for you to take along!"

He did not wish anything to remind her of the shock. "Leave the devil his share," he said quickly. "He mustn't be tampered with too much. Let that food be ransom for our lives."

"Then I'll buy you something else in the city," she persisted. "You must take along food, and it must come from me. For luck."

He was amazed at her single-mindedness, her determination not to relinquish her plan, just as though nothing had happened or changed. Where, he wondered, in this girlish body was the source of the strength which had given her the audacity first to break into his Auschwitz world and pull him out, and now to send him back to those Auschwitz terrors? Looking at her, he saw the blurred boundary between the darkness of death on the road outside and the radiance of life glowing from the nakedness of her body. And she, laughing with delight, entwined her arms about his neck. "Come, my hermit! Tomorrow you'll be leaving me," she murmured huskily by his ear. "Tomorrow . . ."

As they walked out of the house, Harry took her by the arm. "I hate this dust, the way it settles on your shoes," he said to distract her from the sight of the alley. "God knows when they're going to get this road paved."

"Masha must have put lunch on the table by now. Not very nice of us to be late," she said.

He smiled, and in his smile was the reason for their lateness. With her hand in his, they reached the busy city streets. Here and there, people were crowding around gutted buildings. Again he contrived to divert her attention.

"Harry, just look at Allenby Road," she said. "You'd never know there had been a bombardment here, any more than you could tell by looking at us." And, indeed, the city moved at its usual pace. The Jewish community, inured by years of Arab rioting, had quickly adjusted to this first bombing of Tel Aviv by Egyptian pilots.

All of a sudden she pressed against his arm. "I'm trying to forget it but it keeps coming back, banging inside my head," she said, staring ahead. "Every time I remember that bomb." She was silent. Then she said, "I can't understand it. Even now, I keep seeing the bomb falling right on you. But actually it fell closer to me than to you. Let's walk faster, Harry." Her voice had a strange edge. "It's so odd: whenever I think of that bomb hitting you, I feel as hungry as a wild beast. Come on, let's hurry to Masha's."

They turned onto David Artzi's street. A quiet short street. At the far end, people were crowding around. Across from the house a civil-defense vehicle and an ambulance were parked at the curb.

They came closer. "What happened?" they asked the crowd of curiosity-seekers.

"A bomb hit the roof of this building. The whole family was wiped out. They've only lived there a short time. A man, a woman and a baby."

Lying on the stone floor of the city morgue were the victims of the air raid. Here, there was no weeping. Here, the mourners were as still as the gathered limbs of the dead. Galilea stood at Harry's side. He dared not touch her, dared not support her. As though if he did, he would insult her. Still as a stone she stood beside him, their eyes on the white shroud on the ground, which oddly, asymmetrically, covered the Artzi family.

"Well then, Aunt Geegee . . ." Not Aunt Geegee any more. David was lying under the white sheet on the floor. "You can see the whole of Tel Aviv from our windows," he had laughed with pleasure.

Here, weeping had no place. Here was the other, impenetrable side of weeping. Masha, who had not been reborn until she pronounced the name Felix.

Again it flashed through Harry's mind: if it had not been for Felix, he would have drowned in the river at the frontier.

Strange, each time he thought of Felix a preposterous question came to mind: Why had Felix sprawled on the hood of the truck throughout the mountain drive? As if everything else puzzling him had been resolved, and nothing remained but this one question. He had wanted to ask Felix that when they got to Treviso, and again when they met in Naples—and again at the Seaside Café. But, for some reason, on none of these occasions had it seemed appropriate to ask such an odd question. On his way to Felix's for lunch, he had thought of it again. Now he asked the shroud-covered body: Felix, why did you sprawl across the hood of the truck that time? Suddenly he remembered the Star of David painted on the hood. And now his question did not seem so bizarre. David Artzi, this mangled body, was he not the Star of David itself?

Galilea stood rigid beside him. Her thick hair fell over her profile so that he could not see her face. What was going through her mind? "Whenever I think of that bomb . . ." her words came back to him, "I feel as hungry as a wild beast."

He stared down at the sheet covering the Artzi family. Masha couldn't believe the doctors in Italy when they told her she was going to have a child. He stared at the shroud and saw the ghastly secret peering from Masha's blue eyes, the secret he alone knew. He had never asked her whether she, like his sister Daniella, had been in the Nazi House of Dolls. But to him Masha was like a halo surrounding the face of his sister Daniella. His blood was crying for vengence. Yet its image eluded him. Was it the face of the German baby hidden in the cellar of the German home, or was it Renée's face lying still beneath this white shroud. Was it the smoke gushing from the crematorium chimneys of Auschwitz, or was it the nuclear cloud hanging over the heads of all living flesh?

Daniella was dead. Masha was dead. Where was the vengeance for the death that was *there,* and where was the vengeance for the death that was *here?* Now, for the first time, he repudiated his plan to leave Galilea and write. It was loathsome to him, this writing—anathema. In the secrecy of that lonely cabin among the citrus groves, would he find refuge from the viper of revenge in his soul? Where was the desert to which he could run to escape it? Where was the whale that would swallow him with the curse of God on his head? He would always be vomited forth—even as Auschwitz and the river and the bomb had vomited him forth.

Galilea whirled around to face him. Silently, she gripped him by the arm and led him toward the exit.

23

A grayish-green rectangle of morning was framed in the window of the cabin. Harry's open eyes were staring into space. He had not closed them all night long. Now he could make out the sacks of fertilizer stacked along the cabin wall, he knew that behind the grapefruit trees day had arrived. Sliding down from the bunk he had put together under the rafters, he walked over to the plank desk by the window. His eyes lifted wearily to the calendar nailed on the wall. Another day! Picking up the stick beside his pen on the desk, he dipped its point into the black ointment he used to dab on the trees' stumps after lopping off withered branches, and smeared a black X over yesterday's date. Another withered day chopped away. He had already marked fifty-two crosses on the calendar. Like a black column they advanced upon him, all the days, all the moments of the days, a countless enemy host without end, converging upon him from the pages of the calendar, from beyond visible horizons. How much longer could he continue to retreat from them? A column of gravediggers dogging his footsteps day after day, night after night. This morning he plunged the stick deep into the ointment with a new fierceness; the ointment streaked down to the bottom row of dates like a black nightmarish tear.

On the desk, the pages covered with writing lay ready for the fire. Ready since last night, before he climbed into his bunk. The iron shears weighting them down appeared to him like the beak of a vulture ready to strike. Next to the shears, the matches. Everything ready. Fifty-two days of his life—fifty-two days in which he had tried to find a substitute for revenge—his solace. All to be put to the flame. No miracle possible.

Fifty-two days and fifty-two nights. Once these pages were burned, would he have the strength to begin all over again?

His hand reached for the matches. He felt it tremble. He leafed through the pages again. Words. Hollow words. Dead words, not scorched with the smoke of the crematorium. Frigid words, their iciness preserving nothing of the eternal fire burning within the Auschwitz mountain of ashes. Vacuous lines. Silent corpses. Where in them was the quiver of life? Where were their screaming voices? Where was the choked cry beyond the hermetically sealed door of the gas chamber?

He flung the pages to the floor in revulsion. *Auschwitz! Where can I run to escape you? And where can I hide from your memories?*

He knew that as long as these pages remained in the cabin, he could never begin again. He bent down. One by one he picked them up and carried them to the door of the cabin. He walked out.

The new day had spread across the treetops. Grapefruit gleamed among the green leaves like milky bulbs of light. He walked along the main path, which ran the length of the grove from one gate to the other, heading beyond the row of trees in front of the vegetable plot he had planted for his food supply. As he passed the jackals' lair, Mother Jackal's head poked out, her bleary eyes puzzling at him: Where are you off to so early in the morning, Kind Feeder from the cabin? And what is it that makes you look so gloomy? He doesn't even throw us a glance today!

He was past the trees. His rubber boots glistened, wet to the knee with the dew of the wild grass. He had been neglecting the grove lately; in places the weeds came up higher than his neck. He picked up some of the border stones between the vegetable beds and carried them a distance away from the fruit trees to set up a circle for the bonfire. He sat on the ground beside them with the pages in his lap. He touched a match to the first ones.

The pages twitched and writhed as the flames lapped at them. And when the paper's white body was consumed, the words leaped like a negative from the blackened pages. The words stared at him. They were his own. Mute witness to all the days and nights he had undergone here. They stared at him as if it were painful to part with him: Why do you do this to us?

Page after page he wrested from his lap and cast into the fire. Burned sooty flakes of paper, flying upward and away. Black ashes and pale ashes. The paper consumed becomes ashes. But words, where do the words go?

This was how they had been burned in Auschwitz, those whose bodies had turned to ash, whose lives had been unlived. Where did their souls go? He knew that as long as the soul of his words did not become one with the unfinished lives endlessly hovering in space, he would continue condemning the paper beneath the words, sending it up in flames.

He looked at the last pages in his lap, then in one swift gesture brought them to the fire. *Oh God, give me the words to match the mute and haunting sorrow in their eyes!*

He rose from the bonfire. His hands felt so empty now. The emptiness seeped through him. He was back at the beginning of the road. All the time he had spent here was gone as though it had never been. Again his feet were stuck at the crossroads. Which way was he to go? He felt as helpless as a child who has lost his way. For the first time since he had been here, he knew how much he needed Galilea. Not to talk to, only to be near. Like a dying man silently

sucking air from an oxygen tank, he would inhale her courage, her confidence. "Stay away as long as you like, even
for a year—until you finish," she had said. Well, today he
had finished. Could he let her see him this way—in defeat?

He followed the irrigation pipeline through the Jaffa
trees back to the cabin. Today the inspectors from the fruit-
marketing company were supposed to come to see about the
spray. Taking a magnifying glass from his pocket, he held
it up to a leaf on one of the trees, looking for traces of citrus
mite. The leaves were swarming with ladybugs. It looked as
though they had already devoured the citrus mite. He
wished the fruit-marketing people weren't coming today. He
had to get ready for them. The way he looked they might
take him for some kind of caveman.

He went back into the cabin and took out his shaving kit
from the suitcase, raising the mirrored lid. A stranger's
face—a frightening face—looked back at him. He ran his
hands over the full beard of the stranger in the mirror.
The moustache drooped over the upper lip, tangling with
the wild growth of beard and hiding the mouth from view.
He looked about the cabin, searching for some remnant of
himself. A light suit, cut in the latest fashion, was hanging from the rafters in a zipped nylon bag. A pair of white
leather shoes at the bottom of the wardrobe, a blue silk
shirt draped over the shoulder of the suit, and on the shirt
a bow tie. His eyes darted from one piece of wardrobe to
another. He needed to convince himself that he was indeed
Harry, Galilea's husband, meticulous in his appearance, not
this thick-bearded stranger staring at him from the mirror.

Suddenly he was seized by an urge to put on the suit,
even if only for the day. To be clean-shaven and neatly
groomed. To appear again in his own town, among people
who did not know him, where no one would realize what
face and what days he had shed.

His eyes moved from the mirror to the nylon bag to the

Auschwitz garb lying on his bunk—he could no longer tell which of the three was his real self. Which was he, and which was the mask? He searched for himself in the three worlds, but in none of them could he find himself.

He didn't know whether he could muster the courage to show himself at home. But as surely as the inspectors from the marketing company were coming, he knew that he would go home today.

He picked up soap and a towel and went outside to the water barrel standing beneath the dripping tap.

24

. . . Today for the first time I felt the child kicking at the wall of my belly. Harry's child in my womb. Today he has announced that he's alive. Now I have Harry with me day and night. Alive in my womb.

Is it a boy or a girl? Or twins—oh, let it be twins! If it's a girl, I'll name her Daniella. Though Harry doesn't know about it yet, and I have no idea what he'll think. And if it's a boy I'll call him Monish. And the two people Harry loved so much will be brought to life again.

And if Harry isn't home yet when it comes time for the baby to be born, I'm still not going to interrupt his work to tell him.

I live in total isolation these days. And I can't get over my discovery that I don't need company around me all the time. The isolation strengthens my sense of partnership in Harry's work. He insisted that he didn't want me to shut myself off from the pleasures of life in his absence. But even my beloved can't seem to grasp that being alone with him, even if it's only in my thoughts, is the ultimate pleasure for me. Where else but here in our home could I sense Harry with such complete awareness? Every object here has been touched by him; in every corner he has kissed me.

Beginning today, I'm not even going to visit my parents. I'll spend all my time alone with the baby. Harry's baby. Our child. What are you waiting for, you little character? Come on, kick Mummy hello! So you won't? You're just like your father, stubborn as a mule.

I'm burning with curiosity to know what this child in my belly looks like. Does every pregnant mother feel this way? With all these new scientific discoveries, how is it they haven't come up with an invention that would show me what the baby looks like, would let me see Harry looking at me from the baby's eyes.

He worried me terribly the last time he was home. Even though I was prepared for it, when I saw his face so haggard and lined I felt shaken to the core. He didn't say a word about his writing. He hardly spoke at all. Then he left as suddenly as he had walked in. I knew from the beginning it would be like this. Still, I can bear up under it. I haven't the slighest idea what goes on when he's writing, but when he was here I could sense the heaviness of the burden. He seems to be torturing himself for leaving me all by myself for so long. And that frightens me most. His worrying about me must interfere with his work—and then he has to stay away longer; the longer he's away, the more he worries, and on and on in a vicious circle. At least I got him to tell me where he's hiding out—though his very telling me confirmed my worst fears. "If you need me," he said, "call at once." Of course I won't. But I will write him a short letter to slip under his cabin door—just the way I put my first note under his cellar door. Harry needs me very much now. My letter will be able to say what I cannot. But he mustn't see me. What point is there in our being apart if it disturbs him so much? My heart picks up an alarm. I'll write now. Coming, my love.

25

His head between his hands, Harry sat at the makeshift desk he had set up under the window sill of his cabin and stared at the blank page before him. He had been sitting this way for three days, unable to summon the will to edge his hand over to the pen. Day and night, no difference. As if the hand were struck with paralysis. Would this numbing vacuum never let go of his brain?

Renée, in a single leap, came to nestle on his shoulder. Her tiny body rubbed against the back of his neck to appeal for a caress, at least a glance.

He had found the kitten outside the cabin. As if the mother of this foundling had decided that her baby would be better off here with this recluse. One night, bent over his desk, Harry had heard a whimpering, like a newborn infant's, from behind the door. He rushed to open it and found her lying on the ground, an abandoned waif, her tiny body shivering with cold, her cries heart-rending. Scooping her up in his palms, he brought her inside and laid her down on his bunk. Her little body was pure white except for a tawny crescent on her forehead, from the left eye to the ear, as though her mother had gazed too long at the quarter moon when she was carrying her. It was not until dawn that Harry had noticed a second spot on her foreleg. The moment he adopted her he named her Renée, because of her whimpering which intruded upon his thoughts just when the face of Masha's baby plagued his mind's eye.

Now Renée was demanding her due, clamoring to be petted. He wasn't writing anyway. It interested him to see how with patient training a creature like this could be taught to behave. Now Renée never bothered Harry if the pen was in his hand. He wondered whether she would also learn in time that man is not a cat—that a man could very well be active though sitting perfectly still.

He was suddenly angered by the purr rumbling in her belly by his ear. He wanted to shake her off. He was hot with anger, not really at this little white creature but at the thoughts that had settled like leeches in his brain to suck the marrow of his days and nights. Wasn't Renée appealing to him for exactly what he was begging of his thoughts? Didn't he need the very same pittance of compassion and understanding as this simple creature?

He placed a gentle hand on the kitten's silky fur and turned his face toward her tiny head. Her forepaws floundered in the tangle of beard on his cheek as though she had miscalculated and thought it was something solid, her arched tail all the while brushing against the hair at the back of his head. He looked tenderly into her eyes, with all the compassion his own soul thirsted for.

Tammy lighted on his window sill, cooing good morning. This was her daily visit with Harry, paid every morning with the regularity of a clock. Harry reached into the box of seeds, and Tammy flew over to perch on the end of his fingers, which were cupped around the seeds like a bowl. It had taken Harry many days to train her not to be afraid to enter a strange man's cabin. Come on, little dove, don't be frightened, no one here will steal your virtue. She was truly a little flirt, captivating from head to toe: her head crowned with a vermilion shawl, her lids done up in blue mascara, the tips of her tiny feet painted pink, her puffing bosom covered with a white mini-blouse, and her shoulders mantled in a cape that ranged from the sun yellow to purple. A designing little tease, with an audacious tail tipping up behind her. Such a beauty should be afraid to traipse around all by herself—but Tammy, no need to worry about her. That mistrustful red beak would discourage any molesters.

In no hurry to leave, Tammy lingered for a while on his fingertips. As if it would not be in good taste to gorge oneself and then immediately fly away; courtesy demanded an extra few moments with one's host. Tammy too had learned manners these past few months. She perched there, looking him over with a round bored eye, waiting for a tidbit of gossip for dessert. Renée's purr by his ear swelled into an angry rasp of jealousy.

Suddenly, as Harry stared down at the dove perched on his left finger and the kitten on the shoulder of that same left arm, he realized with a blinding clarity what had been numbing his mind, holding him back from writing the most difficult chapter of the book. He was paralyzed with hate. And hate, by its very nature, is barren. Hate is darkness. Hate drags your soul into its abyss of poisons. But the chapter he was trying to write, the chapter about his anguish, had to burn pure and clear, had to soar above the abyss of hate, so that like a beacon it would shine through the night; his agony should glow with a white heat, purging everything it touched, even hate itself.

Not through dark air of poison but with the pure red of fire would he reach the end he had vowed to achieve. As long as he cannot make his right hand, with which he wishes to write, be like his left, on which he had trained a dove and a cat to coexist, the pure fountain of creativity will be sealed. What would his own iota of hatred be, added to the apocalyptic hatred which in Auschwitz had reduced his world to ashes? Rising to his feet, he sent the dove out the window and lifted the kitten down from his shoulder.

She looked at him briefly from the floor. Again Harry was struck by how tiny she was. All these months she had grown hardly at all. As if she came from pygmy stock.

He suddenly realized that if Tammy had already come in for breakfast it was time for him to shift the sprinkler lines in the grove. His eye went to the tape measure on the desk. He should have long since measured off and pruned the stubs, which were already cutting into the grafted scions. Day after day he kept postponing the work he needed to do on the trees with the excuse that he had to finish the chapter first. And the wasted days drifting by horrified him. A whole week frittered away staring blankly at the pages. In this state of self-chastisement, what frightened him was the sense of his utter ineptitude. He wasn't even fit for the grove. Everything slipped through his fingers; he made a mess of everything he touched.

His eyes rested on the blankness of the sheet, and another wave of vertigo washed over him, as if looking over a precipice into a bottomless chasm. Furiously, he shoved the tape measure into his pocket and stomped out of the cabin without a glance at Renée, trailing behind him.

One by one he shut off the taps on the sprinkler lines and transferred the pipes to the front rows. Once the soil had soaked up the irrigation water, virtually no trace of the irrigating was evident—like a mouth wiped dry after drinking. He was the only one in the whole region who watered his grove at night. Twenty-four hours around the clock, he was awake. He looked up the hill to the water gauge on top of the tower. So early in the morning and the gauge was already at the half-empty mark! With this water shortage, the trees would soon be parched. The pressure was so low, he'd have to water the grove during the day too; nighttime wouldn't be enough.

Walking in among the Jaffas, he found some consolation

in how well the "eyes" he had grafted had taken; they were beautifully healthy. He passed from one tree to the next, measuring twenty inches above the grafting point and marking it for pruning. The sap and vigor of the graft had been received. The wound of coupling had healed over. The graft was green and succulent, and the tree's body had not rejected the infusion of new life. This tender scion would become a fruit-bearing tree, and the aging parent stock would regain its youth with the new injection of life.

He moved from tree to tree, measuring and marking each tree with a nick. He would work down to the end of this row and then go back to prune them. That way he'd save time. Removing the bandages from the grafts that had healed, he placed props under the young shoots that needed buttressing.

He got as far as the sour-orange section. Around the jackals' lair was a stir of activity in preparation for some feast. The patriarchs of two neighboring clans were busy plucking a chicken whose carcass they had dragged from somewhere. From inside the dens their offspring were watching, impatient little heads peeking out, their sad watery eyes quivering with anticipation. They were too busy today to pay attention to their patron from the cabin.

He stood watching them, and his eyes filled with agony at the sight of the jackals. The pain of Auschwitz and the pain after Auschwitz impaled him like two poison-tipped arrows—the death *here* which had engorged Masha and Renée and the death *there* which was the essence of Auschwitz. What had death fed on *there*? And what did death feed on *here*? The light of brotherhood was bestowed upon these two jackal heads. *Why, O Creator of jackal and man, have you hidden this face of Your Light from man?*

His eyes smarted as if he were standing in blazing heat and the grove all around him were being sprayed with sulphur. He saw the rows of skeletons marching to the crematorium, and he saw the jackals. The images were superimposed, one upon the other—twofold, transparent, one succeeding the other. In a rage, he flung the tape measure away. Where could he run from this anguish? Where would he find refuge from hate? He walked into the thick of the trees; the dried-out twigs scratched at his face. A strangling weed was twining around the loins of a tree. The untended grove had become a jungle.

At the edge of the path, he saw Renée standing under one of the taps, her head tilted upward and her tongue reaching for a drop of water. Suddenly her white fur bristled as though she were caught in a gust of wind, her tiny body rearing back, forepaws petrified in mid-air as she stared hypnotized with terror at whatever was ahead of her. Then, on the other side of the tap, he glimpsed the head of a snake slithering out of the weedy overgrowth. Horrified, Harry stood riveted to the spot. Man and snake stood opposite each other—primordial enemies, with a hatred between them as ancient as Genesis. At the dawn of Creation, each had gone his own way, dividing the earth between them: the one to lord over its surface, the other to be king of its nether reaches. Then by what right did he come here now to drink of the upper waters gilded with sun? The snake's jaws opened. "Renée!" the cry was pulled from Harry as he lunged for a tree prop to slash at the enemy.

Too late. Glassy-eyed, Renée lay beneath the tap. The snake had vanished in the thick of the wild grass. Harry swung wildly all around him with the stick. Blindly, he stamped on the grass and smashed at the ground with the stick until it had broken into pieces. One after another he ripped up the sticks propping up the trees, continuing to beat the underbrush savagely and senselessly. It was all his fault! Why had he been so careless? Why had he neglected the grove so the weeds could get that high? Why had he moped around the cabin for days and weeks on end, staring at those blank pieces of paper, allowing the snakes to take over the grove? Why hadn't he cut down the weeds? The grafted shoots snapped as he pulled away their supports. He was ready to rip up the whole grove just to get at the snake hole. The blood pounded deafeningly in his ears. Maddened by his lust for revenge, he stormed into the thick of the grass higher than his chest, leaving himself exposed to the serpent's bite. He would confront the snake!

In his frenzy he found himself outside the grove. Limp and beaten. He dragged on beyond the trees until he came to the bonfire stones on which he had burned the manuscript. The stones were rimmed with soot. He stared back at the grove. From the distance the trees seemed to have closed ranks to form an impregnable wall barring his way back. He felt as though he had been banished from the grove for having allowed the snake to reign. He stood looking down at the bonfire stones, a memorial to his days and nights. The black soot was all that remained of his writing. And there in the grove the snake prevailed.

Stumbling back along the road dividing the cultivated from the barren areas, he was shaken with guilt that he had named the kitten after Renée. Everything around him seemed weighted with symbolic meaning. Staring at the dirt road, he saw it as the bombed alley near his home; in his arms Galilea was numb with shock. He did not know where to turn. Everywhere, dead ends: Galilea, home, the grove, the cabin with its blank pages—all locked and fenced off from him. And he dragged along, desolate, shunned by everyone.

Hunched over, he wandered through the rows of trees like someone who has strayed into an alien grove. He did not lift his eyes to the trees his own hands had implanted with new life.

A terrible yearning for Galilea welled up in him. She was the only one who could give him the strength to keep on—just as she had when he had come home after burning the first manuscript. But this time the way to her too was barred. He couldn't go to her again empty-handed.

Ahead of him was the donkey, tied to the trunk of a tree. At the sight of him, she brayed a neck-stretching, buck-toothed welcome, then immediately fell silent, almost as if she sensed his misery. Harry gathered her head in her arms. He felt the warmth of life in the animal's neck, and he envied her. Bending down, he put a few handfuls of fodder into her bucket and proceeded on to the cabin.

As he turned left, he saw the tap, and next to it the pair of yellow jackals standing over Renée's tiny corpse. He shrieked at them as they fled in terror for their lives from his hail of rocks. He couldn't bear to go near her dead body. Skirting around it, he went on into the cabin.

Again he was sitting in front of the pages, his head in his hands, staring at the blankness. Like a bobbing boat lost in a timeless ocean, his thoughts drifted toward desolate shores.

He woke from his reverie and saw a sealed envelope that seemed to have dropped out of the blue. He stared at it, unable to comprehend what it was. He looked up at the window above his desk. How had the envelope gotten here? He opened the envelope, and inside he saw Galilea's hand.

Beloved,
Forgive me for breaking into your solitude. I couldn't do otherwise. Ever since your last visit I've been tormented by the thought that because of me you have no peace of mind. And this is what I must give you back to you. Like Rabbi Akiva's beloved, who sent him away for twenty-four years so that he might find peace for his spirit and his way in the paths of the Torah, I pray that you will draw spiritual peace and healing from your writing. Like Rachel his wife, I too believe that only

in retreat and seclusion can you find this peace of mind. I envy Rachel for having to shear her hair and sell it for bread when they were parted. It was not given to me to offer such a sacrifice. Allow me at least, beloved, the privilege of my own meager one —this daily sacrifice of your being away from me—and I shall be the gladdest of women.

You had the wisdom to raise me to the understanding that even when we are apart in body, we remain inseverably joined. Never have I felt as strong as I do these days: I have your life in my womb. This way, beloved, you have realized your first vengeance, made manifest in skin and sinew. But only your labor of loneliness will bring to light your second vengeance. Together, therefore, let each of us attend to his own task in this our vengeance, for it is a sublime privilege we have been granted . . .

He soaked his face in the letter and it washed over him like purifying water.

26

Night retreated. He did not know how many nights had now departed. Dawn was pale in the window of the cabin. He had written the last line of the book. He sat immobile, his eyes on the rising light as he slowly returned to earthly time.

The new day cast its light upon the pile of pages on the desk scribbled in a dense hasty hand. Only now did it strike him that he had reached the final line. The final line! And with it came the full impact of the significance of this day: today he was going home.

He snuffed out the kerosene lamp. His eyes lifted to the calendar. Today—what was today's date? The black *X*'s were lagging far behind. They had stopped somewhere on a page of the season past, unable to catch up with him.

His mind was clear and his body as light as air. His destination lay homeward. And an odd sensation filled him. He was like someone preparing for a journey to a distant foreign land. In his absence, the city and its people had become strangers to him, their ways almost forgotten. And the obsessive anxiety rose in him again—the fear that his strangeness would attract attention. He began making sounds, then isolated syllables, fragments of words, sentences. His long silence made the words sound eerie and coarse to his ears, as though some strange person were speaking. Unused to hearing his own voice, flesh-and-blood voice of this earth, he no longer recognized it.

He left the cabin. In the grove the trees glittered with blossoms, and their fallen petals covered the ground. The path unrolled at his feet a carpet of white buds. He stood there inhaling the deep fragrance. "Spring!" His voice reverberated through the festival of trees, and the birds accompanied his exclamation like choir boys spreading a tapestry of hymns before the cantor.

He walked along the flower-strewn path, and on both sides the branches extended him chalices brimming with wine. Veiled brides in tiaras of blossom, the trees flanked his path.

Turning back to the cabin, he went inside and pulled down the nylon wardrobe from the rafters. He took out his suit and picked up the bow tie, on the back of which the tiny key was pinned. He looked at the key that Galilea had enclosed with her first letter, the first human gift he had been given after Auschwitz. He replaced the bow tie on his suit. He opened his shaving kit. He picked up soap and a towel. Then he undressed and walked out naked into the dawn to wash himself in the water barrel. Making himself ready for the city. Its people. Galilea.

Harry had hardly begun climbing the stairs to their apartment when a neighbor, coming down, beamed at him: *"Nu,* Mr. Phoenix, is it time for congratulations yet?"

Harry was bewildered. The folder containing the manuscript was pressed under his arm. For a moment he had forgotten that life had continued in the outside world.

The neighbor persisted. "Your wife has already given birth?"

"Oh, excuse me . . ." Harry stammered, and he wheeled around and ran down the stairs to the nearest taxi stand. "To the maternity hospital!" he called to the driver.

The corridors and wards of the hospital were jammed with the beds of women in labor, and their wails mingled with the cries of the newborn babies in the nursery. Instead of a series of individual beds within each ward, he seemed to see one gigantic bed stretching from wall to wall, and the white caps of the nurses floated back and forth like sails on a horizon.

In the midst of this corridor-long confusion of beds and emergency stretchers, Harry searched for Galilea. He bumped into other people, and other people collided with him. His way was blocked by a woman heavy with child who clutched at her belly with both hands, her face contorted with weeping. "Doctor! Doctor! Why do you have to have pull to get anything done in this country?" She was complaining bitterly to the man in light suit and white shoes, a folder tucked under his arm, whom she mistook for a member of the medical staff. "See that one there? She came in two days after me, and they whisked her right off to the delivery room and wheeled her out again in a few minutes, baby and all! And look at me, in such pain for three days, and nothing! Oh, Doctor, I can't take these pains any more!"

Harry grabbed one of the doctors rushing by. "Excuse me, please. Professor Glick's daughter is supposed to be here. Could you . . ."

"She's up in the Chief's room," the doctor replied brusquely. "We had a bed put in there for her. Walk down the second corridor, then turn right and you'll see a sign on the door . . ."

Harry paused a moment in front of the closed door, then quietly pushed it open. Some men and women were lounging in armchairs. Flowers. A white bed. And the low hum of talking which, at his entrance, came to an abrupt stop— as though the newcomer brought the stillness of a vacuum into the room with him.

He stood at the foot of the bed. Galilea's face was immobile. Silently, their eyes met.

Galilea reached out toward the nurse by her bed. "Show the father his daughter," she said.

From the crib, the nurse lifted a small white-wrapped bundle and placed it in his waiting arms.

Cowled in white, peering up at him with stunning suddenness, was the face of his sister Daniella. With the eye of a camera he saw her: diminutive, focused, exact. Just like the day they had parted in Kongressia, Poland, when Harry promised her he wouldn't take long to bring her over to Palestine. The identical blue eyes. As he looked into this face, the Daniella he remembered in the ghetto was wiped from his mind. As if Daniella had never known the ghetto, had never been locked up in the Nazis' House of Dolls. It was as if she had leaped from their moment of parting at the railroad station, the end of summer 1939, to cling to the folds of the present moment. He could hear himself calling to her out the window of the express train: "Dani, I'll bring you to me in the land of Israel!"

One by one, the other visitors left the room. Harry straightened up. Walking over to the nurse, he returned the baby to her arms and she put the baby down beside Galilea. Harry handed the folder to Galilea. She opened it and saw, in bold handwritten letters, the title of the new book: DANIELLA.

PART TWO

And when I passed by thee and saw thee wallowing
in thy blood, I said unto thee: In thy blood live!
—Ezekiel 16:6

27

The water tower among the groves was suddenly torn from the hill and hurled into the air, its sides splitting apart, water gushing umbrella-wise from the cracks. Harry ran until he thought his lungs would burst. "Water! Water!" he screamed, and his eyes opened in terror.

The bedroom was dark. The cry still trembled on his lips, resounding in his ears as though he had actually screamed in his sleep. His hand felt the bed by his side. Galilea was missing again. He did not know what to make of the weird dreams that had been hounding him lately. He felt exhausted from his dreamed flight of terror. His heart was pounding as hard as if he had actually been running.

Harry brought the watch on his wrist to his eyes, straining to read the phosphorescent dial: a quarter to five. If he hurried, he might make the first bus. He had to get the orange-pickers started. A vicious winter this year. The fruit was in danger. The rains kept up. If only the cold winds didn't bring hail.

A short ladder of light penetrating the slits of the shutter was projected from the street lamp onto the wall across from him. Harry gathered up his clothes, holding the shoes in his hand. He'd put on the shoes beyond the front door so that he wouldn't disturb Galilea and the children sleeping in the next room. Passing the window, he glanced outside. A long sheaf of rain strands, like the bundle of fibers in a broom, shimmered under the street lamp. The wind swung the lamp to and fro, and the lighted sheaf swept over the puddle with the long broom of rain. A hard winter, Harry mumbled to himself. If this rain didn't stop by dawn, the pickers might not be willing to climb the ladders at all.

The floor beside the bed was littered with newspapers. Harry picked his way on tiptoe, and the papers under his feet made a grating rustle. The house was choking with newspapers. Galilea couldn't get to sleep unless she had all the evening papers by her bedside. Her day began with the morning papers and her night with the evening papers: Has anyone been killed by the *Fedayoun*? Have more victims been blown up by another mine?

In the hallway, he heard gasping sobs from the children's room. He dropped his clothes on the floor and dashed in. The night light in the bathroom cast its red glow into the room, and watching over the children from the sofa between the two cribs lay Galilea, whimpering in her sleep.

Harry wanted to smooth her forehead, to awaken her from this fitful sleep with a kiss. But he knew from experience that her crying would grow ten times worse once she was awake, and then the children would wake up too, making it impossible for Galilea to get back to sleep. So he would only be precipitating the beginning of another painfully haunted day of sobbing. The pattern never varied. Lately, Galilea hadn't been able to sleep without pills, and her day dragged on until she was totally exhausted with weeping and dropped off into a pit of sleep, only to emerge from it into another endless day of torment.

The children were sound asleep in their cribs, the boy's foot dangling between the bars. Harry carefully tucked the little foot back under the quilt. It was time to buy the kids new beds, he mused, real beds. Monish was growing like a beanstalk. Though a full year younger than his sister, Daniella, he was already as tall as she was.

Almost every night lately, Galilea had been jumping out of bed and dashing into the children's room to see if they were still alive, then staying there to ward off whatever danger might lie waiting. She would have liked Harry to stay with them too, but she knew how hard his day's work in the grove was and how much he needed his few hours of undisturbed sleep. It was impossible to tell what had triggered Galilea's fearfulness. It seemed to have begun after the birth of her second child, when Harry had just finished his book *Monish* and Galilea had become as familiar with it as she was with his two other books. It was then that the first symptoms of her anxiety became evident. For two years of torment she had kept her fears a secret from him. If only she had confided in him at the outset, he might have been able to sterilize her fear, to root it up before it had spread. No one in the whole country was as terrified of the *Fedayoun* as she! Why should such dread be concentrated in Galilea, of all people? It was as though she imagined that the Nazis had been metamorphosed into *Fedayoun*; just as they had murdered Daniella and Monish back *there,* so they were plotting to snatch the lives of her own Daniella and Monish *here.* Little by little her anxiety for the lives of Harry and the children had bloated into a malignant growth. The bigger the children grew, the more beautiful they became, the deeper her anxiety, and, with the increasing frequency of headlines reporting the *Fedayoun* murders, the blacker the imaginary danger—as if it lay in wait for her family alone. As if the fate of the entire nation were concentrated in the nursery of her children.

He stood over Galilea, still undecided whether or not to wake her. He couldn't bear to see her tortured in her sleep. The crying did not subside; heavy indistinct phrases were convulsing in her throat, as if she were pleading with someone, begging for mercy. No one would have recognized this Galilea, and it had been years since she wanted to see anyone. She hardly ever went out of the house now. All day long she stayed in bed, or stood at the window watching tensely to see if Harry would come home from work safe and sound. When he was gone, everything else was wiped from her mind but the one horrendous thought: Any minute they would come to tell her that he had been killed. It terrified her to pursue this thought to its end, but the moment Harry was out of the house it pounced on her, grabbed her by the throat. Then only food had the power to help her breathe again. But once she had eaten, the bitter tears began to flow again. A vicious circle spinning her round and round.

If they could have seen her now, not one of her acquaintances would have believed this was Galilea. As though she had planned the destruction of her beauty as a sacrificial exchange for the lives of Harry and the children. All traces of shapeliness were lost in the rolls of hulking flesh. She hid chocolate bars all over the house and kept food in the linen closet and in the pockets of her dresses and coats. The house had become a mess of newspapers, medicines and sweets.

Harry's hands trembled as he covered her, drawing up the blanket she had thrown off in her sleep. At once the weeping stopped; turning on her side, she sank into a peaceful slumber.

Harry went into the kitchen and closed the door behind him so the light would not disturb the sleepers. Under a newspaper on a corner of the marble counter, he found a pile of egg shells, the remains of Galilea's nocturnal feast, her foolproof method of inducing sleep after waking in terror at midnight. More than ten broken egg shells. Two empty margarine wrappers. The oversized skillet, as deep as a pot. He lifted the lid of the breadbox. Of the two loaves of white bread that had been there when he went to bed, only a miserable butt was left. Looking at the remains of the bread, Harry imagined Galilea's struggle not to down it all—at least to leave him enough for a sandwich to take to work. Haggard and shaken, he stood amid the ruins of his life. His eyes surveyed his surroundings. *Why has this happened to you, my precious love? Why you?*

A deluge fell from the skies. The universe was nothing but trickling water. Harry stood on a ladder among the branches of a tree. The rain fell in slender strands, but the drops of water spilled heavily from the leaves overhead, as if he were standing under a shower head.

As he dropped the picked fruit into the pouch hanging on his hip, its weight pulled his body down on one side, and the strap cut into his shoulder. The rain water had bloated the fruit, and as the heavy pouch at his side filled, it upset his balance. The drops of water fell onto his eyelids, and a thick dark fog hovered among the branches. His hands were damp and frozen, but without letup he continued to snip the fruit with the shears. The truck would be coming any minute now to haul the fruit to the packing house. Two hundred and eighty-eight boxes to a truckload. The crop must be saved. The wind was knocking down the fruit, and anything left on the trees would be ruined by the frost.

The pickers in his vicinity were climbing down from their ladders to empty their pouches into the field bins. Their eyes met in question: Does it make any sense to go back up? It was neither desirable nor possible to pick in such rain. They were ready to give up a day's pay. Watching Harry climbing in among the branches to the top of the tree, they couldn't make up their minds whether to continue working or dash for shelter under the cabin eaves.

Harry's hands were scratched and bleeding from the thorns on the branches, and the rain came pouring down on them. He felt no pain and he ignored the cuts. The eyes of the laborers looked up at him in puzzlement. Did he really think he could fill those eight tiers of fruit boxes for the truck all by himself?

Harry pushed farther into the branches. He did not want to be seen. His head felt feverish, and the tears streaming down his face mingled with the rain and sweat. As he cut down the fruit, Galilea's bed floated before his eyes. He saw the children pleading with their mother: "Don't cry, Mommy! Where does it hurt you?" And Galilea sobbing as she clutched them to her: "It hurts me in my soul . . ."

His head jutted above the upper branches. In their denseness the treetops seemed to be spread in a blanket beneath him, and above his head the weeping skies of rain and fog sprawled like a cloak of mourning. Whenever a thick fog rolled over the Nazi camp, the Germans didn't march the Jews out to the hard-labor area. Not because they felt sorry for the Jews, but because the fog would hamper the sentries' aim should any Jew think of escaping. One prayer was on every prisoner's lip then: Never let the fog lift! It was their only chance to rest, and the damp chilly fog had the warmth of a mother's lap in which they could rest their heads for a little while. How intensely they hated the first ray of sun that pierced the curtain of fog. To each of them, that sun was more evil than the Nazis.

Could the Auschwitz hunger and the Auschwitz anguish have been absorbed into Galilea's blood from his books? *"It hurts me in my soul . . ."* After that terrible night when the *Fedayoun* smashed into Aunt Nina's home in the village of Sharon, Galilea could not be consoled; no medicine or drug had the power to calm her. Day and night she stuffed food down her throat. Impossible to understand how a human belly could hold so much food. The unrelenting pain of the compulsion to eat screamed from her eyes, the eyes of someone drowning, gagging on mouthfuls of sea water, with no one around to save him. Eating quieted her only for a moment; then her hunger would erupt all the more savagely, sending her rushing into the kitchen, where she would slam the door behind her so that no one could see her as she was being raped, as she was being violated by the compulsion to eat. Sometimes they could hear her weeping from behind the closed door, and Daniella would plead with her outside the door, "Mommy, I won't go to school today. I'll stay in bed with you and take care of you, just like a nurse. Please don't cry, Mommy . . ." And Monish would press his face against the wood of the door: "And I'll bring you anything you want from the store . . . I'll stay with you too until Daddy comes home from the grove . . ."

Suspended in fever, he stood at the top of the ladder, grabbing the oranges one after the other, cutting them and dropping them into the pouch, snip-drop, snip-drop. The chilling rain washed off the sweat mixed with his tears. *Oh God, have mercy on her and the two little ones . . .*

Winter days, and the grove was distant from the city. Harry left home in the darkness of morning, and in the darkness of night he returned, every day transferring to six buses, back and forth.

Every evening, short of breath, Harry would hurry back. The moment he reached the corner of his street, he would look anxiously toward his house: What if a crowd is milling around and what if someone comes running out to inform him that Galilea has put an end to her torment? It was futile to try to defend himself against these thoughts; like wormwood, they had taken root in him. He was afraid to think them through, but they burrowed inescapably in his mind.

Their building was no longer an outpost at the city limits. Tel Aviv had long since moved farther northward. New streets pushed through from one day to another, hives of residences and business districts. The barren waste which the windows of their apartment had once overlooked was now a brisk noisy metropolis. Their neighbors were newcomers from the far reaches of the Diaspora; none of them would know that only a few yesterdays ago a girl as sun-filled as a butterfly had dwelled there, a girl whose name was Geegee.

Harry's hand shook as he opened the door to his apartment. Lately, this moment—the opening of the door—had become the most frightening. He tried to force calm upon himself. In a demonstration of composure, he took off his coat in the hallway with slow deliberate motions, his steps carefully relaxed as he approached the bedroom. As always, the children ran to meet him, and he searched their mute faces. So that he would not infect them with his anxiety, this time too he did not inquire about their mother. He still clung to the vain belief that by ignoring Galilea's illness he could undo it. He persisted in a game of make-believe: here he was, coming home, and finding his world as whole and as normal as it had ever been. He hugged the heads of the children nestling against his body, and with a feigned serenity, he led them into the bedroom.

The bedroom floor was the usual clutter of newspapers, and piled high all around—on the night tables, at both the head and foot of the bed—were Escoffier and Larousse cook-

ing encyclopedias, volumes of baking and pastry confections in French, English and Italian. Publishers from all
over the world, admirers of Galilea's from the days she had
been associated with them because of Harry's books, sent
them from time to time as tokens of friendship. Dust
jackets with photographic displays of mouth-watering delicacies. And strewn around in the midst of this chaos were
Galilea's medicines in glass tubes, cellophane wrappers,
jars and gelatine capsules next to water glasses turned on
their sides owing to Galilea's lack of control over her hand
muscles, weakened with obesity; not to speak of empty
boxes of candy and crumpled pieces of chocolate foil which
she had thrown on the floor—this, the normal appearance of
Galilea's room these past few years.

"Hello, precious!" Harry greeted her. He bent over and
held her head between his hands. "I have a surprise for
you, dearest."

"I bet the next thing you'll say is I look terrific, 'touch
wood . . .'" Galilea mimicked his usual compliment. "And
you, on the other hand, dear husband, look like a real
Auschwitz Mussulman! This has got to change. Either you're
coming home every day for lunch or you're not going out to
the grove again. That grove can rot, for all I care, if it
needs my husband's health to survive! And today I concocted a brand-new dish for you. It's absolutely magical.
A gastronomic symphony! I spent the whole day in the
kitchen. Did I say kitchen? I should say lab!"

She was off on a flight of fancy. Her mind was lucid and
quick, composing recipes and inventing methods of preparation. Harry listened attentively, his head resting on her
breast as her fingers ran through his hair, while her mouth
stewed and sautéed and baked and fried endless delicacies.

Across from him, on the edge of the bed, was the evening
paper. His eye fell on an item: "Today in the Negev, at

Kilometer 127 of the Beersheba-Eilat highway, a bus ran into a mined ambush. The *Fedayoun* opened fire. The driver and three of the passengers were killed. Bloodhounds have traced the tracks to the Gaza Strip."

Harry reached for the paper to get it out of sight, but immediately realized the inanity of his impulse. As if by getting rid of the paper he could get rid of the terrorist murders! And what about tomorrow, next month, next year? Would the situation ever change? Could he keep shielding her from the daily reality of the news?

"Good God!" Galilea started. "Look at me feeding my husband on theories when I should be serving him food. And that emaciated pack of bones lying there not saying a word. Quick, get off me! The mere thought of that heavenly dish I cooked up for you today makes my mouth water." Her puffy eyes laughed up at him.

Harry was cheered by her elation, even though her mind had not once strayed from its obsessive preoccupation with food. He helped her lower her swollen legs from the bed— one, then the other—and picked up her housecoat from the floor to help her on with it. This oversized housecoat was the only thing she could squeeze into. No one in the house had seen her in anything else for a long time now.

Suddenly, as she looked at Harry and the children with their arms around him, her eyes widened in horror. She saw them lying mangled under a white shroud on the floor of the morgue, like David Artzi's family. The Arab enemy had slaughtered her family. Straining to conceal the vision of terror from Harry, she pushed her head into the pillows and burst into a terrified wailing.

Shivering as though they had been caught in a wave of fierce cold, the two children stood by the bedside. Harry bent down to his son and asked him in a whisper whether Grandpa or Grandma had visited today. "Yes," the child whispered back, "but Mommy wouldn't let them into her room. She didn't want to see them."

Dazed, Galilea turned her head to Harry, her face swollen with weeping, staring through him to unfathomable distances. Then her arms reached out for him. He buried his head in her embrace and she held him tightly against her body. "Harry, I'm so tired . . . I can't stand this torment any more . . ." The words were distorted as if she had lost all control over her throat muscles. "I can't stand to see how I'm torturing you and the children. Oh, Harry, I don't know what's happening to me . . ."

He lifted his head. "What makes you say things like that! You'll see, you'll be well again, and everything hurting you will go away like a bad dream."

Daniella climbed onto the bed and took the plate off the night table to begin spoon-feeding pieces of fried egg into her mother's sagging jaws. "You'll see, Mommy, I'm going to make you all better."

Harry sat Galilea up in bed. Monish held slices of white bread in his hand, and for every swallow she took from the spoon, the child put some bread into his mother's mouth.

She was quieted by the food, and the tears now flowed gently down her cheeks. She swallowed them with the food. "Harry, I'm making your life miserable." Her voice was muffled as she chewed. "I'm making my sweet family miserable. I don't know what's the matter with me. I'll never get better."

"But, Mommy, you see, you're already getting better," said Monish. "You've already stopped crying . . ."

"Harry," she said, clasping all three of them in her arms, "the children have set the table for you. Look what's come over me, my love, I'm not even fit to serve you food. Go, Dani baby, serve Daddy his supper. He hasn't had anything hot to eat all day. Go, Harry; Dani has set the table especially for you. Please go, I beg you. You'll see how beautifully the children have set the table."

Harry sat at the table, properly and formally set in his honor. The knife in his hand sliced the bread, and his throat tightened. He was afraid to look at his little girl sitting across from him. "Why don't you dip the bread in the sardine oil?" the child asked him.

He wanted to ask his daughter whether she had done her homework. Daniella was the best pupil in her third-grade class, and her face was an exact replica of his sister Daniella's. He suddenly saw himself sitting with his sister on the steps of the ghetto soup kitchen, and he could hear her saying, "You put on my sweater this minute, Harry. You have such a long way to go to get back to your Jew Quarter. I can't understand how Sanya lets you out like this."

He dawdled with his bread in the sardine oil and could not bring it to his mouth. The last bite he had taken was lumped in his mouth; he could not get it down. He wanted to tell her to go in to her mother—he didn't want Daniella to see him this way—but even this he could not get out. Nobody in this house had yet seen him in tears.

As he retired to his corner in the living room, its emptiness so stifling that it choked him, Monish quietly drew close, school books in hand. "Mommy fell asleep," he informed him in a whisper. "I've been waiting for you to come home. Now I can get my homework done." Harry sat him in his lap. The boy brought his lips close to his father's ear to entrust him with a secret: "Today Mommy burned all her pictures from the old album. I saved one for you." He held out the picture and tiptoed away to the nursery to do his homework.

Before him was Galilea in a bikini, smiling with all the joyful exuberance of youth. She stood at the top of the shale hill on the seashore of Tel Aviv, her head tilted to the wind ruffling her hair, and in the background was a sky of snow-white clouds.

He turned the photograph over. "In memory of our unforgettable Sabbath eves at the sea in Tel Aviv." Harry examined her handwriting and the date. He had taken this snapshot himself to preserve the memory of that time.

Those Sabbath eves when they used to meet every Friday afternoon by the sea. Masses of bathers milled around them on the beach, but they saw no one. They swam out to sea, away from the crowds; then back on the beach they would climb to the isolated spot atop the ancient shale hill. When Sabbath descended, they would walk along the promenade, their fingers interlaced, the last to take leave of the sea. The shops would all be shuttered by then. Hasidic Jews in fur hats hurried past them to welcome the Sabbath. And they, in the sanctity of their love, moved at a leisurely pace toward the privacy of their cellar.

He turned the snapshot from one side to the other. On the one side was her handwriting, and on the other the bronze gleaming contours of her body. Why was she so intent upon destroying all the photographs, all the memories of that time? What demon drove her to efface the beauty of her body? When had all this happened—and why? How had the Auschwitz hunger gotten into Galilea? Only in Auschwitz had he known such ravenous hunger.

He heard Daniella's footsteps approaching the living room. He hid the picture in his pocket and wondered why he did. "I washed all the dishes." The child spoke in a hushed voice. "Come put us to bed now."

He lifted his little girl into his arms. She clung to his neck, covering his face with kisses as he carried her into the nursery. He took off her shoes and undressed her. He knew how much the child needed now to be the pampered, not the pamperer. He pulled on her nightgown, then lifted her into the bed, her arms tight around his neck. "Tomorrow too, you have to leave so awfully early in the morning to go to work?" she pouted like a grownup pretending to be a child. His head nodded against the curve of her neck. "Bring Monish to bed too," she said. "And then you can tell us more about the adventures of Chum Pum."

Harry darkened the room and sat on the sofa between their beds. He was wondering if tonight again Galilea would leap from her sleep in terror and lie down here to protect her children.

"This time, children, I will not tell you about Chum Pum but about a special princess and her two little angels. Once upon a time there was a very, very beautiful princess . . ."

28

"Get out!" Galilea screamed at her mother, clenching her hands into fists. "I won't have you hanging around here!"

Daniella was standing in front of the tall candelabrum with a lighted candle in her hand. Like a golden cape, her hair flowed down over her shoulders to her waist; her frock was white, her feet in white socks and shoes, and on her head was a silver paper crown.

Ceremony of the First Hanukkah Candle. Twilight had come already, although it was still quite early. All day long Galilea had toiled in the kitchen frying the pancakes in preparation for the Feast of Lights, wolfing them down, hot or cold, while she worked. Even so, the trays were stacked with pancakes for the guests.

On this particular evening, Galilea's parents and family were gathered in her home, a rare occurrence. Her parents had had more than their share of suffering of late. Yet with Galilea so relaxed after her weeks in the hospital, it was possible to believe that things were back to normal. Thorough medical examinations and tests had indicated that nothing was basically wrong with Galilea, "although sensitive and highly intelligent women sometimes do suffer traumatic reactions to childbirth, or to the intense shock of an experience beyond the ordinary, during which their emotional stability is temporarily disrupted," Dr. Wieselthier had explained. "It's not unusual. It is to be expected that she will recover fully."

Monish, dressed in pristine white, was standing beside his sister, the prayer book open on his palms, about to begin the recital of the blessing over the First Light. For days the children had been hard at work polishing the menorah and decorating the living room with strings of lights in honor of the Feast of the Maccabees and, even more, to welcome a ray of festivity finally allowed into the bleakness of their home.

The family stood around the candelabrum. Madame Glick's eyes glistened with tears of joy as she looked at her granddaughter. "Like an angel!" She pressed her lips to Daniella's head with a kiss of pride that could no longer be withheld. "My little child . . ."

"She's not your child!" Galilea turned on her mother with a sudden shriek. "Daniella's mother was burned in Auschwitz! No one here has the right to be Daniella's mother! No one! No one!"

Harry attempted to restrain her in his arms, but Galilea struggled fiercely to pull free. She was trembling all over. Harry shouted in her face, "It's not your mother's fault that the other Daniella's mother was burned in Auschwitz. Do you hear me, Galilea? *It's not your mother's fault!*"

"Why did they murder Daniella's mother *there*? And why did they murder Aunt Nina *here*?" Galilea cried in desperation. "The *Fedayoun* will kill us all one night. You'll see! Give me the children! I've got to hide my children! I want to save them!" Breaking loose from his grip, she began beating her head with her fists. She flung herself down at his feet. "Forgive me, Harry, I wanted to give you back your Daniella and your Monish. I have cheated you, Harry. They're going to burn every one of us like they did in Auschwitz! Not one of us will be left! Like David Artzi! Like Masha and Renée! They'll throw a bomb at our house too!"

Galilea was thrashing about on the floor in a wailing lamentation of the flames of the Auschwitz crematorium and the *Fedayoun* who would set their house ablaze. "They'll break in through the windows to get us . . ."

Professor Glick bent over his daughter, ostensibly to caress and calm her, and deftly jabbed her flesh with the needle concealed in his hand. She did not seem to sense or feel it. Harry lifted her from the floor and carried her to bed. Strangled cries of agony still struggled within her.

"Our celebration was a bit premature . . ." Professor Glick sighed heavily as he stood by the dark window, staring out.

Harry ran all the way to the home of Dr. Wieselthier, head of the psychiatric department of the state hospital. The doctor's wife opened the door, eying him as though he were some rude intruder. Couldn't he see that this was the doctor's private residence, where the doctor was not to be disturbed? "Dr. Wieselthier only sees patients at the hospital office," she said curtly.

Harry quickly told her who he was and on whose behalf he had come. He knew that this woman's life had been saved on Professor Glick's operating table. He was flustered. He should have said right away that he had come about Professor Glick's daughter.

She ordered him to wait in the hall and walked off. As she slid open the doors, a long table festively set for the Hanukkah banquet was revealed, with guests seated around it. The room was light, and outbursts of carefree laughter filtered out through the doors, which slid shut behind the woman. Harry sat in the hall, gripping and ungripping his hands. He felt miserable, and shameful, humiliated.

Dr. Wieselthier stepped out of the dining room with a look on his face that indicated clearly his displeasure at this intrusion. Harry rose and speechlessly followed him into the study. Dr. Wieselthier closed the door. He neither sat nor offered Harry a seat. "My wife is not feeling well again," Harry said.

"In that case, I would recommend more intensive psychiatric treatment."

"That's why I came to you," Harry went on, "because my wife insists that you treat her. You are the only one she completely trusts. Actually, she's much better since she's been home from the hospital."

"I couldn't even consider it," Dr. Wieselthier dismissed the suggestion. "I'm up to my neck in work. All my hours are taken."

"But you are familiar with her case," Harry pleaded. "She's Professor Glick's only daughter and so precious to him, you know that. You can't imagine the horrible tortures she goes through day and night. And you treated her before and succeeded. She wants you to take her back into your department."

"Out of the question. I can't even begin to consider it." Dr. Wieselthier emitted the verdict with a burp bubbling up from his interrupted meal. "You wife doesn't need hospitalization. Moreover, my department is not the place for her sort of demonstrations. We have examined your wife thoroughly, and indeed I am familiar with her case. Her neurosis is most likely the result of some trauma whose roots cannot be found except by deep analysis, certainly not by hospitalization. I can do no more than recommend a few doctors to you, though, as a matter of principle, I usually don't do that. Try them. One of them might be free to take her on for extensive treatment."

Standing beside his desk, Dr. Wieselthier kept shifting his weight from one foot to the other, impatient to be done with this caller and return to his guests. Harry saw the doctor through the blur of Galilea's tormented face, the faces of his children, the pall of mourning over his home. How could he go back to her now that her only avenue of escape had been cut off? Harry put on the desk a sum which only the most distinguished physicians ask as a fee. "Pay him immediately," they had instructed him, so that Dr. Wieselthier would not mistake this call for a reciprocal gratuity owed a colleague.

With a nervous hand, the physician shoved the money back at Harry. "I don't consider this a visit," he said. "We've hardly talked three minutes."

"I interfered with your leisure and your dinner," said Harry, turning to the door.

"Half will do then; that's what I get for consultation." Dr. Wieselthier said, dismissing the matter with obvious distaste.

"No!" Harry said with conviction, looking the psychiatrist straight in the eye. "This was a visit, Dr. Wieselthier, a fully completed visit . . ."

As they walked out into the hallway, Dr. Wieselthier handed him a slip of paper with the doctors' names.

List in hand, Harry hurried through the streets looking

for the addresses. Lights glared from the crowded cafés. Crossing the avenue, he was almost hit by a taxicab. Passers-by on both sides of the street froze at the screeching of the brakes. He walked on in confusion, and as he crossed the next street against a red light, a policeman ran after him but at the sight of his face let him go. He had already been to two of the doctors listed and had come out no better than with Dr. Wieselthier. Everyone was overloaded with patients. This was his first encounter with the world of soul healers. He would never have imagined that in this restless gay city so many souls were in search of healing. Now he too strained to read the name plaques on buildings, searching for a healer of mind and soul, rushing desperate through the streets of the city to find help for Galilea.

He entered the office of the last one on the list. He was drenched with sweat, and his heart was hammering in his chest. The doctor, a stoop-shouldered elderly man, reached languidly for the thick appointment book on his desk. Its cover was shiny with use. The doctor took his time, contemplating the appointment book before opening it as if he were reciting an inaudible incantation over it. Then he slowly began leafing back and forth through the pages.

Please help me this time, God, so I don't have to go back with empty hands!

"I will be able to take you in ten months." The doctor drew out his syllables languidly.

"Not me. My wife," said Harry.

"It is all the same, sir, all the same," the doctor drawled.

"But my wife needs help immediately. She's in very bad shape," the trembling words escaped him. "Dr. Wieselthier referred me."

"I am all taken up." The doctor resumed his idle flipping of the pages. "Everything is taken. For the time being, have her come over once so that I can meet her. Tomorrow evening between seven and eight. One of my patients has just had to cancel his appointment. I'll have an opening for you in ten months."

Sick with disappointment, Harry went down the street. Now where? Who could he turn to? He thought of Friedel. At the age of eight, this girl had been placed in a convent only hours before her entire family was taken off to Auschwitz. In the convent she was taught the rules of self-mortification, how to conquer the evil urges of the body. Crawling on all fours to scour the tiles of the convent, Friedel was instructed by her superiors that when she felt as if her spine would break, that was the supreme moment of trial; at such a moment she must concentrate all her being on the torments of the Crucifixion. Only thus would she purge her body of sin, and may God keep her from being led astray by carnal thoughts at such a moment. At the end of the war, when the boys of the Jewish Brigade, like Felix and his comrades, spread through Europe searching for Jewish survivors, Friedel was brought to Palestine, completely alone in the world, her seventeen loveliest years crucified and burned upon her soul.

Harry knocked at the door of her rented room. The only person Galilea was unable to help was herself. Years after the convent, Friedel had been struck dumb, and when she and Galilea had shared a room in Dr. Wieselthier's division of the hospital, it was Galilea who had been able to help her regain her speech.

He stood in front of the door to her room, waiting for it to open. Both Friedel and Zivah were still outpatients at the hospital. He wanted to find out who was treating them, and, most important, if the hospital doctors were available for private practice. A rustle came from inside. Someone must be in there. His ear caught hushed whispers, but the door remained closed. Or perhaps in his emotional turmoil he had only imagined that someone was there. He couldn't just stand here waiting. He decided to go on to Zivah's.

Zivah had been born into wealth. Her father was a prominent politician who never found a free moment for his daughter; in effect, she grew up fatherless. As she got older a blind hatred of her mother, who shut herself up at night in the bedroom with Zivah's father, had developed. On the eve of her seventeenth birthday, perhaps out of a wish for revenge or perhaps to frighten her parents into paying attention to her, Zivah had swallowed the whole supply of Luminal tablets that her father used to put himself to sleep after the tension of his long meetings. The doctors had worked tirelessly to return life to her body. After this experience, Zivah had rented a room in a stranger's house and severed all ties with her parents. They were relieved to be rid of her—and on the face of it both parties might have rejoiced in this solution were it not for Zivah's insatiable hunger for men, the end result of which was to make her parents' lives a worse hell than ever.

When he entered her room, Harry found Zivah in a mood more tense than usual. He could not get her to say a word. He spoke to her, but she did not seem to hear him. On the table were two glasses and a bottle of prepared Martini mix. She paced back and forth like a caged animal, constantly glancing at her wrist watch. Harry felt like an intruder. He simply wanted to ask her if she could concentrate for a minute to answer a question; if not, he would leave. How could Zivah fail to remember the time when she had been ill in their house and Galilea had fussed over her like a sister? Now it was Galilea who was sick. Very sick. And all Harry wanted was some information. Zivah's behavior infuriated him. He was about to pick himself up and go, when from outside a key turned in the door. A young man walked in, his hair blond and curly, a briefcase under his arm. Seeing a strange man, the newcomer stopped short in the doorway, then, quickly regaining his composure, he handed Zivah the key. "You left this on my desk," he said, and withdrew.

Zivah ran after him. In a little while she was back. "That was my doctor," she said.

"Why didn't you tell me right away you were expecting a visitor? I wouldn't have bothered you, not for a minute," said Harry, striding to the door.

Zivah slung her coat across her shoulders. At the building entrance she extended Harry a hasty hand. "Forgive me," she said, "I'm terribly mixed up right now." And she was gone.

Harry crossed to the sidewalk opposite. From a distance he could see the healer of Zivah's ailing soul waiting for her on the corner, the man familiar with all her weaknesses and sexual vulnerability. Zivah approached him with quick steps; turning around, the two of them hastened back to her room.

Harry stood there, unable to take a step. Was that what soul healers were like? But this was robbery of the soul, the most abominable of robberies, a thousand times worse than stealing pennies from a blind beggar's bowl, more evil than the theft of the shroud off a dead body. And he was about to entrust Galilea into such hands!

Across from him the light in Zivah's room went dark.

Not knowing where his feet were taking him, he wandered aimlessly along dark streets. Then somehow he found himself back in front of Friedel's door.

Shocked though she was by the look on his face, Friedel expressed delight at his visit. She got out a bottle of French cognac and poured him a glassful. Harry pushed it aside. "Galilea is very sick," he said.

"Why didn't anyone tell me?" Friedel demanded. "And

who's with her all day? I'll rush right over to her. Why didn't anyone let me know?"

"Galilea needs a good doctor. She needs intensive psychiatric treatment. Are you happy with your doctor?" Harry asked.

Friedel's face lighted up. "Oh, *my* doctor!" she said, with an ecstatic look. "He'd treat Galilea for nothing!"

"I don't want anything for nothing," Harry almost shouted.

"Now take it easy, dear, take it easy," Friedel smiled secretively. "Very soon now I'll be Dr. Sakko's wife. We're about to get married, you know, and my husband ought to feel privileged to treat a friend of mine for nothing."

Harry was stunned. "But doesn't Dr. Sakko have a wife and children?" he asked.

"It won't be long now till he gets rid of her, and then I will become his lawful wedded wife," she proclaimed triumphantly.

"Did he actually tell you that in so many words?" Harry asked.

"My doctor doesn't have to tell me. I wasn't born yesterday. If he didn't plan on marrying me, he wouldn't be coming to my room, now would he? I'm madly in love with him!"

Harry jumped up and bolted out of the room. He felt sick to his stomach. He was afraid to be alone, just as he was to enter his home and meet Galilea's eyes. His feet took him to her parents' home.

Madame Glick hurried over to him when he came in, but drew back when she saw his face, "Has anything happened to Galilea? How is she?"

"She's better," Harry lied.

"Thank God! From now on everything is going to be fine," Madame Glick said, leading him into the salon. "We've already found her a doctor."

Opposite Professor Glick a man was seated, his strong, youthful face crested with snow-white hair. His topcoat was draped across shoulders, and his suede gloves rested on his knee. "Our son-in-law," Professor Glick said, introducing Harry to Professor Barlevy.

Barlevy was one of the best minds in the field of psychiatric research and one of the most profound interpreters of Jung; a man who on principle would not accept private patients, because in his opinion it was not desirable for a financial relationship to be established between psychiatrist and patient. However, when Professor Glick asked him to come, he had responded immediately. He listened attentively to all that was said and, weighing every detail, suggested a doctor residing in the officers' quarter in a suburb of Tel Aviv. It was true, he said, that he was not conveniently located, but there was no one else he could recommend. Professor Glick took the hint. Realizing how late it was, he did not detain his colleague any further and warmly expressed his appreciation for the gesture of his visit. All three accompanied him to the door.

Harry was silent.

Madame Glick wiped her tears with her handkerchief. "Why does my daughter hate me, Harry? Tell me, Harry, when will she stop hating me?"

"When she stops hating herself," Harry replied.

The maid peered cautiously into the salon. "Midnight snack is on the table," said Madame Glick. "Harry, come join us."

He asked to be left alone. He couldn't eat. All he wanted was to sit there by himself.

No sooner had he sunk back into the corner of the blue divan than, like a kaleidoscope, the pictures began whirling through his exhausted brain. He saw Galilea sitting at the oval table, as she had been the first time he visited her, her chestnut hair falling across one side of her face, her dress

clinging to her curvaceous body. Then, suddenly, out of
the silence, he heard her say, "Marry me . . ." His thoughts
were like chips of color, falling and shifting: *"Stay away as
long as you like, even for a year . . . until the book is finished . . ." "I saw the bomb hit you. Arabs! . . ." "Renée! The
snake! . . ." "Whenever I think of that bomb hitting you, I
feel as hungry as a wild beast . . ." "What can we offer them
when our souls are ash and our bodies are as ravaged as
scorched earth . . ." "Don't cry, Mommy, I'll take good care
of you, just like a nurse . . ." "She's not your child! . . ."
"They'll burn every one of us like they did in Auschwitz . . ."
"I cheated you, Harry! I wanted to give you back your Daniella and Monish . . ." "They'll break in through the
windows . . ." "Sensitive women are likely to have a traumatic reaction to childbirth or to the intense shock of an
experience beyond the ordinary . . . beyond the ordinary . . .
beyond the ordinary . . ."* Then the black smoke billowing
from the alley, and centered within it the provocative silhouette of a girl, framed against editor Levitan's opaque
door. *"Open Sesame. . . . Sesame . . ."*

Harry sprang up from the divan and rushed to the door
without stopping to say good-by. He ran home, his lips
moving as if he were praying: *We must try by putting our
strengths together . . .*

29

"Dr. Garden, you're not even listening to what I'm saying."
The words tumbled heavily from her mouth, as if her
tongue and lips were paralyzed. *When will this awful*

*headache go away? Have I actually spoken these words or did
I just think them? All the time I keep talking and talking,
but no sound reaches my ears.*

"Dr. Garden, can you hear me?" she asked.

Dr. Garden looked up at her. His hands were clasped
around his coffee mug as though he wanted to warm them
against it. His voice came from far away: "I've told you
more than once, Galilea, that not only do I hear every
word you say, but I register it like a tape recorder—both for
me and for you. But the moment you are silent, the tape
recorder is silent for you as well. That is why you should
try very hard to say whatever comes to mind, to talk without any inhibitions, even if it seems incoherent. Don't try
to force any order on the flow of your words."

*Am I silent? My father never used to listen to me. He
was always too busy with his patients. And my stories only
bored him.* "Dr. Garden, do I bore you when I go on and
on about the same thing?" Her voice was monotonous, slow,
like final emptying drops.

"Your purpose in coming here is not to entertain me,"
he said, addressing her with a firm directness. "Please just
go on talking and try not to suppress anything. You're intelligent enough to understand the importance of what I'm
asking you to do."

But she did not understand what he was asking her to do.
That was exactly what she had been doing, talking to him
incessantly in plain everyday language. Her eyes did not
move from his hands folded around the coffee mug. *Ever
since I can remember I loved Papa's hands. But his hands
were always busy with patients, or else he was out of the
country altogether. . . . Now all they do is preach at me:
"Say whatever comes into your mind." Every time my parents went abroad, they deposited me at Grandma's. "Force
the food into her mouth if you have to!" Grandma used*

to say to Aunt Anna, "and if she doesn't want to eat, we'll throw her to the Arabs."

Outside the window, the railroad tracks running from Egypt to Syria gleamed along the wadi. The tall smokestack of the German factory Wagner projected above the tracks. *That's where the German quarter was. That's where the German kids always used to come from to throw stones at our windows. And when I read in Harry's books about the crematorium in Auschwitz, it was Wagner's smokestack I saw in my dreams. . . . "Just swallow down the food and the train will be right along, and Mama and Papa will wave at you from the train window."* Had Harry known what train his father and mother were in when they were taken to their death? Harry never spoke about his past. And he didn't allow her to ask him any questions.

I live with a sphinx. Harry's face turns white whenever a question about his past slips out of me. I live with a man who had half of him cut away. He came to me from the planet of Auschwitz—as if he had fallen from outer space. He's half-man, half-enigma, and I can't penetrate the enigma no matter how hard I try to imagine Auschwitz. The only thing I understand from his books is the hunger of Auschwitz; all I can feel is their hunger. Only in this did I manage to get close to Harry. Not in anything else. Nothing else. All this time I've been knocking in vain—trying to penetrate my beloved's other half, the cut-away half, the enigma. I want him whole, Dr. Garden, the way he used to be before Auschwitz, before the Nazis. But every time I dare get close to the secret of his past, the insane hunger lunges at me, fixing me with the stare of a Mussulman, and I get terrified and run away. "You're running away." "You're running away from yourself" is all they can preach. Dr. Garden, my husband was a Mussulman in Auschwitz!

Her teeth were chattering.

*I brought God's anger down on myself by cheating Harry.
I shouldn't have been so greedy for happiness. Oh, what big
ideas I had about how I would win the battle. I wanted to
make up to Harry for everything the crematorium had
robbed him of. I wanted to give him back his Daniella, his
Monish, the joy of living. And I ended up making whatever
is left of him just that much more of a wreck. I can't stand
watching Harry suffer because of me any more. Because of
no one but me.*

Her knees were shaking, as though it were freezing cold.
The hunger in her brain was ripping her to shreds. She
wanted to reach out to the doctor for help, but she could
not move her hands. "I'm hungry . . ." she whimpered,
"hungry . . ."

She saw Dr. Garden rise from his chair. Leave the room.
Her eyes clung to his back, imploring him not to abandon
her. She wanted to promise him she'd talk as much as he
wanted, about anything, anything at all. If only she could
get some control over her paralyzed tongue. All this time
she'd been talking and talking. Couldn't he hear her? She
saw Dr. Garden come back to the room and resume his seat.
She heard him speak; again his voice seemed to come from
a great distance. "There's nothing for a person to be ashamed
of in feeling hungry," he was saying gently, "and there's
no reason to be afraid of this desire for food."

. . . she was standing on the footstool by the window in
Grandma's home, too small to see over the sill. Aunt Anna
was shoveling spoonful after spoonful of food into her
mouth, prodding her to eat, distracting her with stories:
*". . . and so, by night, the Arabs of Jaffa came to slaughter
us all, and they had long sharp knives in their hands. But
we were big and strong because we ate lots and lots of butter
with our bread and ate up all the egg. Do you know what
else we did? We took a long cord and made it go from one*

house to the next, through all the houses on our street, and in each house we tied a bell to this cord. And every time the Arabs came close to one of our houses, the Jew inside would pull the cord in his home and all the bells started ringing together in warning. Then we all began to scream and shout. Oh my, how frightening it was! You can't imagine how frightening. Come on, swallow that food!" And I swallowed the food, as I swallowed the fear that the train would flash by and this time again my parents wouldn't be on it. As I swallowed the fear of the Germans across from our window, and the fear of the Arabs of Jaffa. To this day I don't know the Arabs of Jaffa. Don't know them. If only I could talk to them. Like I did in Egypt. From my heart. Explain to them. Listen to them. Must talk to them. But my tongue feels dead. All these words in my head, why are they stuck in my throat? I can hear them so clearly. There's no end to them; they stream on and on the way bare feet of the Arabs used to come toward me in the Egyptian desert. Who is the Sergeant Climp who stands again between me and the Arabs with his whip? What uniform does he wear this time, and what language does he speak? Why shouldn't Harry's children be able to live together with the children of the Arabs? Why not? They're brothers by race, aren't they? The same race Hitler tried to exterminate. Why can't we know one another? Tell me, Dr. Garden, what can I do to save my home? If only I could vomit up these thoughts that are driving me crazy and vomit up the hunger in my throat that won't let the words come out!

The tears streamed from her eyes. Food was the only thing that could calm her now. The hunger whipped her like a ruthless enemy. She was drained of all strength. She had only one wish—that the doctor would listen to her, even though the words could not pass through the barrier of tears in her throat. She wanted him to *see* her words just as she could see them, even if she could not get out the sounds. She wanted him to know that she had lost all glimmer of hope that she would ever get well. "Dr. Garden, help me! I want to get well . . ."

He lifted her to the couch. "Dr. Garden, don't leave me! . . ."

The door of the doctor's office opened a little way. Someone in the doorway was holding a plate; on it was a wedge of cake. Dr. Garden walked over to the door and, taking the plate that was offered, he brought it to Galilea. Sick with mortification, she felt her hands reaching out for the cake. She stared at her outstretched hands. "Look at my hands, Dr. Garden!" she cried hoarsely. "Like the hands of a monster, like someone with acromegaly! Dr. Garden, why do you just stand there—like my father. Not saying anything. Can't you see me? Can't you hear me?"

Deliberately, Dr. Garden put the plate down beside her. "I do see you, and I hear you." His voice rang with authority. "But you must remember that I'm no more than your mirror. You'll only see what you show the mirror; don't expect to see what you refuse to show. Try to go on, try to keep talking, and don't hold anything back. Reaching for that piece of cake doesn't make you a monster. And I assure you, you don't have acromegaly. Why are you so ashamed of eating a slice of cake? You want to eat that cake, don't you. Why all these inhibitions here in the office with me. I want you to feel as free here as you do in your kitchen at home behind the locked door."

Trembling, she reached for the plate. Tears of shame still swelled at the rims of her eyes. She chewed and gulped the cake like a spanked child whose misdeed has not penetrated to his consciousness and who is not pacified by food offered to him. "Dr. Garden," she mumbled, "Harry never says he's hungry." Yet his books told of nothing but his hunger in Auschwitz, that Auschwitz hunger which had grown in her like a malignancy. But in Auschwitz Harry wasn't served cream cake on a platter. Then how could she gorge herself on this cake dripping with cream? Betray Harry this way in front of Dr. Garden? But deep in her gut was an iron determination to cross the same road of torment that Harry had crossed—to be equal to him, to be worthy of him. Harry's body had been bloated with hunger; her body was bloated with overeating. Now they were equal. Hunger made them one. Her whole body began to tremble. Anxiety rose in her throat, and she gagged on it. Bits of description from Harry's books fluttered around in her brain; howling within her was the terror of that starved Auschwitz prisoner who, in his sleep, had bitten into the flesh of his shelfmate's calf; the terror of the insane hunger that had driven him to such a point. Horror rushed through her: Could that anonymous biter have been Harry? Had the hunger of Auschwitz driven him to plunge his teeth into the living flesh of his shelfmate? Now Harry never said he was hungry. Was it possible that Harry's hunger was tearing at her guts?

Her eyes lifted imploringly to Dr. Garden. "Is such a transference possible?" she murmured. She wanted the doctor to empathize with her, to understand that she was not to blame for her illness, to *help* her. The hunger never subsided, never even for a minute let go of her. She wanted to escape to a world of nothingness, to sink into unknown depths, to become a being whose eyes were shut even beneath their open lids. She was tired, so tired.

The words oozed from her mouth, shapeless and blurred. "Dr. Garden, when I see the trees changing with the seasons I feel the anguish of time . . ." *Remember my joy, Harry, when they planted the trees in the little garden in front of our house? In no time, the poplar grew as high as*

*our window. Now I am so frightened of trees. Their
branches are hideous arms reaching out to strangle me. Like
the withered arms of the Mussulmen in your books. I can't
even remember trees green with leaves, Harry. Nothing in
the world is green and blossoming for me any more.*

Harry was sitting by her side. She gazed at him with
compassion; her eyes closed. Somebody inside her was talking, talking, talking . . . *Every person must fulfill his life's
purpose, and once he has, he must die. I made you keep the
vow you swore in Auschwitz; I made you the father of
Daniella and Monish. I have fulfilled the purpose of my
life; now I am destroying everything I have built. You sit in
your cabin far away from me, but I know how useless it is,
your sitting there, because your thoughts are with me. In all
the years of my illness you haven't written a single word.
You have betrayed your vow. And I am to blame.*

*Don't mourn over me, beloved. At last I'll be able to rest
from my torment. Be comforted by this. I have no strength
left to be strong for you. I don't want you to remember the
sick Galilea. When the children are grown, take them to our
cellar and tell them how beautiful their mother once was.
They don't know . . . Walk with them to our hill over the
sea—let them see that too. Remember the letter I slipped into
your cabin? You told me afterward that my letter gave you
the strength to go on writing. Now I shall write you another
letter. Not existing, I shall help you, as I once helped you by
existing. I'll go to your cabin just this once more, to see
you just once again. Dr. Garden, I want to go to Harry's
place. Just once more . . .*

30

In a paroxysm of rage, Harry swept the papers off his desk, and they scattered all over the cabin floor. He grabbed up the remaining pages on the desk and in a black fury tore them to shreds, smaller, smaller, smaller, as if he could make them disappear altogether. Then he kicked the pieces into the dark corners of the cabin to get them out of his sight.

Today, once and for all, he was going back to Galilea. And he wouldn't hear another word about getting on with the damned writing. It was all his fault! He had brought it all upon Galilea. She was as compulsively drawn to his writing as to her accursed food, and both were like opium to a drug addict.

In a blinding light he could see the thread running from her shock following the bombardment of the alley to the most recent of the *Fedayoun* raids. It was perfectly clear. How could he take her back in her consciousness to the beginning of the shock, and pull it like a thorn out of her soul? He blamed her Auschwitz hunger upon himself. He had opened the world of Auschwitz to her, and she had walked into the heart of his books as someone might wander into a laboratory of poison gas. He should have realized that Galilea was defenseless against the fumes of the crematorium. Only those who wore masks over their souls, who were immune like himself, could enter there. Then why had he allowed her to become so involved in the translations of his books? For days and nights on end, she had dug

deeper and deeper into the pit of horrors, her lungs absorbing all the undiluted poisonous essence of Auschwitz. Why
hadn't he seen what was coming? She knew by heart every
description in his books; each line, like a powerful venom,
was alive in her blood. For every phenomenon of her present world she had a counterpart from Auschwitz; for every
event *here* she had drawn on a simile from *there*. The *now*
that she existed in ran parallel to the plane of Auschwitz,
and her vision of the end *here* was patterned on the end
there.

He kicked at the shreds of paper still under his feet; he
hated them. He hated the curse of Auschwitz dogging his
footsteps like a shadow. They ought to keep him under
lock and key, quarantined in a valley of lepers, so that he
could not spread the deadly germs he had carried in him
since Auschwitz.

"Everyone who comes out of Auschwitz is like a bucket
full of pus," Professor Glick had warned his daughter before
she was married. And she, without flinching, had said,
"Then I'll push my head right into the bucket and suck it
until it's drained." She had sucked the pus all right. Now he
was healthy and Galilea was sick. How right every word of
her father's had been!

"That girl gave Harry back his first smile ten years before
it was due," the writer Menuhin had said. She had poured
every drop of her life's joy into him, and she had absorbed
all the darkness of his grief. Not life added to life, but life
given for life.

Harry walked out of the cabin. He couldn't stand another
minute in this place, with the rags of his writing in every
corner of the cabin. He loathed this place, where for some
insane reason he had thought he could extract the essence
from the pit of darkness and bring it up to the light of day.

The grove was sweltering in the heat of summer noon,

and he inhaled the hot air. He glanced at his watch. The company Piper should be coming around soon to spray the trees. The grove was being eaten up by the Mediterranean fruit fly, and now the citrus rust mite had joined in. Terrible blights had struck the grove this year! The whole crop was in danger. The curse of God was on him wherever he was. Today he was going home. In any case, he shouldn't be around while they were spraying. The spray was so noxious that it destroyed not only the pests but their predators, which were as necessary as air to the trees. After the last time, the stench of the jackals' carcasses had been unbearable. The poison had destroyed every living and crawling creature around. The moment he heard the buzz of the plane, he'd have to clear out.

He went in among the front rows of trees and bent over the fruit with his magnifying glass. His heart sank. The tree was as swarming with vermin as a mangy old dog. An army of ladybugs wouldn't be enough to destroy them. It had been two weeks now since he had informed the spray company. At that point the fruit could still have been saved. But the whole country had been hit by this plague, and the pilots were working themselves to exhaustion. No wonder they had had so many fatal accidents lately.

He walked over to shift the sprinkler lines. Hardly any pressure in the pipes. Right there was the worst danger this country faced. City people paid it hardly any attention. The country would dry up for lack of water. The natural water sources were gradually disappearing all the time. And for the past five years there hadn't been any rain worth mentioning. Nine months out of every year coppery skies hung overhead.

With a heavy step, he trudged toward the grove gate. If the plane didn't show up again this time, he thought, the fruit was really doomed. He raised his eyes to the water tower on the hill; the gauge indicated that the reserves were almost gone. The bleached concrete of the water tower reflected back a glaring gray, and the blazing heat shimmered before his eyes like incandescent veils. The dream he kept having came into his mind: the water tower rising skyward, breaking apart, and the water gushing forth. His heated brain tried to interpret it. What he dreamed at night might well be a fulfillment of his daytime craving for water. That was all it was, wishful thinking. But for now the concrete dome jutted into a scorching sky, and inside it was almost dry.

He heard a droning in the blank stillness of noon. A dot on the horizon, the plane appeared behind the water tower. Another moment and like a bird it tore away from the water-tower roof, looming larger and larger as it approached the grove. Harry passed through the gate to the dirt track. Good God, was the pilot out of his mind? Why was he flying so low? He was bound to hit the iron arch over the gate. The pilot leaned out the cockpit and waved wearily to Harry. The whole universe seemed listless in the swelter of noon. As if not just the pilot but the engine of the plane were longing for a nap. The Piper swept right over his head, almost within reach of his hand, and the pilot released the spray switch. A long whitish jet trailed behind the plane. Like a train on its track, the plane appeared to be riding its own jet. Gradually the swath spread and thinned into a transparent cloud, sucked up in among the treetops.

The Piper banked to the north, vanishing in the direction of the neighboring groves. Then, flying back in over the dirt track, it returned to the second tree lot, and the pilot took off over the barren fields to the groves beyond the water tower. He'd be back in a minute, spraying until he had crisscrossed the whole checkerboard of citrus groves in the area. Harry raised his head to the blazing horizon, squinting against the glare. The plane blurred in the hot vaporous air, almost disappearing behind the transparent shimmering veils. He followed it, the thoughts dripping in his tired brain: How many hours had this pilot already put in today? Hard to understand how he didn't faint up there with all those fumes. If it were up to him, Harry would have passed a law that spray pilots work only four hours daily for a full day's pay. But try to get that out of the company. Their first concern was profits. They were delighted with any pilot willing to slave longer than his regular eight hours a day. The epidemic of fruit flies that had hit the country was as profitable to the spray company as a bumper crop is to farmers.

Suddenly his eyes opened wide. From the other end of the dirt track, a figure wrapped in a black coat was approaching. Galilea? Or a heat mirage? The figure stopped short, apparently just as startled by the sight of him. With this distance between them, it was impossible to tell whether or not it was Galilea. He stood rooted there, not sure whether or not to run toward her. Now she was raising her hand over her head. It was Galilea! A split second before he started running toward her, a shattering blast broke upon his ears. He wheeled around and at the roof of the water tower saw a giant black bird taking off, then immediately plummeting, enveloped in dense black clouds. In a wildly erratic course, it skimmed over the uncultivated field and then, with an ear-splitting sound, burrowed into the dirt track, smashing against the iron gate of the grove. Thick clouds of black smoke and flames billowed up against the sky. Hurtled from the cockpit, the pilot came running across the field to Harry, feeling his body all over for injury. Harry shoved him aside and broke into a run to the other side of the crash. He emerged choking from the thick smoke onto the dirt track, running on and on to the head of the road, to Galilea lying in a crumpled black heap on the sand.

He threw himself down beside her and lifted her head. She opened her eyes. For a moment the lids squinted shut as if she were blinded by dazzling light, then they opened again. She stared at Harry in wonder. She lifted her eyes higher, from him to the treetops, and out of the depths of the revelation, the cry broke from her: "You're alive, you're whole . . . Oh, Harry my love, the trees are green!"

And, fainting, she sagged back.

Neighbors from the surrounding groves came running. They helped him lift Galilea into the wagon. "It's nothing," the farmers reassured him. "She'll be all right in no time. It's just the shock."

Harry hitched the donkey to the wagon as the people gathered around to advise him: "The hospital in Petah Tikvah is the closest one around." Harry jumped into the wagon. With one hand he held Galilea's head pressed to his body; with the other he held the reins. She opened her eyes. Both sides of the road were flanked with groves. "Again you were saved, my love. Again on a road of sand," she murmured. "The trees are green again."

He turned off the dirt track onto the highway to Petah Tikvah. He prodded the donkey. *The trees, my precious, are green again!*

PART THREE

There is a bird called the phoenix
He lives for a thousand years,
And at the end of a thousand years
A fire from his nest consumes him.
But he grows his limbs again.
And lives again.
                              —Genesis Rabbah 19:5

31

When Galilea arrived at the hospital, the bed next to hers was occupied. Harry was too upset at the time to take note of the girl lying in it. But during the course of his daily visits to Galilea, he grew accustomed to Liza's eyes, like hot coals set within a long skeletal head. Liza never interfered or uttered a sound during his visits to Galilea, though he knew that Galilea took care of her like a sister; often when the doctors failed to reach her, Galilea would succeed.

Now a starched sheet was pulled taut over the smooth mattress. The white exposed emptiness proclaimed a vacant bed. No mistaking it. Lisa had reached the end of the road.

Like an open conduit, the flow in the hospital proceeded. Life and death ran into each other here, like busy salesmen in a railway station, each with his suitcase of invisible wares. When someone died, all the surfaces were wiped clean. Rubber wheels muffled the sound. Stretchers glided in blank silence. As in a revolving door, those departing and arriving alternated with a constancy that was never inter-rupted. Now and then someone would take his destiny into his own hands, determine for himself which station along the road would be his last. Liza for one.

Now, in the high-ceilinged white room, Galilea turned her eyes to Harry. He saw the resolve in her gaze. A tremor of pleasure washed through him. Talking no longer had any place. Words had dropped between them like empty husks. Only their peeled, inner kernels looked out from Gali-lea's eyes. She lay covered with the blanket up to her chin, gathering her energy for the future; dormant strength quickening in her body; thoughts stirring to action. Some-times, before your eyes, a green shoot will sprout from the face of a rock. A wonder wrought by nature's hand. The supreme authority.

Today when Harry had come, he found a chair waiting for him beside her bed. Galilea did not want to go out for their usual walk today. Sometimes they had walked as far as the grove. Mostly, he would do the talking and she would listen, absorbing the inner meaning of things. Yesterday, as they parted, she had said, "I feel as if I have crawled out from under the debris of a wreckage. How I wish I could wash away the ugliness of my body." She was still ashamed of her bloated body, but only as if it were a temporary bald spot, which one hides from others until the hair has regrown. A distinct sign of recovery. "Remember our shower after the bombing by the Arab plane?" she had said. "We washed away the filth from our bodies so quickly then." And he added, but only to himself: *The shock was not washed off all that quickly.*

Yet now, no one better understood what had happened than she. Sometimes a person is revealed to himself under the eye of a microscope. And then he is imbued with a different spirit. He acts in a different dimension. He suddenly sees the connections. Because it is he that the events have struck. Javelin-like, the thunderbolt has impaled his being, his soul and body. And sometimes he will convert it into light to show his way.

Harry had long since forgotten there could be such concentration of light in Galilea's eyes. Her eyes had spoken to him exactly this way during her first visit to the cellar. Radiant with resolve. Beyond words.

Now the circle had closed. A single invisible path was marked in her soul, leading back and forth from the Auschwitz fear to the fear of the Arabs. Both were ready to destroy her. But now that she saw them clearly, she would not flee from them any longer.

The resolution was bright in her eyes. The summation had been come to earlier, constructed in the course of their daily strolls.

"I can't remember a thing of what I went through during my sessions with Dr. Garden," Galilea had said. "It's all wiped out. Except for one sentence that sticks in my mind: 'You must look reality straight in the eye!' "

The connection between the Auschwitz fear and the fear of the *Fedayoun*—that was reality now.

Between these two fears the human being, son of a divided country, stands like a gaping wound, with anguish burning in his divided soul.

"And what of the Arab living with his own people in his own village in Israel?" Galilea had said. "Isn't his soul also torn in two? Isn't he suspended between two fears just like I was? This Arab, what do we know about him?"

The face of Ahmad, who worked with him in the grove, rose before Harry. Harry had made his way through the entire farming community, going from house to house in search of a room for him. At first each had agreed—until they learned it was for an Arab. They had not even seen the man's face, but terror was in their eyes, terror of the stereotyped image of an "Arab"—fifth column—and the stereotype wiped any resemblance to a neighbor from the face of Ahmad, son of this land.

The stereotype of "Jew" with which he himself had been marked, the tattoo stamped like a trademark on his left arm—how intimately he knew the taste of labels.

In the ghetto the question used to gnaw at Harry: How had it happened that the Pole, the neighbor of the Jew, would take pity on a scrounging dog, but a runaway Jew from the ghetto who begged the Pole to take him in for a night to save his life would be driven away like Satan or a witch who should be burned at the stake?

He had found the answer here, in the Jewish farm community. The suspicion lives beyond borders and climates, and is revealed in the eyes of man.

For as long as a thousand years Jews had dwelt on the soil of Poland, and their Polish neighbors never came to know them as one gets to know a fellow man. The children of Poles believed, in all good faith, that the Jew, beneath his clothing, was shaped like a devil, with cloven feet like the hoofs of a goat. For as long as a thousand years two peoples dwelt within the bounds of one country, and their children never came to know one another as human beings. Until two distinct odors crystallized: the Jewish odor and the Polish odor. To the nostrils of the Polish neighbor the odor of the Jew was more repellent than the smell of his own bedbugs; what exuded from the Jew was the stench of the accursed crucifier of God.

And in the eyes of the Jews of the farm community was the terror of whoever bore the name "Arab."

This was the connection. The revelation was in Galilea's eyes. She was the confrontation. The two had met in her soul.

She had overcome the consequences of the decision she had made in his cellar. Could she now face the consequences of this new decision?

"In the Egyptian desert," Galilea had said, "in spite of the presence of a foreign exploiting power, I found an immediate understanding with the stricken Arabs, a common language. And today, couldn't we possibly find a direct common language in which to speak to our Arab neighbors in spite of all the foreign powers exploiting the anguish of this divided land?"

"You must look reality straight in the eye."

He saw the sheet pulled taut over Liza's empty bed. Liza had never mentioned to anyone what Nazi camp she had come from. She had taken her secret with her. From the time she was joined to a man in matrimony, all the passageways of her body had become blocked. The secret sealed within her had rejected food, the sustenance of life, until they were forced to feed her intravenously. Then one night she had walked into the bathroom, slashed her wrists, and with the blood spurting from her opened veins Liza had unburdened herself of the secret.

He was staring at the empty whiteness stretched across her bed, and he thought of the girl in the stable on his way from Auschwitz.

"What can we offer them when our bodies are as ravaged as scorched earth . . .

"How can either of us lie beside a woman or a man and at the same time exist in a world which they can never enter and we can never leave? . . .

"There is no one on this earth who can understand us, except ourselves. . . . In what language could we explain to

them? . . . Now there is nothing I am afraid of any more except living as a woman with a man. . . ."

Starting, he turned to Galilea. "What did you say, precious?"

"It's pointless for me to stay longer in the hospital. It's only an excuse not to be seen looking like this. I'm thinking of taking a trip for a time. I want to come back to you the way I used to be. I'm not running away from myself, beloved. I'm returning to myself."

Beyond the open door the white shadows of orderlies passed to and fro. Hands on wheel chairs. Soundless. Their white silence brushing back and forth across his field of vision. Stretchers gliding in blank silence. Departures and arrivals in a constancy never interrupted.

32

"Like drifting smoke, the lesson of Auschwitz will disappear if man does not learn from it. And if Auschwitz is forgotten, man will not deserve to continue to exist." With slow, deliberate steps, Galilea walked among the rows of trees in the grove, the words Harry had spoken here in this very place resounding in her ears. She heard them as distinctly as if Harry were walking beside her.

She had learned the moral and the lesson to be gleaned from Auschwitz. In the shade of these fruit trees it had been revealed to her.

The words which in Dr. Garden's office could find no

outlet were set free among these trees. Harry had rolled away the heavy stone at the mouth of her soul, and the thoughts dammed up within had burst forth, clear and flowing. "Every day," he had said, "like Creation itself, our life is renewed with each good deed we perform. God created the world in its virginity, and handed it to man that he might spread time over it. There is no creature but us in the whole universe who has the power to weld the links of time into one continuity. In this we are more powerful even than the gods, who cannot choose to do either good or evil."

Now it was clear to her what she was called to do and the path she must take to do it. And with clarity came relief. Now she knew: she would open her home—which fear had boarded up—as the first house in the Jewish city to receive the Arabs as guests. Face to face, as they had been in Egypt. No Sergeant Climp—no matter what the insignia on his cap, his language, or his motives—would come between her children and the children of the Arabs, the sons of this land. The Auschwitz fear and the Arab fear had stemmed from one source in her soul. And here among these rows of trees Harry had helped her see it.

Day after day, Harry had taken her here on their strolls from the hospital. And little by little, one hour and still another hour, a day and still another day, the light had pierced through the darkness of her confusion until finally the truth had dawned. The skies turned blue then, and the trees became green again. The miracle was worked in the shade of this grove, among these sun-splashed trees. Only Harry could have brought it about. The secret of the strength which had helped Harry outpower Auschwitz was revealed to her here, and during their solitary walks he taught her how to use it.

Tirelessly, Harry would repeat over and over the words he had used when they stood together in front of editor

Levitan's door: "Let us try by putting our strengths together . . ."

Today she had decided to come here by herself. On this
day of release from the hospital, she wanted to be alone, to
look into herself in solitude. Like someone who has been
leaning on a cane and now is walking without assistance,
she was conscious of each step as she set out on the new path.
When Harry came to the hospital, he would learn that she
had left, and he would suppose that she was at home. But
Harry and the children would have to begin to get used to
being without her for a while. She had decided to go away.
Alone. From now on, not even Harry should see her in
this condition. No one she knew would see her again until
her appearance, like her soul, had returned to what it had
been. Now that the light was back in her eyes, she was
shamed by her appearance. Like Eve once her eyes had
opened to see her nakedness.

The aroused power of her soul quivered within her and
lightened the steps of her heavy body. Feelings which had
been paralyzed for years were stirring.

The tally had been made; her soul's accounting was complete. Now everything was as clear to her as the blue sky
overhead and the green leaves of the trees. Harry had given
her the key—the very same key she had once given him.

Near this tree, Harry had unfastened from his jacket the
key she had given him, the key he wore always. Attaching
it to the lapel of her coat, he had said, "May the same gate
to life open for my beloved!"

Slowly, very slowly, hope was reborn. Layer upon layer,
the nightmare was unearthed—examined, clarified, understood. And with understanding the glimmerings of solution
began to emerge: Harry had come to her from the world of
Auschwitz; she was the gate through which Harry had
passed to cross into life. But Harry had carried his mission
out with him from Auschwitz—unlike herself, who had

imagined her own mission to be accomplished on the night of November 29th. There, on the hill, she had believed it possible to find happiness on an island unto itself. The first Arab bomb had shattered this illusion. The walls she had erected around her home crumbled, and she stood in the midst of the rubble and ruins, defenseless, vulnerable to every danger. It was then that the miasmas of Auschwitz began to swirl around her. The sick poisons seeped into her —just as they had infected the inhabitants of Auschwitz. Like them, she gave in to absolute despair. And if she had actually been in Auschwitz, she would never have returned. But Harry was filled with the strength of the oath he had taken: Auschwitz must not remain an island sealed· away from mankind, an island on an anonymous planet; it must be revealed to the world. This was what had forged his will to armor. That the steadfastness of his spirit had safeguarded his body was now incontestable. But she had floundered like a Mussulman in the depths of Auschwitz, with nothing to protect her soul from its terrors. In the whole world there wasn't enough food to satiate the ravenous hunger of Auschwitz preying upon her. And as there had been no help for the desperate wraiths of Auschwitz, so there was none for her in her desperation.

"If man does not learn from Auschwitz . . . he will not deserve to continue to exist . . ." Here among these trees, the purpose which would justify her own existence was revealed to her. *No man is an island unto himself.* How awesome and mysterious were the ways of fate. She had brought Harry back to life with the springs of her joy; now he had rescued her soul from its torment. No doctor could have helped. Because she had not been sick. It was the world and the time that were sick. And once she had understood the task that lay ahead, all her old energy and will surged back.

She came out from under the trees. From the sky above,

the drops of the first rain were beginning to fall. She looked up at the brightness of the sky, and the raindrops washed across her face. Walking with her face upturned, she breathed deeply of this purity, and with each step she seemed to be walking along the blueprint of the days to come.

By the cabin she came to a standstill. She opened the door and went in. In front of the plank which Harry had used as a writing desk, her eyes fastened on a black splotch of ink soaked into the plank. The first time Harry had brought her here from the hospital, he had led her to this plank desk, pulled out the pen he wrote with, and, clenching it in his fist as though he were gripping a knife, he plunged the point of the pen deep into the plank. The ink splattered over the wood and was absorbed into it. "How can I continue to write when I see the poison of Auschwitz streaming into you?" She was shaken. She could not believe what she was hearing: he was making a counter vow, renouncing his Auschwitz pledge, the secret of his survival! She felt as if he were stabbing the point of the pen into his very heart. A renewed determination quickened within her. Now she bent silently toward the smudge of ink, bringing her lips to it: *Beloved, I shall put a new pen in your hands.*

33

The cable had arrived the night before: NOVEMBER TWENTY-NINTH FOR BIRTHDAY RETURNING HOME STOP FLIGHT NO. . . . For over a year Galilea had been away, and the postcards had come from all over the world. The day after her return from the hospital, she had pulled down a suitcase from the loft and packed it with the barest minimum of clothing. All she had said was: "I'm leaving for a while, Harry. I'll write you from wherever I am." And Harry had not questioned her. She would explain in her letters, he had thought. But there were no letters, only postcards from cities around the world. The messages were brief: "Hello from Rome," "Kisses from Florida," "Regards from Lapland." And he had not even been able to write her because he never knew where she would be. None of the cards had hinted at her next stop, or how long she would be staying. Obviously she preferred not to receive letters, if only to be free of the obligation to explain. The sketchy messages made it clear that if she were not afraid of upsetting her family, she would not even have sent the postcards.

Like pigeons from a dovecot, the first passengers emerged from the doorway of the plane, their gaze on the blue of a new world. The customs hall was humming with the commotion of the arrivals. Atop the long counters, a colorful array of dresses, suits and undergarments flowed over the rims of opened suitcases past the eyes of the custom inspectors, like fish leaping from a narrow stream. Each passenger stood by his open suitcase as though his private parts had been exposed to the official eye of the inspector.

Daniella was straining on tiptoe to catch a glimpse of her mother in the distance. Necks craning, the expectant crowd pushed forward toward the narrow opening to the closed customs hall. The children impatiently bit their nails: "Do you see her yet, Daddy? . . ." One by one the passengers were coming out of the customs hall, a flow of tourists: businessmen, rabbis, athletes, glamorous actresses. But no sign of Galilea.

Madame Glick tried to contain her nervousness. "Take my arm, Mike," she said to her husband. Harry hoisted Monish onto his shoulders, and the boy towered over the crowd. "See anything, Monish?" his sister called up to him. "Now pick me up too, Daddy!" Harry lowered Monish and lifted Daniella. Monish wouldn't leave his sister alone: "See anything?" And Daniella, on high, was just as excited: "Daddy, why isn't Mommy there?" Their questioning eyes clung to faces and figures. Was that her now? Or maybe this one? The mother they remembered wore a faded house-coat over her huge fleshy body, her face was bloated, and her eyes peered out from under a tangle of hair in constant anxiety. Their eyes searched the customs hall to find her.

Between the customs counters another beautiful woman was making her way toward the exit, the porters wheeling her luggage along behind. She walked a few steps past them, then swerved around on her high heels and flung her arms up to Daniella, riding on Harry's shoulders. "Mommy!" the child cried.

She was tall. She was willowy. No more the disheveled hair of the tormented years, or even the old hair style that used to fall along the curve of her cheek, but a new chic coiffure. Looking at her, no one would have recognized the young Galilea, much less the Galilea she had become in recent years.

Only in the depths of her eyes was the agony of the pre-vious years discernible. Under her glamorous appearance, Galilea had succeeded in camouflaging the scar from every-one but Harry. In this, they were now alike.

The airport porters struggled to load her suitcases into the trunk of the Buick. "Papa, let me have the car keys!" Galilea said suddenly, turning to her father. "I'll be your chauffeur."

Madame Glick gasped: Never in her life had Galilea driven

a car! Without hesitation, Professor Glick handed the keys to his daughter. "It's about time I had a chauffeur of my own," he said, smiling.

Galilea started the car, stealing a sidelong glance at Harry sitting beside her. Their eyes met. Daniella leaned forward from the rear seat and wrapped her warm little arms around her mother's neck. "Mommy," she purred in her ear, "You must come to school tomorrow. I want everyone to see you."

The car pulled smoothly away and turned onto Defense Highway. This was the road that led to the quarter where the officers lived. Almost every day she had taken this road to Dr. Garden. For how long? Two years? Three? The nightmare had faded from her mind the way a dark shadow disappears with the advent of light. She must make sure of the dates: When was the first trip to the doctor and when was the last? One thing, though, was vivid in her memory. Whenever she took the Sheroot taxi to Dr. Garden's, she had always had the feeling that her "I" was waiting for her in Dr. Garden's reception room; it was only the shadow of the "I" that was traveling to meet and merge with its source and substance, sitting there in anticipation of her arrival. She would tremble with expectation. Soon they would meet, and for the hour of the session she would no longer be two halves of one being, severed one from the other. As a child, when it was dark on the street, she used to move from one street light to another, delighting in seeing how the two shadows of her body would advance and merge on the sidewalk—the one projected by the street light ahead, the second by the light in back of her, again to separate and then meet, according to the rhythm of her gait. And every time the two silhouettes would overlap, like the hands of a clock, she would stop for a moment. A moment that eventually became an hour, the hour with Dr. Garden.

She used to imagine her life during those trips to the doctor—restlessly rolling black ocean waves, one swallowed within the other, never reaching shore; like rootless seaweed she was buffeted about in the foam of the breaking waves. Only when she was inside Dr. Garden's office, only then was the seaweed cast up upon the shore, lying there exposed to the doctor's eye.

Now once again she was traveling the same road. This time, whole and unfragmented. Was it Dr. Garden who had helped her? But no doctor could have helped her. Because she was not the one who was sick; no disease was in her. Forces outside herself, the times, they were the sickness. Would the obscure connection between the Auschwitz tragedy and the present tragedy of Arab vengeance, as they both confront each other upon this land, ever be understood? It was in her soul that this confrontation had raged: the Auschwitz terror and the terror of the Arab hostility. The two were one. But they had divided her soul in two. Could she ever explain it to anybody? Would anyone see this Gordian knot and understand?

Now she was on her way home. The streets of Lydda were bustling with activity. Probably none of the people who lived here now remembered that Arabs had once lived in these very houses. *"You must look reality straight in the eye."* This was the reality she must face. She had looked directly into her terror of Auschwitz, and she had overcome it. Now she would look this reality in the eye. She would open her home to the Arabs, and she would go into their homes. So that the Arabs too would see the reality and recognize its anguish, and then together they would try to overcome what fate had forced upon the two peoples of this land.

"Do you remember this road, beloved?" Galilea asked.

He had been thinking of the time when he would sometimes go with Galilea along this route to Dr. Garden, and he was astonished that their thoughts were so congruent. He gazed at her profile. She was new. Ungraspable. Like swift currents, the different periods of his life since that first evening with her surged through him, each leaving its own taste and smell in his mouth. Moments when they had soared to heights and moments when despair itself seemed to weep.

"Yes," he said, "it seems like the same road."

The trees on either side of the highway swayed together, their branches interweaving. Driving through a tunnel of green, Galilea reached out for Harry. Their fingers tightened around each other. A feeling almost forgotten yet familiar filled him. And she breathed deep of the ·arched green overhead.

34

Like sucklings sated at their mother's breast, the children fell asleep in deep contentment. Harry took down from the storage closet the suit he had worn on their first evening together. Galilea too reached up to the shelf in her closet to bring down the dress she had worn that night, which she kept along with her wedding gown. And she was neither elated nor surprised to see that the dress fitted her youthful silhouette perfectly.

They put out the lights and tiptoed out of the house.

A full moon lighted their way and cast on their faces its silvery glow. No more than burning candles could dim the light of day could the street lamps diminish the moon's streaming light. They avoided the bright crowded streets and walked without knowing they were walking.

At Magen David Square everything had changed, just as Tel Aviv itself was no longer what it had been. But in their eyes everything seemed exactly as it had been on that night of November 29th, the night of the balloting at Lake Success, Galilea's birthday night then and her birthday night now.

Galilea came to a stop at the spot where she had stood then. Harry moved on to the pedestrian safety island in the center of the square.

Her eyes were fastened on Harry's back as he stood there alone; she remembered the square thronged with people—heads at the open windows, on the balconies, on the sidewalks around. Again she visualized the people listening in the hush of suspense to the radio announcer reporting the results of the balloting at Lake Success. People embracing one another, each of them realizing how little he could comprehend the greatness and awe of this moment. Where was Harry? Why wasn't he here with her at such a moment?

She saw Harry in the center of the square, as she had seen him then. Quietly, she drew close to him. The moon illumined his face. What was he thinking in this moment of isolation? Her hand found his, as it had then. They turned and walked silently away, their bodies trembling with anticipation. They walked to the hilltop. . . .

They were still lying in their embrace, still riding the trail of iridescence imparted by the sky-rocketing moment of love. "Beloved," she breathed, "my body trembles just as it did the first time you touched me."

"We're back on our hill," he said.

The blocks of buildings which had sprung up all around the hilltop over the years had vanished from their sight. Once again there was nothing but the face of the full moon and the twin stars sparkling from Galilea's eyes, the heaving of the silvered sea, and she in his arms. But unlike the first time, her gaze now revealed the scar of past fears. He knew the pain from such memories coursing in his own veins. As if understanding his look, her lips whispered: "Like you in Auschwitz, I was in my own hell for five years."

"And now we have found each other again," he said.

"This time I am the one who has come to you from a long way off," she said. "I ached for the smell of your body, beloved. Across seas and continents it haunted me and wouldn't let go."

"I embraced that filthy old housecoat of yours," he said. "I kept your cookbooks beside my bed and searched them for traces of your fingers. Why didn't you write even a word about yourself?"

"I wanted to return to you chastened, as you first came to me. Now I'm not afraid any more to rejoice in my good fortune. The devil's had his share of me. And I've given him the same number of years from my life as you gave Auschwitz. I stayed away in exile for a year in order to complete the term. Now, as equals, we both deserve our happiness."

He looked at her, then jumped to his feet. "To the sea, precious!" he cried out.

The path of moonlight on the sea reached out from horizon to shore, and they floated along its length. As they swam, their hands combed the silvery ripples, and the gentle sea smiled on them.

They lay back on the sea's rippling carpet; above them was the fire sparkle of the stars. Alone, in a universe all their own. They were the breath of God in a moment of love. Male and female whom God had created.

She floated on his open palms. In his arms she turned to face him. "Like then, beloved . . ." she breathed in his ear. And like then, no longer seeing sky or sea, they themselves became the sea, they its tempest.

35

The spacious living room was crammed with Arabs and Jews sitting shoulder to shoulder, cross-legged in Oriental fashion on the carpet; others stood on the balconies, filled the hallways and spread out into the back rooms. Galilea's door stood open to any Arab in Israel.

Harry sat in the corner of the room, squeezed between guests who were unaware of who he was or his relationship to this house. The editor of a respected morning paper, this evening's principal speaker, was addressing the gathering, but Harry's ears still burned with the heated argument he had overheard earlier, before the influx of guests began. "All those cherished Arab friends of yours you're ready to give your life for, given the chance they'll butcher you and your kids," Galilea's old schoolmate had sneered, "and once they're done with their slaughter, they'll go to bed and sleep without a care."

"How can you say such horrible things!" Galilea had gasped.

"What do you mean 'how'? Have you forgotten that's what they set out to do? Only they didn't quite make it. Oh, what a holy bloodbath they'd have given this country if we hadn't managed to drive them back."

"But now we sleep without a care," she had cried.

"Oh no we don't! And people like you are one reason why."

Harry rubbed his face with his hands as if he could erase the nightmarish exchange, but it was futile. From his corner he watched Galilea listening tensely to the speaker be-

side her, and his eyes moved among the rows of people, resting on the faces of the Arabs who frequented their home.
"Given the chance they'll butcher you and your kids . . ."

A young Arab rose to his feet. It was his turn now. Excited, ready with his reply, he waited for the refreshments
to be over. Daniella and her friend Jasmin from the Arab
village were picking their way between the rows, trays of
baklava in their hands—Daniella, with golden hair cascad-
ing over a blue dress, Jasmin's black curls set off by spotless
white. Like Daniella, Monish would occasionally invite his
friend from the Arab village to these evenings. "At the
mere thought that my child is liable to hear something like
this from a Jew," the Arab who witnessed the fight between
Galilea and her schoolmate had said to him, "I feel as if
I'm going out of my mind. It would tear him apart, poison
him beyond saving." He said nothing more, but the shock
lingered in his eyes.

". . . and as for the second question raised by our distinguished lecturer," the Arab speaker continued, "permit
me to point out that every political party, without excep-
tion, treats us the way they treat cows: fill their troughs
with fodder just so they keep on giving milk. Because all
the parties have one and only one concern: that slip of paper
the Arab drops into the ballot box on Election Day. If it
weren't for the ballot not one of them would give a damn."

Harry looked at the hands of the young Arab who sat
pressed against his side; his left hand was cupping an ashtray as the fingers of his right hand ground out a cigarette
butt—grinding, grinding. He was one of the construction
gang working on the Hilton Hotel, who had come to Galilea's home this evening. But what about after they left here?
Where would they find a place to spend the night? Renting
a room in the city was quite a problem for an Arab. He
looked at the brown arm of the hand holding the ashtray—

muscular, traced with lime. He wanted to raise his glance to the young man's face, but didn't.

". . . the distinguished speaker asked, and not without sarcasm: 'When did the Arabs in this country ever have it so good?' By the same token I could of course ask: And when did the Jews in this country ever have it so good? Allah! How long are the Jews going to go on thinking that time has passed by the Arabs of Israel? Why even the Arab in Egypt isn't what he was like in the days of Farouk!"

All around Harry the people were absorbed in the tense dialogue between Jew and Arab. It was better, he mused, that the thoughts festering in the hearts of the Arabs were brought out into the open here in this house rather than back in the Arab village, where they could not even be refuted.

". . . my friends, our country has been through an Arab-Jewish war. Most of us Arabs were no more than children at the time. But our government has already made peace with today's Germans, arguing that the younger generation is not to be held responsible for the deeds of the fathers. Jewish logic has decreed that the new generation of German children is no longer 'German' but German. Only we and our children go on being 'Arabs,' forever under suspicion. If we are indeed a fifth column, I'll be the first to admit that the attitude toward us has been much too kind."

Fifth column. The horror-show of the hanging of Jews in the ghetto square suddenly rose before him. He saw the faces of the Upper Silesians, Hitler's fifth column in Poland before the outbreak of the slaughter. Afterward, they were rewarded with the houses and businesses of those who had been hanged. And he, standing among the Jews forced to watch the execution, he had studied the gloating faces of the Silesians who had come out to see the ghetto Jews hanged. He remembered how they had been before

the war: peaceful citizens, merchants, neighbors of the
hanged. What was it their eyes saw as they followed the
writhing of the bodies on the gallows?

Fifth column . . . His eyes roamed over the people seated
on the carpet, guests in his home, and the question pierced
his brain: *That placid face over there, is he?* . . . *Or could
this face here . . . ?* But then, he might not even be an Arab.

Another young man was seated on the other side of him.
The points of his shoes gleamed up at Harry. The sleeves of
his immaculae white shirt were ironed to a sharp crease.
Harry's gaze groped along his profile: Jew? Arab? No mark
but the name on the identity card to distinguish one from
the other. Their eyes met. He wished he'd speak so he could
hear his voice. He examined his outfit—sharp, city style—
and remembered his old preference in clothes, how he had
dressed to keep the refugee from being recognized. *"And
thou shalt love the refugee as thou wert once a refugee."*
Who here was the refugee and who the citizen? Who was
the stranger and who the native? Who was the newcomer?
And who was obliged to love whom?

Daniella was moving among the guests, emptying ash-
trays. He saw his little girl flushed with the warmth of hospitality, and then, like shattering slivers, her face was
smashed in the mirror of his soul. *"Given the chance they'll
butcher you and your kids . . ."* And throbbing in his tem-
ples were Mahmoud's words: "Something like this from a
Jew . . . would tear my son apart . . ."

He got up and picked his way among the crowd on the
carpet. Infuriated glances were turned on him for the dis-
turbance. He squeezed through to the doorway and bolted
toward the street.

36

Unhurried and assured, the sun moved in the height of its twilight glory toward the sea. Soon it would dip into the shuddering scales of water. Galilea turned the car sharply onto the road leading east. Harry sat by her side, his back against the seat as he listened tensely to their guest in the rear.

A drug-like heaviness dominated the horizon. Sweltering dusk. Behind the hills evening lay in wait, its net already cast over their crests. The brilliant fragments would be gleaned one by one. Steadily, the evening spun its web against the withdrawing sun. At such times emotions are lured to the hazy and the unknown. The mind withdraws. Until it is difficult to express a lucid opinion.

"May I invite you to join us at the Arab village this evening?" Galilea had said to the official of the Bureau for Arab Affairs. "There you can observe firsthand how we work, On the way there we'll be able to continue our discussion."

The official had called at their house earlier that day to caution Galilea about the hazards involved in her Arab activities: "These matters," he had said, "are of an extremely complex and delicate nature, and, considering the present situation, only experts in the field can be permitted to deal with them."

Galilea had arranged for an Arab-Jewish gathering in an Arab village this evening. A scholarship would be presented to a gifted village girl to enable her to continue her studies. Rabbi Zakin, touring Israel with a group of two hundred

American young people, had responded to Galilea's request to sponsor the scholarship. A large crowd was expected, and the American Jewish youth would have the opportunity to see life in an Israeli-Arab village. An experience of undeniable value.

Turning east at this evening hour, you draw closer and closer to twilight. This is the nature of things. Yet somewhere in the distance you sense a constant watchfulness, biding its time. Gossamer veils descend and unfold, veils which will thicken into impenetrable darkness. This may be the enemy's plot. Veils strengthen the illusion of peace.

The buses coming from Jerusalem with Rabbi Zakin's group would be at the next junction, and the convoys from the south would be waiting there too. Together, the festive crowd would enter the village. Tense, straining slightly to one side, Harry tried to grasp the implication of what was being said. "And this is why it appears to me," the man in the back seat was saying, "that it is precisely your pure intentions and impeccable reputation that have induced a certain type of individual to infiltrate your home. The motivation of this type is quite different from what their glib talk would have you believe. Their motives are far removed from the goals you have set for yourselves. These people, Madame, are out to exploit your naïveté, your idealism and your kind heart."

The bus-stop signs along the road string the highway with the names of settlements, old and new. Some, bloodstained, mined by the *Fedayoun*, are engraved upon the memory from the morning headlines. And yet another sign will soon appear: BORDER AHEAD. Then you must turn right. The barren wilderness comes into view. Hidden among the rocks, the border guards keep watch. Twilight sucks at the gaps in the rocks. Like witnesses whose testimony is recorded on archival scrolls, the jagged scars in the bare limestone are engraved with the annals of innumerable conquests. Mists enfold the mountaintops. You draw ever closer, and the unknown steps forth to receive you. Perhaps you are actually returning through the substrata of time to the quarry of your origin.

"Naturally," the man behind Harry continued, "we are well aware of the kind of gathering you hold in your home— that is, the dialogue between Jews and Arabs. It is a difficult and important task you have undertaken. The idea is marvelous but not without its dangers, considering the two elements participating in these encounters. On the one hand respectable Jews—academicians, authors, scientists and so on, who enjoy visiting the salon of Madame Galilea, which, I suppose, reminds them of the literary salons of peaceful Europe in another era. As far as they're concerned, the purpose for which you've set up these evenings may very well be secondary. And the Arab guests on the other hand, some of them leaders and intellectuals of the Arab minority. We know every single one of them, and we also know what X or Y has been secretly preaching to the Arab community long before they were ever guests in your home. And just as we took seriously what they had to say then, so we must investigate with equal intensity their motives for planting themselves in the very heart of Jewish society. The danger is the front they're putting up. Who do you think is ready to shelter the saboteurs infiltrating the country and mining our highways? Do you really mean to say that you don't see the subversiveness and hostility in the heart of the Arab?"

"We brought peace unto you . . ." The countryside rang with the singing voices as the buses carrying Rabbi Zakin's youngsters passed them and raced on into the mist shrouding the road to the Arab village. A fresh spirit swept across the dreary landscape. Galilea could not contain her rising excitement, and the words poured forth. "I'm by no means blind to the pitfalls," she said. "But there's one thing absolutely sacred to me: as a Jew, the stereotype of 'Arab,' 'Negro,' 'Jew' is taboo. I open my eyes every morning beside a man whose arm is branded with the label 'Jew,' and I'll fight the stigma of 'Arab' with my dying breath if I have to! And even if the Arab population has suspicious or subversive characters, it's not my responsibility to track them down. That's your job, your responsibility—you the authorities. As a Jew and a citizen, my obligation is totally different. The ghetto heritage of my people's suffering obligates me to go to the Arab villages and bring them the simple human greeting *Salaam Aleikum*."

The caravan of cars filled with guests for the evening of brotherhood in the Arab village was following along behind them. They saluted one another with their horns. From the north and the south they had come, from wherever Galilea had organized homes to welcome Arab and Jewish circles, the gatherings modeled on her own in Tel Aviv. "People in this country," she liked to say, "are ready for the idea. They've only been waiting for a sign, an example to follow." The stream of eastward-moving light from the caravan of cars illumined the road. The impetus of what she was saying carried Galilea along: "A new generation is growing up in this country, among us as well as among our Arab neighbors. Shouldn't we be the ones to break the cycle of hate so that the new Arab generation within the country can become a living bridge to our neighbors across the border—or should we sit back and let hatred take root in the new generation as well?

"Do you hear me, Dr. Pelli?" Her head was tilted against the wind, and her voice rose with emotion. "Do you see this man beside me? I don't know another person who has as much right as he to hate the whole world, but from him, of all people, I learned to hate hatred. Can you understand me, Dr. Pelli? With hatred you can only destroy, not build. Even a powerful army cannot be maintained on

hatred, only on love—love of country, or love for your own
life and the lives of the children you left back home when
you went to the battlefield.

"Do you understand me? I'm not telling you anything
new, I know. How did you put it before? 'Exploit my
naïveté and my kind heart!' You may very well be right.
But when it comes to love and hate, let me, in my naïveté,
say to you that our striking power all the way back to the
War of Independence has not stemmed from hatred for the
Arabs but from love of our land. Even today we don't hate
the Arabs of Egypt, Syria, Iraq. But we do love our country. And that is the miracle and secret of our strength. A
country has a soul too, and we must act in such a way that
the country will love us as well."

This way! This way! the voices were calling. The shafts
of the headlights picked up swarms of children in the darkness of the entrance to the village. They were waiting to
direct the guests to the meeting place in the village square.
"*Shalom! Shalom!*" they shouted in Hebrew as they scrambled onto the cars to earn a few yards' free ride as guides.

The children of the Arab village, for whom this must
have been their first encounter with Jews, were not afraid.

37

With nightfall the visions return, reawakened to hover in
the dark, like rocks giving back to the darkness the heat
soaked up from the day.

In Auschwitz, when he had lost all hope, he would go

out into the blackness of night and put on the dome of the heavens as his cap. In the silence of loneliness, existence flickered over yonder like a lost firefly. And the eyes spun webs to ensnare it.

He had long since come to terms with his visions. He saw them as fellow wayfarers, conspirators sauntering toward him. Their obscure slang was one he understood well. They hailed from the same province. He had once imagined that with the upheaval they had sunk into the abyss. But there they were, riding the carousel of time, coming full circle past him, only to return again, some with a changed face, some with a hidden face, but in the gaze of each one the same mute demand: Let him see his signature upon the writ and be reminded of the day the pledge is due!

Now, as he looked up at the hills above the village square, remembrance was released by the string of lanterns burning there. The women of the Moslem village, who by custom were kept separate when the men met together, had gathered on the hills, their children with them. Only as the eyes became accustomed to the dark and pierced the distance could their presence be discerned: cloaked in night, flanked by the lanterns, they stared bewildered at the scene.

With danger approaching, night moans in your ear, as it moans in the ear of the waylayer lying in ambush, a sough of nameless grief that knows no cause. But the echo within you responds in its own language.

Beyond the string of lanterns, beyond the no man's land where darkness spreads, what form, what appearance does danger now assume, whose smell is wafted here with every breath of wind? At night in Auschwitz, the string of lights along the electrified barbed-wire fence would whisper tales of a nameless world somewhere out of reach, beyond the fence. A world that might hold humans, whose shape and image still flickered out of the recesses of memory.

Only later did you learn that those who had imprisoned you were human too.

Beyond the hills, what lies hidden in the depths of the night? *"Who do you think is sheltering the saboteurs infiltrating the country and mining our highways?"*

Hundreds of heads gathered in the square. Row upon row. The light from the lanterns spilled over them—a lake within the girding darkness. Voices raised in glorious singing, as if they were discovering new meaning in the old worn-out words: "How good and how pleasant it is for brothers to sit together . . ."

Village elders in white *keffiyahs* and bespectacled American youth, sitting side by side. Between them oceans and lands, yet less separating than the distances which separate the Arabs and their neighbors in this small land. Now they were united by a pure tremor, a tremor born of the pain of hostility.

The moment you join your voice to the chorus of singers restraints fall away. Inhibitions drop. Boundaries burst. Singing in chorus you can say what could not be said otherwise. Then sing again, sing some more. What a shame to lose what is now at hand. Everyone knows the meaning of the words. Eyes to eyes say it, throat to throat responds. Then sing again, and still some more.

What is the night hiding in its depths, and what will dawn on the morrow?

"We will never forget this evening we take away with us from our trip to Israel. Now we know that in the Holy Land Jews and Arabs can live together."

The foreignness of the language coming from the loudspeaker is absorbed in the village air. Interpreters stand on both sides of the teen-age speaker from Rabbi Zakin's group. Sentence after sentence is being translated from English, now becoming Hebrew, now Arabic. Without knowing the language, the heart still drinks it in as if it contained vitamins which must be swallowed. The air is disinfected against the virus of cynicism. Here only one of the two can prevail: grace or hate.

"I just don't know how to say it. But the scholarship you are giving me is from Jews. We are poor. Now I have the chance to be a teacher one day . . ." And again sentence by sentence, this time into English, then Hebrew. The scholarship girl could meanwhile catch her breath and, embarrassed, cut a path through the maze of words to the next sentence. "I always wanted to be a teacher. Now that you have done such a thing I want to even more . . ."

And the speeches in a trio of tongues continued. Jews speaking, Arabs speaking. And Rabbi Zakin delivering a speech. "The hour," they said, "demands a dialogue, face to face . . ." "Our two peoples," they said, "must come together through personal acquaintanceship . . ." "All it needed," they said, "was one person to take a stand, to be first, to begin. Not on orders from the government, of course. Not in order to make converts for political parties . . ." On and on, in the same vein. As if the occasion needed rhetorical platitudes to keep it down to earth, and thus prevent it from soaring into a higher sphere where they themselves already were.

The village youths, who came often to Galilea's evenings, were insistent with the guests: the tables were waiting, laden with food. In their eyes was an apology for not feasting their guests on a banquet of lamb in accordance with their tradition of hospitality. They had been told that Rabbi Zakin and his group were prohibited from eating meat not slaughtered according to Jewish Law.

The village dignitaries, bronze faces cowled in white *keffiyahs,* moved leisurely on the edge of the square, lacing the boundary between light and dark. Dissolving and ma-

terializing. Their relaxed step confirmed their seigniory.
Lords on their own terrain. Now and then the light from a
lantern exposed the hermetic silence sealing their faces.
Eyes would meet, then a desert sandal might crush a cigarette
butt into the ground. So many foreign languages had taken
over their square. No communicating except through an
intermediary. Even so, there was no way of expressing what
the mother tongue was so adept at hiding. No traps could be
laid in one's own language. Back to the hermetic silence then.
Only their youths could decipher the parchment of their
faces. But the youths were dancing with the Jews in the center
of the square. Circle within circle. Hands clasped in hands.
A night bewitched, and the yearning in the heart clinging to
its magic—so that you might even be persuaded to think:
what if the shepherds of the Tribe of Isaac had danced with
the shepherds of the Tribe of Ishmael on this very square?
And more such farfetched questions.

*"A new generation is growing up in this country, among
us as well as among our Arab neighbors. Shouldn't we be
the ones to break the cycle of hate . . ."*

It is here for your eyes to see. You cannot ignore it. You
feel the pulse of change. And you yourself are only a detail
in the *vitrage*. What is happening has resulted from what
has been made to happen. What sense is there in probing
the complexities behind the spirit of this night? What is
before you now is real, and what is real is bound to
seep down to the roots of motives. This is not a wildlife
reservation. You are standing waist-deep in a vat of fermen-
tation—and change—in the process of distillation—is rising
to the surface.

A new generation is breaking free of the village fossiliza-
tion. They are building the city with their tight-lipped
humility and sweat. The temptress draws them to her. Now
she has come to them, to the obscurity of their remote vil-

lage. Tel Aviv has come, and New York. A tantalizing aroma, painful and intoxicating. Circle within circle. Hands clasped within hands. Rays can penetrate even unto the roots of a malignant disease. But refracted rays will only spin a mirage. A seductive night. Momentary and fleeting.

38

The Arab house was filled with cigarette smoke. Family and friends had gathered there, some to pay their respects to Galilea, others to bid farewell to the scholarship girl, Jumana. "I'm so happy you're spending the night under our roof," Jumana had said. At dawn, they would leave together for Nazareth. Uncle Hussein, her guardian since the tragic death of her parents, would escort her, and Galilea was to attend to the financial matters at the boarding-school office. "What a lovely aristocratic face that girl has," Galilea was saying to Harry.

Outside, the night was black. Darkness had emptied the village square—as if the departing guests had taken away with them all the trappings of joy.

The Arab women had long since gathered up the lanterns and taken them to their homes. The village resumed its own rhythm. Only in the home where Galilea and Harry were invited for the night was coffee being pounded with a pestle in the kitchen, and food prepared. One might at first have imagined that the exhilaration which had pulsed

through the village square would carry over to the inti-
macy of this home—like the spirit of festivity found in the
relatives of newlyweds at the end of the wedding celebration.
And, indeed, things did look that way to begin with. Until
the old mother's story suddenly halted in order to clear a
passage in her throat, for the tears were rolling down the
furrows of her cheeks, dumb and heavy like a tank lumbering
along its tracks. Then she went on with the story, tone and
rhythm just as it had been till again the story halted. The
throat was blocked. Then on with the story. Then a halt.

The only sound was the pounding of the coffee in the
kitchen.

The vaults, so to speak, had opened, the keys to which
are passed down by heads of family from generation to
generation.

A sudden and cruel transition from the earlier atmos-
phere of the village square. Or perhaps not that sudden. A
direct outcome. The way one thing leads to another. Or perhaps even a token of trust. The family scar was now speaking. Pain had shed its skin and the viscera were laid bare.

"My daughter, America is far away? Yes, far away. Look
out the window. There, behind the hill, is a village. And
there is a path. I used to walk on it, back and forth. Just
close your eyes, and like me you will be able to see the village. It is so near, but it is farther away than America. I
saw your Rabbi from America, may Allah grant him long
life. Only my son who is over there in that village I cannot
see. For twenty years I have not seen my son. I am old. I
shall die, and I will not see my son."

From a corner of the room, the pale blank eye of the
television was staring at Harry. Israel was still without television stations, but most of its Arab villages had sets. Harry
had turned on the television when he came in, and at once
hosts of Arab army battalions came marching across the set,

their legs swinging high in that Nazi goosestep he could never forget; right-face, and all their eyes were turned on you: "We're coming back! We're coming back!", the Arab battle song sounded. Then the scene cut immediately to a full-faced Nasser among a battery of microphones, then to a raging sea of heads screaming through bared teeth in their frenzy. It was a catapulting transition, as though a cruel hand were thrusting you toward the bared pain that had now emerged from the vaults within this Arab home. And once it had been laid bare, the suddenness of the transition was no longer perceptible. Boundaries blurred. Now you had entered into the prevailing climate. Invisible paths had led subterraneously from the unprecedented experience that swept you away outside in the square to this exposing of the wound. The way bait dissolves caution and lures the hunted animal out from hiding.

There were some among them who lowered their eyes as Hussein spoke. Especially the young ones. They felt uncomfortable that such matters were being spoken of in their presence. Perhaps they preferred that such things remain locked away inside the vaults; perhaps they preferred to forget them altogether, to swim at last in the stream of the new life. The scorch of the words could be seen on their faces. Hussein was exposing the family shame in public. They were sorry they had come now; yet to get up and leave was unthinkable. For Hussein was speaking of his own flesh and blood—of his father, his brother.

"How old was I then, *Yamma?*" Hussein asked. And the old mother, her eyes upon the darkness at the window: "Maybe you were eight, my son."

"Father threw himself down on the straw in the barn. 'I shall not leave my home!' Remember, *Yamma?*"

Harry blurted out, "And why in fact did everybody run away?" The question seeming oddly out of place.

"It's true that the village was at war with the Jews then. But Father was an old man. All he did was to give the village fighters ransom money to buy a rifle. He himself did no fighting. And maybe he was afraid that if the Jews won they would butcher his sons. And when he did cross with us to the other side of the border, it was as if he hadn't crossed at all. He turned and looked back in the direction of his home. Then lay down in the middle of the path and died. Attallah and I stood over his body. Attallah refused to go back. There was revenge in his eyes. Even if no one else in the whole world takes his side, I will stand by him. How old was Attallah then, *Yamma?*"

"Maybe ten, my son." With her eyes upon the darkness in the window.

You could see the border blazing in the living body. It cut through the heart of this old mother. And like a suppurating sore, it dripped its pus into the roots of the next generation. Jewish-Arab brotherhood. Dialogue. Person-to-person encounters. Friendship. Brothers together. What hadn't they spoken about outside, what hadn't they sung about? Yet inside, the border dividing. A line of fire that could not be extinguished. Fanned by foreign powers who needed the flames, needed the border. If the border did not cut behind the hill, Hussein's brother Attallah might well be sitting with them now. Wouldn't the exhilaration of this evening still be felt then?

The youths found a hold for themselves in the demitasses of coffee clutched in their hands. They hung their broodings on the handle of the cup, a lighted cigarette between their fingers. It was an obligation to listen when family elders talked. All the more so when bleeding dignity had the floor.

And from the corner the pale bleary eye of the television stared at Harry. The screams of the Arab throng still echoed

here. Even with his eyes closed, he could see them marching: "We're coming back!" Suddenly the question rose in
his mind: *Attallah, Hussein's brother—isn't he one of those
who come back in the dark of night to mine our highways?*

Harry shot a glance at Galilea. In her eyes, as she listened
to Hussein, the scar seemed to have been ripped open. The
fear submerged within was staring out like an ogre rearing
up from its dungeon, ready to break loose and smash everything in sight. On the way here in the car she had been
biting her lip as she listened to the government official:
*"Who do you think is sheltering the saboteurs infiltrating
the country and mining our roads?"*

"Allow me, Hussein," Harry said. "In all sincerity, I
value your frankness with us as a sign of trust and respect.
I have heard your bitter words about the attitude of the
Jews toward the Arab workers in the city. Who of us here
is not aware of the efforts being made to improve the situation? The facts are well known. But now, permit me to ask
you in the same spirit of frankness: If, for example, it happened that your brother Attallah should appear on your
doorstep one night with a saboteur's pack on his back, do
you suppose that you would shelter him for the night?"

The demitasses stirred between the fingers of the guests.
A heavy silence fell between questioner and questioned.
Rather, between two elements—between two peoples. A
silence that had to be broken. The question had been asked,
and it demanded an answer no less direct. It could not be
evaded. It was not only this moment that was threatened; it
hung over the whole of this divided country, this country
torn in two.

"I know what you mean," said Hussein, his voice heavy
with dejection. "But I would understand you even better
if you'd tell me this: If you were in my place and the brother
you hadn't seen for twenty years—since you last stood to-

gether over the body of your dead father—if he should appear suddenly one night on your doorstep with a saboteur's pack on his back, tell me, would you turn him in?"

And Jumana, a silent plea her only protest. She stood there with her suitcase gripped in her hand, a searing pain on her face. Nothing more was said. Nothing more could be said. Everything was clearly understood. Surrender yourself to the arms of the blind Stygian waters, and the current will carry you where it will. This was the reality you must look straight in the eye. A burning wound in the soul of divided man in a divided land. More and more Jews and Arabs would come to Galilea's salon for evenings of brotherhood and friendship. More and more homes would be opened, north and south. More and more rallies would be organized in Arab villages. Dances would be danced. Songs sung. Speeches delivered. Scholarships granted. But all the while an old mother in the dark of night would be staring toward a village beyond the border, waiting for her son to come back to her before she dies, even if he carries a pack of explosives on his back.

The beds must be prepared. Tomorrow at dawn they would depart. The guests began drifting out, in their eyes a mute apology like the one that had spoken from their eyes earlier, when they were denied the privilege of preparing the traditional banquet of lamb for their honored guests. Their hands were limp and sweaty as they departed. They had no words. More likely than not, once outside they breathed free.

39

Behind the morning mists, the east caught fire in a flush of crimson. Soon the sun would be up. "It's lovely to catch this moment," Jumana said. But there was no time to linger. Hussein had figured that he would just be able to take Jumana and still manage to be on time at his job in Tel Aviv. He didn't work by the hour, so even if he began his day at eleven he would still be able to fill his quota.

Since he had bought the pickup truck, he could get back to the village more often. No need to sleep in the fields. And if he felt like staying in town to see a movie, he could easily park the truck in the field. "I sleep like a king in my truck," he said. But now he wanted to get there quickly. And if he took the shortcut between the two neighboring *kibbutzim,* they could get right onto the highway in a direct line to Nazareth.

Galilea started the car. In all the excitement of the night before, they'd forgotten to raise the top, and the seats were soaked with dew.

The truck pulled away, Jumana turning her head and waving to Galilea and Harry behind her. Her raised hand was bidding farewell to the home and village she was leaving. Would she come back at the end of the four years? There was a haunting sadness in the girl's gesture. *"I always wanted to be a teacher. Now . . . I want to even more . . ."* What would Jumana be teaching the children four years from now? Harry wondered. But immediately he pushed these thoughts aside. He didn't feel like pursuing them now.

They drove past the square. The tables, stacked with empty bottles, still surrounded it. Benches in rows. The speakers' table. *"How good and how pleasant for brothers to sit together ..."*

They left the village. The sun had not yet risen. In the east, dawn was still battling the shades of night on a bloody plain of fire. "There'll be a *khamseen* today," Galilea said.

And he felt content to be by her side. Galilea could not have slept very well last night, but he didn't ask her. Better to avoid stirring things up. A new day. Magnificent dawn. She would begin to sing soon, he expected, as she always did on long drives.

They were riding along a dirt track. From this point, the truck would turn off onto the road between the two *kibbutzim*. Hussein was quite an expert on these roads. It was while he was still working around here that he had bought the TV set. "I used to make pretty good money in those days," he had said. Until the word got around that the money was better in construction work in Tel Aviv.

A balmy freshness rose from the fields sparkling with dew. Galilea could never sit at the wheel for long without singing an accompaniment to the rhythm of the engine— in Yiddish, in Hebrew, in anything. A film of sleep was still on her eyelids, but already she was beginning to feel exuberant.

And ahead of them Jumana's excitement was obvious; she was utterly unable to sit still in the truck. Her face was turned more toward Galilea than toward the road. "Sweet child," Galilea said. "We must make it a point to visit her from time to time. Look at that delighted face. Shall we sing something, Harry? In Arabic? So Jumana can sing with us. 'We brought peace unto you ...' "

The prickly cactuses on either side of the narrow road held out handfuls of ripe sabra fruit. But there was no time for picking. Time is master of its own course, and the chips bobbing in its current flow on toward their destiny. Jumana, her face turned back to them, was clapping her hands as she sang out joyfully. Glorious dawn, filling the heart with expectation. Her dream was coming true. Even at a distance you could see her rapture.

And as it was seen . . .

The truck was torn from the road. Flung high in the air. The camera of the eye just managed to transmit to the nerve-center of the brain the truck's acrobatic tumbling through the air.

Then—nothing.

Blackout. Burned celluloid. Unmeasurable in the yardstick of time. Chips flung off time's course.

Eyes opened. Perhaps they shut for an instant; perhaps they did not shut at all. Senses short-circuited. And the link of time which had jumped the track snatched them up, tumbling with them across to the unknown. At the point of no return, stupefied, the eyes stared the way an embryo stares. They saw the front wheels of the truck jutting up in the air within a hair's breadth of them. A gravel of glass splinters all around them. And still they had not grasped what had happened. Perhaps, were they to be asked, they could have named the objects they were staring at, names without meaning.

Galilea was the first to come back. The hood of the overturned truck lay across the crushed hood of her car; the wheels in the dawn air had barely stopped spinning.

"Harry, what's happened!"

There was no possibility of getting to Hussein from underneath. Only part of his jacket was visible. The fury of the steel had swallowed him up. In a daze, they remembered Jumana and ran to the other side. Without the obstruction of the steering wheel they could reach her body.

Harry carried her in his arms. They were between the two Jewish settlements. And he didn't know which one was closest. Perhaps he should leave her and run for help. Or perhaps wait for a car to pass. Vaguely he recalled that Galilea had already run off in the opposite direction. No life stirred in the girl's mangled body. Yet every second might be crucial. He was carrying her in his arms, his legs buckling in his frantic haste. He must be injured too. The blood was running from his head down his face, and his hands were not free to wipe it away. Thoughts of terror storming his brain were lucid. What he saw was removed, far away from the scene. Or perhaps it only seemed so. His eyes were on the path ahead and on the water tower jutting out above the treetops. Any second his feet might set off another mine buried in the road.

"If your brother Attallah appeared on your doorstep with a saboteur's pack on his back, would you shelter him for the night?"

He had no control over his spinning thoughts. He could no more stop them than he could keep his feet from running. Would Galilea overtake him with a car or something or would he get there first on foot?

He felt as if he were carrying his own body. His arms did not feel to be part of him. Thus had the Red Army soldier carried him from the pile of corpses shot down in the forest on the death march from Auschwitz. Sensations were taking shape in him that had not consciously existed then, that until this moment had not taken hold of him. But once they were aroused, he was emptied of feelings. They were all transferred to the body being carried in these arms that were not part of himself. It was his own body now, he felt, being carried in the arms of a rescuer.

And now, as it had then, the rising sun flared in the east. But this time the body borne by these arms was lifeless.

Design by Sidney Feinberg
Set in Linotype Baskerville
Composed, printed and bound by The Haddon Craftsmen, Inc.
HARPER & ROW, PUBLISHERS, INCORPORATED

69 70 71 72 73 10 9 8 7 6 5 4 3 2